AMBUSH AT PIÑON CANYON

AMBUSH AT PIÑON CANYON

WAYNE M. HOY

authorHOUSE®

AuthorHouse™
1663 Liberty Drive
Bloomington, IN 47403
www.authorhouse.com
Phone: 1 (800) 839-8640

Published by AuthorHouse   09/08/2014

ISBN: 978-1-4969-3806-0 (sc)
ISBN: 978-1-4969-3807-7 (hc)
ISBN: 978-1-4969-3805-3 (e)

CHAPTER ONE

T he young cowboy spurred his horse and rode down on the three men standing at the foot of the worn wood steps leading up to the swinging doors of the Buckhorn saloon, scattering dust and gravel over them. He was off before the horse had come to a full stop, throwing bridle and gloves in two swift jerks. He took three quick sideways steps, the jingle of his spurs jarring in the sudden hush. He froze, half turning, presenting his left side to the three men, his quivering right hand suspended inches above the gun low on his hip.

"Howdy, Higgins," he called in his soft drawl, addressing the shallow-faced man in the center of the trio.

"Howdy yourself, cowboy," the man countered arrogantly; however his eyes flitted nervously to the men on either side of him.

"Where's your sidekick Burton?" The cowboy drawled, eyes shifting from Higgins to the man on his left.

"Bull? Why, I reckon he'll be along shortly. He's been fancyin' te meet up with yu."

"Ah-huh," the cowboy smiled grimly.

"What do yu want with him?" Higgins demanded.

"I reckon I'll deal with Burton later. Right now I come special to see you," the cowboy drawled, "to tell you your time is all used up. Your lowdown scheme has come to a *dead* end."

"The hell yu say!" Higgins sneered, but he again darted an uneasy sideways glance at his companions. "Give me one good reason why I should take stock of anythin' yu have te say, cowboy."

"I'll do better than that, land stealer! I'll give you *six*!" the young cowboy spat and he crouched yet a little more, his eyes seeming to see all three men at once.

"Hold on, McCord, yu best cool down. Think what yu're doin'," the tall slender man on Higgins' left said.

"Ump-umm, sheriff!…you had better step aside. I don't have a beef with you or the law."

"Don't do it, son," the lawman said, hands upraised.

"Sheriff, yu're not going' te stand there and let him throw down on us? Arrest him, I say!" Higgins bellowed.

"This is yore deal, Higgins," the sheriff said coolly, moving aside. "I'm out of it."

"Damn yu, Miller!" Higgins cursed and his hand jerked at the gun on his hip. With blurring speed the pistol leaped into the cowboy's hand, two shots booming almost as one, followed instantly by a third. Higgins went down without a sound, shot through the breast. In an instant the cowboy realized he had misjudged the little man on his left. His pistol was out in a flash, his shot cracking a fraction of a second before the young cowboy's. Both took effect. The little man staggered backward, then dropped heavily to the dust of the street, his bullet, however struck the cowboy high on his left shoulder. He felt the shock, but no pain, but then it was as though his legs had lost the strength to hold him up and he fell to one knee, feeling the hot blood running down his chest beneath his shirt. With great effort the young cowboy stood. His piercing blue eyes raked the crowd that had gathered, gun held low as though daring anyone to step forward. He backed away a pace, glanced over his shoulder apparently seeking his horse. The loud boom of pistols had spooked the animal and it had retreated several feet down the street dragging its bridle. The cowboy seemed to weigh in his mind his next move, measuring the distance to where the horse stood as a strange lightheadedness swept over him.

A boy of perhaps eight or nine abruptly pushed his way through the crowd.

"Jeffery Daniel," a woman cried, "you come back here!"

But little Jeffery either didn't hear or chose to ignore the shouted command, and rushed forward and caught up the reins of the horse, leading it up to the cowboy.

"Here you are, mister," the boy said, staring wide-eyed up at the man his gaze fixed on the red stain seeping through his shirt.

"Thanks, young feller," the cowboy said slowly, giving the boy a crooked smile, which brought a bright prideful flush to the youngster's face.

Slowly holstering his gun, the cowboy stepped into the saddle, and wheeling the horse about, he shot another piercing look out over the crowd, his eyes coming to rest on the tall slender lawman, Hank Miller.

"Sorry, Sheriff, but I reckon I can't stick around," he declared, then touched spurs to the animal sending it bounding down the street amid the subdued murmuring of the crowd.

Below him spread a checkerboard of grass and cedar dotted with gray limestone cliffs fringed with pine angling up with striking boldness into a vast league of black timber. Without bidding the horse had come to a halt, its rider leaning far over the saddle, hand to his bloodstained shirt.

"Well, Sparky, old son, I don't reckon—I can go on—much farther," he muttered through clinched teeth, addressing the tall powerfully-built sorrel.

The day before, he had come upon a long deserted cabin in a little valley. One side of the roof had fallen in, and the outside chimney of yellow stone had partly crumbled away. There he had spent the night and, as he had on the previous two days, he again attempted to treat and bandage his wound, but he hadn't much success given that the heavy forty-five slug had passed clean through his body, just missing, he suspected, his lung. He had concluded that when he found he could breathe without difficulty and had not spit up any blood. But it was the bloody exit wound on his back that he could not easily reach and he was certain it had begun to fester.

Taking the gunshot had spoiled his plans somewhat. He had figured on riding clean away, but that didn't seem possible any longer.

"Well, at least," he smiled grimly, fighting off another wave of dizziness; "Higgins won't ever set foot on the Circle C Ranch."

Facing up to Higgins had been the only way, he rationalized. He could see no other path to justice. He was some aggravated though that Bull Burton hadn't been with Higgins. He would have liked to have settled his hash along with the crooked cattleman. But, with Higgins dead, Burton didn't matter much anymore. Higgins was the one with the money and the brains behind that scheme. Sure, he reckoned, he was an outlaw now; there would be a warrant out for him, but Rick Childers and his pretty new wife would keep their home; he sighed, and was glad, secure in his deliberate and reckless sacrifice.

"Come on, Sparky," he called weakly to the horse, "Get a move on, boy."

The horse, scenting water, started off down the gradual incline toward the creek winding like a broken ribbon, bright here and dark there as it made its way through a rocky gorge to the west. This was wild and beautiful country, this northern New Mexico, but at the moment the feverish young cowboy was insensible to its grandeur.

Wyoming McCord opened his eyes. For a long moment he had no sense of where he was. Slowly he let his head loll to the side, aware now of the pain, a burning in his shoulder. He soon realized that he was in a small dusky-looking room lying on his back upon a narrow bunk. Only feet away was a window through which he could see clouds gloriously white against the deep blue, swelling, darkening, sky.

"You are awake, *Señor*?" spoke a voice thickly accented in Spanish, from somewhere behind him and slowly a head with cavernous eyes, supernaturally bright came into view.

"Who are you, and where—am I?"

"You are at my *casa Señor*. My name is Eduardo Dominguez. You are very sick, *Señor*, from the gunshot," the man said. "I have bandaged the wound. You must rest."

"Water," Wyoming mumbled, licking dry lips.

"Here, *Señor*," the Mexican said placing a metal cup to his lips. The water was cold and pure. He drank thirstily and then closed his eyes and slept.

When he woke he saw that it was nearly dark and he felt hot and flushed. A candle burned on the small table next to his bed casting a pale yellow light. He let his eyes move about the shadowy room. Draped over a chair in the far corner was his shirt and jeans. His boots sat beside the chair and over the back of one side hung his gun belt, and over the other his dusty sombrero. Against the wall to his right was a washstand containing an oven-baked clay washbasin and pitcher. Above it hung a cracked and cloudy mirror in a scuffed wood frame. On the floor in the other corner was his saddle and bridle. His bedroll and pack was still tied behind the cantle of the saddle. The room was otherwise empty of furnishings. The only other adornment was a crucifix hanging on the adobe wall facing the foot of his bunk and in the wavering candle light the image on the cross appeared to move and quiver as though writhing in anguish. He stared at it for a long moment seemingly mesmerized, before glancing away. He listened for sounds and heard faint voices. Shortly, the man Dominguez appeared in the doorway.

"How do you feel, *Señor*?" he asked coming to stand next to the bed.

"I'm—shore thirsty," Wyoming rasped.

"Here, *Señor*," the man said holding the cup to his lips.

"Thanks," he whispered and closed his eyes.

Wyoming woke often during the night, his shoulder throbbing, his lips dry and feverish. He managed to reach the cup of water beside a clay pitcher on the table by the bed and drank, after which he lay staring out the window at the black night, the white stars—of these he was aware, but they meant nothing. Gray dawn came, and he finally slept. It was late in the day when he woke, according to the slant of the sunrays, coming through the window next to his bed. He had awakened to less torture. He dozed off and on, only stirring to drink from the cup by his bed, which had been refilled with cold water while he was asleep. Presently Dominguez came into the room. He leaned over the bed and put a rough and callused hand to the wounded man's forehead.

"Your fever is gone, *Señor*," he said. "Are you hungry?"

"Yes," he acknowledged.

"I will have my daughter Carmelita bring you some food," Dominguez said.

He must have dosed off to sleep again for it seemed only a moment before he heard the soft rustle of movement and upon opening his eyes saw a young Mexican girl. She placed a tray on the table beside his bunk from which emanated the savory aroma of coffee and what he later would discover was rice and beans. He managed to raise himself on one elbow as the girl withdrew a step peering silently down at him. She couldn't have been more than sixteen. Her small tan feet were encased in leather sandals and she wore a plain white skirt that reached to just above her ankles, and a like-colored blouse with a wide rounded neck that lay bare her slender throat and tan strong, shapely arms. Her raven hair, though sporting a bright ribbon, hung loose about her shoulders framing a softly rounded face with large dusky-hued eyes surrounded by long dark lashes. The girl was unquestionably pretty, a little dusky-skin beauty with big expressive brown eyes.

"You must be Carmelita," he drawled grinning up at her. "I reckon you caught me flat on my back."

She slowly nodded, gazing down at him with undisguised wide-eyed curiosity. "Who are you, *Señor?*" Her soft voice held only a slight accent.

"I reckon you can just call me Wyoming."

She smiled coyly, hands clasped diffidently behind her back as she considered him. "Do you work for one of the rancheros? I do not think I have seen you before, *Señor...Wyoming.*"

"Nope, I reckon this is all new range for me."

"*Papá* says you could be a bandit. Are you?"

Wyoming, admittedly, was momentarily caught off guard by the girl's cool audacious gaze and bold question.

"Sorry to disappoint you," he drawled, "I'm just a poor grub-line-riding cowpuncher that got myself in the wrong place at the wrong time."

"Hmm," she murmured slyly, staring straight into his eyes, "I don't think so, *Señor*. You wear that big gun on your hip. I think you are a *pistolero*, and you have come here to hide and get well from your wound," she remarked unabashedly and whirling about, flounced from the room.

Left alone he picked up the fork and took a bite of the steaming hot beans. He managed to finish the food on the plate before the pain in his shoulder forced him to lie back down.

"That girl shore got me pegged," he murmured, "And dog-gone if she ain't a little dusky-eyed beauty. I reckon I could shore go for her in a big way."

The thought suddenly occurred to him that the girl's paw might calculate that there was a price on his head and send for the local law thinking to get a reward. He wasn't sure why he felt so, but something made him think not. He closed his eyes and lay there listening to the night come on. The pain in his shoulder had become a dull ache. Faint sounds reached him through the open window. He heard the hum of insects, melodious on the summer air; and, he thought, from far away the shrill yelp of a coyote.

Had it been only a week ago that he had unceremoniously commemorated his twenty-first birthday? He felt much older. Not even twenty-one and he had killed four men! And one by one in solemn procession the men passed before his memory's eye. He watched them pass by, out of the shadow, it seemed, and he willed them into the past, but he knew it would not be, and a feeling like a sudden cold in his very marrow came stealing over his mind. He pushed away the morbid thoughts, and willed sleep to come.

Wyoming woke to the sounds of voices. They came clear and distinct from below the window only feet away. He didn't know how long he had been asleep, but realized that it must not have been very long.

"Aw, what's with yu tonight, Carmelita? Yu shore air being stingy with yore kisses. Don't yu love me no more?" pleaded a young male voice.

Carmelita made no reply, at least none that Wyoming could hear, but there followed the soft shuffling sound of movement, which lasted several minutes.

"There, that's shore's more like it," panted the same voice, husky with passion. "Come away with me Carmelita, darlin'. Just say the word and I'll carry yu off tonight. We could be married over at Pojoaque in the mornin'."

"There is no priest in Pojoaque," came Carmelita's soft voice.

"Wal, we can ride inte Santa Fe. It's not even a half day's ride."

Carmelita's soft whispered response was too low to make out. It must not have been to the liking of her impassioned lover, however.

"Aw, sweetheart, why not? Yu know I love yu!—Say, who's there?"

"Don't get all riled, kid! It's me, Bard."

"What the hell! What're yu doin' here?"

"Jackson said yu'd rode out te see yore little *Señorita* so I come lookin' fer yu. I've got te talk te yu, kid."

"Couldn't it wait? Yu can see I'm a mite occupied."

"Shore, I can see that, but this is sumthin' important. Send the girl inside."

"Aw, hell," came the man's frustrated sigh after a long moment. Wyoming heard the swift rustle of movement as apparently Carmelita strutted away in obvious vexation.

"This had better be good, Bard!"

"I got a business deal fer yu, kid."

"Aw, is that all! Yu came out here jest te tell me that!"

"Hell yeah! This job's a honey. We stand te make a real fortune on this one."

"Oh, yeah? What's the deal?" came the kid's voice, a little more receptive now.

"The boss turned me on te this deal. Seems there's a newcomer te the range, over to Santa Fe. A greenhorn. Name's Dixon. Jest arrived there a week or two ago. Come from over'n Louis'ana somewheres. He's come te New Mexico fer his health. He's well heeled though and the boss has struck up a deal te sell the *Los Alamos* spread to him, lock stock and barrel."

"*Los Alamos*! Hell, that's more'n a day's ride from here!"

"Shore, but this here deal is worth it."

"It ain't if I got te be away from my little *Señorita* sweetheart—"

"Wal, yu damn shore can't take her with yu. The boss won't hear of it. But shore enough, when yu get back with yur pockets full of greenbacks, that pretty little *Señorita* will shore fall all over yu."

"Ah-huh," breathed the kid, "keep talkin'."

"Wal, the boss is shore slick. This Dixon has agreed te buy everythin', all twenty-thousand head, ranch house and cabins and all—"

"Hell, Hobard, that's old Erickson's place and I shore didn't know he had twenty-thousand head. I figure more like ten, maybe twelve thousand," interjected the kid.

"Shore, me and yu know thet, but thet greenhorn don't. Thet's the beauty of this deal. This Dixon forks out the cash fer ten thousand head of stock thet he ain't got…and then we rustle what's left. Haw! Haw! And thet's where you come in, kid, doin' a little brand burnin'. The boss has buyers south so there'll be some long drives if yu're up te it. What with beef sellin' at more'n twelve a head, we'll shore make a killin.' Are yu in?"

"I reckon, yu can count me in. But I shore don't cotton leavin' my sweetheart fer that long."

"Don't yu fret kid. I'll shore keep her company while yur gone. Haw! Haw!"

"The hell yu say, Hobard!" came the kid's angry retort.

"Jest spoofin' yu kid. She ain't my kind."

There followed the clink of spurs moving away and then all was quiet. Wyoming lay there thinking over what he had just heard. Whoever this fool tenderfoot Dixon was, he was in for a raw deal, and was going to be stole blind. Well, it wasn't any concern of his, he told himself as he gingerly rubbed his sore shoulder. He had gotten himself in enough trouble by getting caught up in other people's business. He ought to know enough to mind his own by now. He closed his eyes and tried to go back to sleep. But his mind remained restless, and it was a long while before sleep finally claimed him.

CHAPTER TWO

Wyoming McCord woke stiff and sore. He had apparently lain too long on his injured shoulder during the night and it was paining him. Sounds came in through the window; the crowing of a rooster and from somewhere distant the bleating of sheep. He sat up and slowly swung his feet off the bed. The tile floor was cold beneath his bare feet in contrast to the soft warm breeze that came in through the window. He became suddenly aware of the delicious aroma wafting into the room from somewhere outside. Slowly rotating his shoulder, working out the stiffness, he crossed the floor to where his clothes lay over the chair. His denim overalls and shirt had been washed, though his shirt still bore the small holes made by the bullet that passed through him. He managed to pull on his overalls and boots. He felt in his back pocket for his pocketbook but the pocket was empty. Then he noticed the pocketbook lying on the chair. It had been under his overalls. He opened it to find the cash—two hundred sixty-five dollars, still there.

"Buenos dias, Señor Wyoming."

Wyoming jerked his head around. He hadn't heard Carmelita's footsteps. He quickly slid the pocketbook into the pocket of his overalls. Carmelita carried a clay water pitcher in her hands and over one arm hung a bright yellow towel.

"Mornin' Carmelita," Wyoming returned.

"Your wound, it is much better this morning, *Señor Wyoming?*" she asked, her dusky eyes staring brazenly at his naked torso.

"It shore feels lots better," he gulped struggling to pull on his shirt.

"I have brought you water and soap and a clean drying cloth," she said, "so you can wash."

He turned to find her nearly brushing up against him, her saucy little mouth inches from his.

"Would you like me to help you?" she asked, with more than a little hint of mischief in her dark eyes.

"Much obliged," he mumbled taking the pitcher and cloth from her, and retreating a step. "But I reckon I can manage."

"If you say so, *Señor.* Are you hungry? *Mamá* has food prepared."

"Dog-gone, I shore am. I'll be there soon as I clean up."

At that moment Dominguez appeared in the doorway and said something to the girl in Spanish. She arched her chin sullenly and marched from the room with a swish of her skirt. Wyoming let out his breath. The girl was a disturbing presence. He found a sliver of soap next to the washbasin and sat about washing. In his pack he retrieved his razor and lathering his cheeks shaved off nearly a week's growth of whiskers. Rinsing, he peered with dubious satisfaction at the youthful, shiny-cheeked face in the mirror.

"Reckon that will have to do," he muttered, ignoring the dull ache high on his shoulder as he dried himself with the cloth the girl had left. It held the clean wild scent of sage.

He took another hard look at his image, before trailing a soft jingle of spurs, he stepped outside onto a dirt patio smooth and hard-packed, enclosed on three sides by adobe walls, which was apparently part of the house. A porch, supported by peeled cedar posts, extended a dozen feet out from the buildings, giving partial shade to the patio. On the fourth side, which faced east, was a wide, open gateway. Chickens puttered about in the dirt and a black and white spotted dog lay sleeping in the shade beneath the overhanging roof on the far side of the patio beside an enormous pile of firewood. Doors and square framed windows were set deep into the adobe walls lining each of the rooms. One of the doors to the room on his left stood partially open, apparently to allow the cool morning breeze to enter. Wyoming noticed that the window frames and doors were old and weathered and the adobe bricks worn by wind and rain, were crumbling along the foundation.

He walked to the open gate curious to take in his surroundings, having no memory of arriving at this place. A draw, grass-benched and thicket-sloped, opened before him, to widen and descend to a colorful valley that spread out to merge into purple range. Sheep in large numbers dotted the green expanse at the base of the slope and their bleating drifted dolefully up to him. He was about to turn and retrace his steps when he caught sight of two riders approaching on the narrow dirt lane some distance away. He watched them for a moment, to make certain they were on their way to the house before walking back to the room. He didn't particularly want to meet anyone. Inside the room he buckled on his gun belt and waited. After some time he heard the sound of horse's hoofs stopping near the gate. Wyoming heard voices speaking low, then one of the riders shouted.

"Dominguez. Where are yu?"

Wyoming had heard that raspy voice before, just the other night outside his window.

"*Aqui, Señor*," Dominguez replied and Wyoming heard him come out into the patio.

"Where's thet pretty little *Señorita* of yurn?"

"She is in the *casa, Señor*," Dominguez replied hesitantly.

"Wal, I shore come te pay her a call."

"I am sorry, *Señor*, I do not think she want to see you," Dominguez said.

"Wal, thet's shore too bad," rasped the visitor. "The kid had to leave sort of in a hurry and asked me to give her a message—Wal, now!"

His voice had suddenly broken off, and Wyoming peeked around the side of the doorframe to see the reason. Carmelita had stepped out onto the patio. She came up beside her father, an eager, expectant look on her face. Wyoming turned his attention to the two men who sat astride horses just outside the gate. One nudged his horse into the patio and Wyoming got a better view of him. He doffed his sombrero, exposing a lean head of dark hair streaked with gray, a swarthy face which, but for its curious awe and smile, would have been a portrait of evil. He had brawny shoulders and unkempt hair low on his thick neck. He rode a dark bay as did the other rider, and Wyoming saw that both were armed.

"Howdy, little *Señorita*," he smiled and replaced his sombrero; hiding the telltale ghoulish eyes, but not before Wyoming had caught the hot glint. Carmelita though, didn't appear to sense any peril at the moment.

"I reckon yu recollect me, I'm the kid's friend; name's Bard Hobard."

She nodded, waited expectantly apparently fascinated by the man's mention of a message from her lover.

"Why don't yu and me go off somewheres alone so as we can talk," he said, his voice changing to something intimately personal. The girl caught it and appeared suddenly to realize the actuality of his lewd gaze. She glanced uncertainly at her father. He spoke to her sternly in Spanish and she slowly backed away toward the house. Hobard leaned back in his saddle, shrewdly recognizing the subtle change in the girl. He spurred his horse, blocking Carmelita's retreat.

"Say, Dominguez, where'd yu get thet fine lookin' sorrel out yonder in the corral?"

"He belong to a friend, *Señor*," Dominguez said slowly.

"Hah! I reckon yu stole thet hawse!"

"No, *Señor*. I take care of it for a friend," Dominguez insisted. Wyoming could sense the new level of alarm that now edged his voice.

"Billy, go rope thet sorrel and bring him up here," the brawny-shouldered man ordered his companion. "Dominguez, yu know what happens to hawse thieves on this range."

"I no steal the horse," Dominguez denied nervously.

Hobard leaned forward suddenly and seized Carmelita's arm and with seemingly little effort drug her up upon his hip.

"*Papá!*" she cried, struggling frantically. The horse began to prance sideways.

"Haw! Haw! Little *Señorita*, yu're too fine a looker to waste yur time on thet wet-faced kid," Hobard panted, reining the horse around. "Come on. We're goin' fer a little ride."

"Stop!" Wyoming shouted, stepping out onto the patio. The piercing command halted Hobard.

"Wal! Who'n the hell's thet?" rasped Hobard, addressing his companion, his swarthy face burning red.

"Let her go," Wyoming commanded moving out from under the porch, but still remaining in its shade.

"Wh-what?" stammered Hobard. The man was at a great disadvantage in trying to hold the struggling Carmelita and keep rein of his skittish horse, and go for his gun, and that fact was plain on his face.

"You heard me!" Wyoming said, and his lithe form sank perceptibly, but even more significant was the quivering hand that lowered demonstrably over the big blue ivory-handled Colt sheathed low on his hip.

Hobard lowered Carmelita to the ground and she quickly retreated to the door of the house where she stood shaking, trembling hands clinging to the doorframe, her dusky face white.

"I don't know who yu are Mister, but yu picked the wrong *hombre* to buck, and over a little black-eyed Mexican hussy." He drew a long deep breath that whistled with the intake. Then arm and voice leaped simultaneously. "Billy! Bore him!" And his hand slapped at the gun on his hip.

In a flash Wyoming's gun was out and spouting red behind a cloud of smoke. Hobard's gun was only half out of his holster when he sagged in the saddle. His horse lunged away to unseat him and throw him heavily to the packed dirt of the patio. Wyoming stepped to the side, his gun now trained on Hobard's companion who was struggling to control his horse. The rider made no effort to draw his pistol. White-faced he held up his hand, open-palmed as with the other he pulled his mount to a standstill.

"Hey, Mister," he said hoarsely, his pale face beaded with sweat. "This was all Hobard's doin'. I got no part in it."

"What's your name?" Wyoming queried.

"Hicks, Billy Hicks."

"Well, Billy Hicks, you pile this stiff on his horse and ride out of here, *Pronto*," Wyoming said. "And if I see you back here, you had better have your gun out. Savvy?"

"Yep, I shore savvy," he choked.

Moments later, Hobard's body slung over his saddle, Hicks spurred off down the lane, the horse with its gruesome cargo in tow. Wyoming followed him out through the gate. He stood watching Hicks depart as he fought down the cold feeling that always came after he had used the big blue-steel Colt. Slowly, deliberately, he ejected the empty casing and reloaded. He took a deep breath and turned then and retraced his steps back into the patio. Dominguez was waiting for him, sombrero in hand.

"Thank you, *Señor*," he said feelingly.

"No thanks necessary, friend," Wyoming grunted, "If I hadn't come here and had you not helped me there'd have been no trouble."

"No, *Señor*, this Hobard, he is a bad man," Dominguez asserted, "He would have carried my Carmelita off. He want to scare me, to say I am a horse thief."

"Ah-huh," Wyoming nodded. The man was probably right, he decided. "This Hobard may have friends, and they may come back. There could be more trouble for you after I ride out."

"Do not worry, *Señor*. I will be ready for them. This is not first time they try scare me. They do not like me have sheep," he said. "Come, the *Señora* has prepared food for you."

Wyoming followed him into the house. Carmelita was busy placing cups and plates on the small wood table. She peered up at Wyoming, her big dark eyes strangely bright. Standing before the large cooking stove was an older woman. She was heating flour tortillas over the *comal*. The heat from the fire made the room clammy. The woman, whom Wyoming speculated was Carmelita's mother and Dominguez' wife, smiled shyly at him as she continued with her task.

"Sit down, *Señor*," Dominguez said eagerly, pointing to a worn cane-bottom chair.

Wyoming looked about and seeing several wood pegs embedded in the adobe wall by the door about head high, hung his sombrero on one of them. He took the seat Dominguez indicated. Dominguez sat down across the table from him and shortly Carmelita placed a plate of food before each of them. Her eyes boldly met Wyoming's as she did so. Wyoming was hungry and the spicy *guisado* dish, though it made his eyes water, was nonetheless delicious. Cleaning his plate, Wyoming peered up at Carmelita's mother.

"Thank you, ma'am," he said, "that shore was good."

She smiled though she obviously did not understand and glanced questioningly at her daughter.

"*Mamá* does not speak English," Carmelita explained and proceeded to translate Wyoming's words. At this the woman beamed.

"Dominguez, I shore do owe you for your kindness," Wyoming said taking his sombrero from the peg. "Maybe someday I can repay you."

"No, *Señor*, it is I who am grateful," he replied glancing at Carmelita.

"Well, then, I reckon I better ride out."

Wyoming stepped outside onto the patio and Dominguez followed him. He offered Wyoming his hand.

"May God go with you, *Señor*," he said. "I will go bring your horse." And he started off for the corral.

Wyoming walked into the little side room where he had slept, and reached for his saddle. A shadow filled the doorway and he turned to see Carmelita.

"Where will you go, *Señor Wyoming*?" she asked softly leaning against the doorframe, hands clasped behind her back as she peered at him.

He shrugged. "Arizona most likely," he replied easily.

"Will you ever come back?"

"*Quien sabe*?" he shrugged.

"I—I will always remember you…for saving me from that—" She swallowed, not finishing.

"Don't mention it, Carmelita. It will only distress you more."

"To say thank you, is—is so small—" she murmured, and her eyes of velvet blackness, shinning like midnight gulfs, fixed upon him.

"Well, Carmelita," he drawled refusing to be drawn in by those eyes. "I'll tell you how you can thank me…make me a promise."

"A promise?" she whispered.

"Yep. Find yourself a good honest fellow, and chuck that rustler hombre who's been calling on you. You deserve better than that."

Her big brown eyes dilated in surprise. "You—heard!"

"Well, I reckon so. I couldn't help it. You were setting right under the window there," he grinned. "And I shore heard enough to be acquainted with what kind of hombre he is."

She bowed her head, shoulders slumping dejectedly. "I know. I heard also this plan. I did not go in the house when Jimmy says. I wait in the patio and listen."

"What's Jimmy's full name?"

"It is Anderson."

"Promise me you'll have no more to do with this Jimmy Anderson."

"I—promise," she replied tremulously.

"Shake on it," he said reaching out his hand.

She sprang away from the door, but instead of taking his hand, she threw her arms about his neck and kissed him soundly upon his lips, a long, lingering kiss, and then she whirled and fled out the door.

CHAPTER THREE

W yoming turned eastward following the road for a short distance, but decided he would be better off on a lesser used path and so turned off the road upon coming to what looked like a passable trail, though dark and overgrown, proceeding in the same general direction. He kept to a trot on level ground and a walk over rough places and upgrades.

It was a big country, exceedingly wild and rough. He climbed a ridge and kept to its summit for most of the morning. He took his time, not pushing it. He saw cattle everywhere, though not in large herds. In the gray of twilight he descended the pine and spruce-timbered slope to enter a gully where water ran over rocks. It was a beautiful white-grassed park, fringed by forest. Peering about the place he decided to camp here for the night. Hunger made him more than usually keen-eyed with the result that he soon espied a rabbit. It ran off a few rods and then stopped and squatted. Wyoming shot it through the head. He skinned and dressed the cottontail and returning to his campsite, built a small fire over which he broiled the rabbit to a nice brown. A touch of salt made it a toothsome meal. The moon rose and cast deep shadows along the forest floor as he rolled a cigarette lighting the smoke with a twig from the fire. Finishing the cigarette, he dragged saddle, blankets and slicker under a thick bushy cedar, and made his bed there. The next morning he was up and after a breakfast of cold beans was once again on the trail.

It was late afternoon. Wyoming let Sparky pick his way along the rocky course of the rapidly moving stream. Mounting a slope beneath the tall pines, he reined to a halt and dismounted. The loneliness and silence of the forest was comforting. He heard the shrill call of a blue jay.

"Well, Sparky, here's where we stop," he drawled as he removed the saddle. "There's plenty of grass for you, so I don't reckon you'll wander off."

From his vantage point on the high slope Wyoming looked out upon the gray-sloped snow-capped mountains to the east. Pure and white, remote and insurmountable, rose the glistening peaks high into the blue sky. A vague, sweet, intangible feeling of familiarity smote him. How they reminded him of the Grand Tetons, lonely, wild and grand. He stood for a long moment deep in thought as twilights shadow closed about him. Shaking his head he set about starting a fire and breaking out a can of beans from his saddlebags, he cut open the can with his jackknife and pouring the contents into a small pan, placed it over the coals. As the beans heated he peered in his saddlebags.

"Two more cans of beans and a can of peaches," he soliloquized thoughtfully. "That should last me until I get through the pass into the high plains. I reckon I'll stop in Santa Fe for some supplies. It's a bit out of my way, but I can't count on always finding game."

Hunger satisfied, Wyoming unrolled his bedroll under a tall pine where the needles were thick and stretched out. Long after dark, Wyoming lay there thinking. He thought of dusky-eyed Carmelita and the long lingering kiss she had planted on his lips, and the feel of her warm body pressing against his. He could have stayed; he knew, but that old longing that had first called him as a youngster of fourteen still tugged at him. Besides, he could never have lasted as a sheepherder. Still, he sighed, taking a deep breath remembering Carmelita's rich black hair and dark, turbulent eyes, and the feel of her soft curves—.

"Aw, hell!" he muttered, pushing the image from his mind.

He had been making his way on his own since his mother died, going from one grubstake to another. He vaguely remembered his father. He died when Wyoming was four, a weak and unhealthy man never having recovered from the horrible treatment he endured in a Rebel prison camp during the late War of the Rebellion. He had a clear memory of his older sister, Abbey, of bright golden hair and eyes shadowed in purple. But she had married young; to a man named Johnson when he was ten and departed for someplace back east. He hadn't seen her since. His first real job was wrangling horses for the "Split T" up in northern Wyoming. It was there he earned a reputation with the blue-steel Colt .45 he carried low on his right hip, and he had killed his first man. It was a fair fight, but it had left him feeling cold all over, and had set him once again to drifting, finally taking a job with the Circle C. The job came easy, for Childers had been hard up for riders, but Wyoming soon discovered few stuck around long. The hours were long, but that wasn't unusual. Rick Childers just couldn't afford to pay what the other ranchers did. Wyoming had stayed on though despite the poor wages. He had stuck with Childers because of…Peggy Hart. He fancied himself in love with her; no matter she was engaged to Childers. Until, that is, he came to realize her love for Childers was true and genuine and there was no place for Wyoming McCord in her heart. Besides, he had nothing of his own but his horse and tack, and the gun he wore low down on his right hip. Oh, perhaps, in a way, she was attracted to him first off, he guessed, but never like a sweetheart; fascinated was more like it, by his cool devil-may-care manner. It was Rick Childers, to whom she truly loved, and knowing that, he had made the choice to ride away, but only after taking the only action he knew to save the two young lovers and the ranch they both cherished.

His mind suddenly went back to the conversation he had with Carmelita the day he rode away, and the promise she made. He hoped she would keep that promise and find a good hard-working honest fellow. That brought his thoughts to Hobard and the cowboy Jimmy. With Hobard dead would that affect their plans to rustle that greenhorn rancher Dixon they spoke about that night under his window? According to the plan Hobard laid out, Jimmy was to get hired on as one of Dixon's riders and then when the time came, betray the outfit. What a sorry mess! He turned over on his side and closed his eyes.

When Wyoming woke the sun was just topping the mountain ridge. He had slept late. He rolled out of his blankets and slipping on his boots, set about building a fire, after which he strolled down the incline toward the creek carrying a small smoke-blackened tin coffee pot. He knelt and scooped up a handful of the cool water, drinking it down. He filled the coffee pot with water and walked back up the slope to his campsite beneath the tall pines and placed the pot on the fire for the water to boil. From his vantage point on the high slope he peered out across the valley below. Santa Fe lay in that direction. Finishing breakfast he washed out the utensils and stored them in his saddle bags after which he saddled the sorrel and started off.

About mid-afternoon, after zigzagging up the steep trail, soft and full of rocks he came out on top of the rim and peered down at a narrow valley and the town of Santa Fe. Beyond lay the purple broken highlands of rock and gorge and forest, and above these rose the black mountains with wave on wave of great rounded peaks illuminated against the blue sky. The scene caused Wyoming to draw a deep breath.

Riding into the town, he crossed over the railroad tracks past the vacant station platform and stockyard pins. People were strolling up and down the sidewalks and narrow streets, sauntering in and out of stores and businesses. He pulled his sombrero low on his forehead, his sharp eyes taking in his surroundings as though he expected to see someone he knew, or, more likely, someone who might recognize him. He decided to get something to eat and then find a hotel room or a boarding house, if that is, there was a vacant room to be found anywhere in town judging from the number of people on the streets.

He had two hundred sixty-five dollars in hard cash, enough he figured to last until he got to Arizona and located a job.

Entering San Francisco Street, he drew to a halt. A large banner was strung between a telegraph pole and the top railing of a rambling adobe structure on the other side of the street fronted by colonnades. The banner proclaimed: **County Fair and Rodeo ~ July 1ˢᵗ Thru July 4ᵗʰ** in big bold red letters, which, he decided, accounted for the increased populace. On both sides of San Francisco Street stood frame and adobe brick buildings. Across the plaza was a single story adobe structure whose long sign across the front proclaimed it the *Exchange Hotel*. Next to the hotel separated by a narrow street was a grocery store. The circular sign on the front of the store read: *Seligman Brothers; Established 1856*. Cattycorner across the street from the hotel was a saloon. Several saddle horses were hitched to the rail in front of the saloon. Buckboards and wagons and black-roofed buggies crowded the narrow street. At the end of the street was an impressive brown sandstone church bearing two tall steeples, which towered over the adjacent buildings. The peeling of bells sounded from the church.

He decided he had better secure a room in the hotel first off. Then he would find a place to eat. His stomach was growling so he thought it could be heard a block away. He rode back down the street to the hotel where he stepped from the saddle and made his way into the building. The lobby was crowded and noisy. Apparently the clerk was accustomed to trail-worn riders and gave Wyoming only a passing glance when he stepped up to the check-in counter though Wyoming could feel other, not so tolerant eyes, upon him. After securing a room he went in search of something to eat. Mounting Sparky he crossed the street and rode down one block to a small café. The place was not large or fancy, but it appeared clean. Tables were arranged against the wall in front of the large front window, and along the center between the window and the eating counter. The café was crowded with customers but he found a place at the counter and pushed his sombrero back off his forehead. Shortly a girl about eighteen approached. She had a ready smile, cheeks bright with color.

"What'll you have, cowboy?" she asked.

"Say, could you rustle up a steak about two inches thick, cooked well, four eggs, sunny side up, some hash browns, and a mug of black coffee?" he replied.

"Coming right up cowboy," she acknowledged and flounced off with an exaggerated swish of her ample hips.

Waiting for his food to come he glanced curiously around the café noticing a couple perhaps in their fifties seated at a table near the window. It was their dress that caught his attention. The woman, handsome for her age, was stylishly clad in an elegant blue dress and the gentleman in a fashionable dark suit. He sported a thick salt and pepper mustache that curled to a sharp point at both ends. Seated next to the woman was a girl of perhaps nine.

"Oh, Henry, I wish you wouldn't go to that gambling place," the woman exclaimed. "That's how all our troubles began—"

"Don't fret so. I've learned my lesson."

"But, dear, you've said that before," she replied plaintively.

"This time I mean it," he insisted.

"Besides, the smoke there, it's bad for you," she continued as though his words carried little weight. "You know the doctor has cautioned to avoid such places."

"I'll only stay a short while," the man insisted. "You know I'm supposed to meet Mr. Hester at six. I'll join you and the girls in our room after that," the man replied, patting her hand. His deep southern accent lacked the sweet-voiced softness of his wife's though it seemed to fit well his refined dress and manner.

Shortly the three departed the café, and moments later his food came and he ate slowly savoring the steak topping it off with a thick slice of apple pie and two cups of coffee.

"Will you be visiting our fair and *rodeo*?" the waitress asked when she brought his check.

"I saw the sign. What's today's date anyhow?" Wyoming asked.

"Today's the 3rd. Fair started already. But there's a big dance tomorrow night the last day of the *rodeo*. Be lots of girls in town for that," she winked knowingly.

"Well, I just might hang around at that," he drawled, trying to remember the last time he was at a dance. He supposed it was two summers ago at the Casper, Wyoming *rodeo*.

Wyoming walked outside feeling good about himself, until he glanced down at his worn clothes and was reminded that he should find a store and buy a new outfit since he figured on attending the rodeo and maybe looking in on the dance. He could spare that much cash. But the day was still young and he decided to take a walk and do a little sightseeing. He strolled west along the street his spurs jingling musically on the board sidewalk. Two blocks over from the plaza he came upon a gambling establishment. Vivid purple letters on the large sign across the front read, *The Monte*. Sounds from inside caught his ear, and struck with curiosity, he entered the large smoky room. Plush carpets covered the floor and elaborate-framed mirrors adorned the walls reflecting the brilliant light of two large candle-lit chandeliers. A number of well-spaced tables were occupied by cigar-puffing gentlemen in dark attire. He hadn't indulged himself in a game of poker in a long time and weighed sitting in on a game, but instead found himself meandering around the room taking in the sights. He paused to watch the faro game and the roulette wheel before coming to a table surrounded by several lookers-on, which usually pointed to a high-stakes game. Peering curiously over their shoulders he espied the southern gentleman he had seen in the little café earlier. His coat was unbuttoned and his cravat hung loose about his throat. Sweat beaded his forehead. It was quickly apparent to Wyoming that lady luck was not favoring him. Only a small stack of chips was in front of him. Across the table from him sat a shallow-faced man in a frockcoat that typified the professional gambler. The man had long slim white hands, flexible, and they manipulated the cards marvelously. Yet when he dealt them out he was very slow and deliberate, as if to show his fellow players that his deal was open and fair. Wyoming began to watch the man's hands intently certain he had glimpsed a furtive exchange but it was so slight and rapid that he wasn't positive. The game seesawed back and forth with the southerner's stack of chips growing smaller.

"Well, suh," the southerner said, taking a deep nervous breath, eyes upon the large stack of chips in front of the gambler. "I'm afraid you're into me for slightly over a thousand. It's time I fold."

"How about one more hand, Dixon," the gambler said smoothly, "you still have chips on the table. Maybe your luck will change."

Wyoming peered with greater interest at the southerner. The gambler had called him *Dixon.* The name caught his attention and his mind flashed back to the conversation he had overheard outside the bedroom window at Carmelita's. 'I'll bet a dollar to a do-nut,' Wyoming breathed, 'this here distinguished looking gentleman is the greenhorn rancher I overheard Hobard talking about. He shore looks the part. Hmm…what do you know?'

"Well, I'm out near that much, but I reckon I'll stay a few more hands," said one of the others, and Wyoming saw a man of sturdy build, in the plain garb of an everyday cattleman. He might have been forty years old. Handsome in a bold way, he had a smooth hard face, square chin, large lips and piercing gray eyes. In a flash Wyoming recognized the cattleman—Hank Ward. It had been two summers ago Wyoming remembered. Ward's absorption at the moment centered on the cards being dealt, but seeming to feel the impact of Wyoming's eyes glanced up. His eyes lit up with immediate recognition, but Wyoming gave him a warning look and an almost imperceptible shake of his head.

"Say," Wyoming interjected, "might a feller set in on this hyar game?"

The gambler glanced up at Wyoming and after a quick assessing glance returned his attention to his cards.

"Sorry cowboy, this game has too high stakes for the like of you," he sneered.

Affecting the guise of one having a little too much to drink, Wyoming pulled out wad of greenbacks from his pocket.

"Wal, dang; this hyar is shore burnin' a hole in my pocket,' he drawled good-naturedly making a show of counting the bills.

The gambler's eyes flickered to the wad of money and Wyoming saw the swift greedy gleam in his eyes before they became hooded once more.

"Well, I hate to take your money cowboy...but if you insist," he smiled amiably. "Any objections gentlemen?" he asked glancing about the table.

"Grab a chair cowboy," Ward said nodding to the empty seat across from him.

A bit boss appeared at the table as though by magic and Wyoming exchanged his ready cash, nearly two hundred dollars for chips.

Sure enough Dixon won the next hand, which brought a jubilant smile to his lips. Wyoming was certain now of what he saw. The gambler was slick, but Wyoming's keen eyes had spotted his sleight of hand. The game seesawed back and forth with Wyoming winning his share and the chips next to him grew. The next deal was the gambler's and the southerner opened the jack-pot, the cattleman Ward raised before the draw as did Wyoming giving the appearance of a pigeon over-confident in his luck. Presently they were all in, which made a high-stakes jackpot of several thousand dollars. Under the hooded gaze of one seemingly inebriated Wyoming's eyes missed nothing, however. Each player called for the cards he wanted.

"Three for myself—to this little pair," the gambler said casually, and he slid the three cards upon the table and laid the deck aside.

Suddenly, like a panther, Wyoming leaped. His left hand crashed down on the gamblers, crushing it flat on the table.

"What the hell!" exclaimed the gambler, but his face turned a greenish livid hue. He had been trapped and that fact was plain on his face.

"Gentlemen, look here," Wyoming said bitingly, no longer the easy-going drunk, and he turned over the gambler's hand. Bent and doubled in his palm were three cards that dropped out. All aces!

"I'll be damn!" exclaimed Ward.

The gambler rose quickly to his feet, jerking his hand free of Wyoming's grip.

"Let go of me you damn heathen cowboy," he snarled, yielding to a passion that perhaps did not rightly interpret the gravity of the situation. With deliberate action his right hand went inside his coat pocket.

"Look out!" Ward warned and the occupants around the table quickly sheered to either side of Wyoming.

"Don't draw, gambler!" Wyoming hissed and even as his voice rang out his own gun leaped into his hand with blurring speed, leveled low.

The maddened gambler stiffened.

"Let go…bring your hand out slow," Wyoming ordered.

The gambler complied; face suddenly ashen, hand and jaw quivering.

"Yu lily-livered cheat!" Ward cursed, "We ought te string yu up right here and now. Get out of town *pronto* before we show yu what we do hereabouts te crooked gamblers!"

The gambler whirled on his chair, knocking it to the floor, and he rushed through the crowded room and out through the velvet-lined doorway.

"Gentlemen, I apologize for breaking up your game," Wyoming said holstering his gun.

"Wyoming McCord!" exclaimed the cattleman reaching out his hand. "Where'd yu come from?"

"Just rode in this mornin'." Wyoming replied as he clasped the man's outstretched hand.

"Wal, wal," went on Ward, eying the young cowboy up and down. "Yu look a mite peeked an' drawn."

Well, Mr. Ward, I reckon I had to do a little ridin'—for my health," Wyoming said with a lazy, cool, little smile.

"Ah-huh," Ward nodded meaningfully. "Wal, it shore is good te see yu."

He turned then to the pale southerner. "Dixon, this hyar is Wyoming McCord. He saved my bacon once—what's it been, son, two summers ago?"

Wyoming nodded. "Something like that."

"...and damn if he ain't at it again. Wyoming, this hyar is Mr. Dixon, hails from o'er Louis'ana. Come west fer his health."

"Henry Dixon," the man said, offering his hand. "I'm sure much obliged, son. At least now I won't have to explain to my wife how I lost all my cash," he chuckled sheepishly.

"I had a hunch about that two-bit gambler," Ward said, "but was never quick enough to catch him." He looked around the table. "Suppose we divide what's on the table an' call it quits," he said to Wyoming and Dixon.

"Agreed," replied Dixon, and Wyoming nodded.

"Gosh dang, it shore is good te see yu," Ward said as his keen eyes took in Wyoming, moving over his dusty and worn clothes hesitating at the ivory-handled Colt low on Wyoming's hip before again meeting his eye. "Say, yu lookin' fer a job?"

"Thanks, Mr. Ward, but I reckon I'll be hitting the trail in a day or two."

"Hmm," the rancher nodded knowingly.

"Gentlemen, if you'll excuse me," Dixon interjected adjusting his cravat and buttoning his vest, "I have an appointment. Thank you again, young man," he said, reaching once more to shake Wyoming's hand.

"Think nothing of it Mr. Dixon."

"Ah, well. Of course," he said hastily and with a formal nod of his head turned and gathered up his portion of the jackpot. Wyoming took his share that Ward handed to him without counting it as he watched Dixon depart to exchange the chips back into cash.

"Dixon thar, just bought a big spread south of here. Don't know the first thing about ranchin' though. Like I said, he came from Louis'ana 'bout a month ago. Sumthin' te do with his health; needin' a high dry climate. He's a fast stepper though. First off on arrival he struck up a deal with Hester—bought a place south of here called, *Los Alamos.*"

"Hester?"

"Ed Hester. Fact is I can't say I hold much regard fer Hester. He's been in a few shady deals, over the last of which he killed a man. In fact, he has several killin's to his credit, and at that he's not been many years here in New Mexico. Came on the scene rather sudden like. Says he hails from California. Talk is he ran a big outfit out there. Bought up the old Turkey Track ranch north of here, then last year acquired the *Los Alamos* spread 'bout ten mile south. There's some question as to how he got his hands on the place. Another one of his shady deals, I reckon. Anyways, he sold the ranch te Dixon. It's beautiful country at the foothills of the *Sangre de Cristo* Mountains; fine range, ideal fer cattle, but Dixon's goin' te find a heap less than the twenty-thousand head of stock he thinks he's gettin'. Thet's where the trick of it comes in. It always does where tenderfeet buy western stock. Couldn't be otherwise."

"Ump-umm. Doesn't Dixon have sense enough to see through this Hester fellow?"

"Nope, I reckon not. Hester has a glib tongue thet I reckon were lost on Dixon. Dang-blast-it, if I didn't take a likin' to the man. I shore hate to see him get fleeced, but I reckon there ain't no help fer it. What he needs shore enough is a hard-shootin' range-rider who knows the game. A feller like yurself, Wyoming," he said, almost as an afterthought.

"I reckon I best not stick around," Wyoming said, fastening his deep-blue eyes on the rancher.

"Ah-huh," the rancher nodded shrewdly. He lay a hand fondly on Wyoming's shoulder. "Dang it, son; it shore is good te see yu! Yu shore yu won't take up my job offer?"

Wyoming shook his head. "Thanks, but I reckon I ought to mosey on."

"Wal, son, I've a hunch yu're what this range needs, and in particular Dixon, I shore wish yu'd think it o'er. It might change yur fortune," the rancher said and his gray eyes gave forth a narrow piercing gleam, hard to meet. "Yu need a place te stay?"

"I got a room over to the hotel."

"Good. I'm stayin' the night there myself. What say we meet fer breakfast?"

"Shore, that'd be great."

"Wal, I'll see yu in the mawnin' then," he said, and turned and walked off.

Wyoming watched the hard old rancher make his way between the tables, his words still ringing in his ears.

"I'll be dog-gone," Wyoming muttered under his breath. "That Hester fellow shore must be the gent Hobard called the boss. It all figures." He shook his head cagily. "It shore was good to see Mr. Ward again, but he shore put me on the spot, what with that talk about me being what Dixon, and this range needs." He smiled grimly. "Well, it's too bad. Dixon shore seems like a fine old gentleman, but I reckon I can't make his poor business deal my concern. It's time I looked out for myself and quit poking my nose into other people's troubles. Besides, as it is I reckon I can't stay too long in one place," he shrugged wondering if he was lucky or unlucky. He concluded it was the latter, for wherever he roamed, unfortunate persons and untoward events centered round him.

Turning in his chips Wyoming was startled to discover he was nearly two thousand dollars richer.

"Well, I'll be! Maybe I ought to rethink my luck. I reckon in Arizona I shore can get a new start!"

Wyoming walked outside. It was still daylight and he weaved his way through the numerous pedestrians crowding the sidewalk back up the street to where Sparky was tied at the hitching rail in front of the café and stepped into the saddle. Reining him about he started off down the street lined on each side with vehicles and horses. He drew up before Carter's general store and dismounted. He stepped up on the board sidewalk and pushed open the door, only to collide with a person just exiting whose arms were stacked high with bundles. The impact sent the bundles flying and the possessor of the packages, a girl, staggering backwards uttering a cry of surprise and exasperation. Wyoming stared. The girl was a petite thing, and young, no more than twenty. She wore a stylish little bonnet that matched the charmingly attractive white dress with sleeves that ended with a tiny row of lace just above her elbows. Still, there were contours under the full-skirted dress that betrayed womanhood. All this he saw in a flash before he quickly doffed his sombrero.

"I beg your pardon, Miss," he exclaimed, "That shore was clumsy of me."

She peered at him with grave, fascinated eyes as though she had never seen the like, and he was suddenly quite conscious of his rough appearance. She had a small oval face, and bright golden curls swept up on her head beneath her bonnet revealing tiny rounded ear lobes. With a frustrated glance at the packages strewn across the floor she knelt and began to gather them up. For a moment he could only stare.

Coming out of his trance, he dropped to one knee and quickly went about helping her collect the scattered bundles. He couldn't take his eyes from her as he fumbled to pick up the parcels, noticing that her hands were small, yet they struck him as strong and capable, with the rich healthy tan of someone who enjoyed the out of doors. Without speaking she took the packages from him and gathering the rest in her arms got to her feet. For an instant her gaze met his. He thought her eyes green but he couldn't be sure in the dim light. He only knew that they had struck him forcibly. She was the prettiest girl he had ever seen in his whole life. He felt more than he could explain. His eyes fell to her ruby lips. What would she do if he kissed her? The very idea was madness, but then he was heading out to Arizona tomorrow. He would never see her ever again. And he had never seen a mouth as tempting as hers. So, what if he did…kiss her? Her arms were full of packages she couldn't slap him. Of course, she could always drop the packages…it was worth the risk. He leaned down and covered her mouth with his. She tasted like surprise and peppermint. He expected the surprise, but the shiver running down his spine at the touch of her soft lips to his stunned him. He broke away just as the sound of footsteps behind her reached him. He took a step back.

"Anna, where—oh, there you are. I've been looking all over for you," the interloper called stepping through the wide inner door. She carried several bundles of her own. Her voice was soft and held a pronounced southern accent. She was younger than the girl staring wide-eyed at him, perhaps sixteen. She had the same pretty oval face and golden curls though and Wyoming realized they must be sisters. For a moment her gaze darted from her sister to him.

"Are you ready, Anna?" she asked hesitantly.

"Y-yes. Come along Angie," she said.

She walked to the door where she paused and glanced back over her shoulder at Wyoming expectantly. He quickly opened the door and she and her companion stepped out onto the porch, never having spoken a word to him. Wyoming stared as they turned down the sidewalk, watching the way the older girl's ankle-length skirt swayed with a gentle rhythm as she walked.

"He kissed me," Annabelle said breathlessly not looking at her sister.

"W-what?" Angelique gasped.

"He kissed me! On my lips. Right there in the store."

"Anna! That cowboy?!"

"Who else?" Annabelle hissed. "And don't you dare look back!" she ordered as her younger sister made to turn her head to look behind them.

Angelique giggled.

"It's not funny. Mr. Ward was right. These cowboys are, well, something else," she said.

Angelique didn't think she sounded too angry.

Wyoming leaned back against the doorframe. The girls had to be sisters and both pretty as a picture but the older one…she had dawned upon him like a glorious sunrise but then he gave a senseless shake of his head. He was riding for Arizona tomorrow; besides, he certainly was not in her league. But he couldn't stop thinking of that kiss.

"Dog-gone," he grunted. What had gotten into him? That was the first time he'd ever stolen a kiss from a total stranger. Thankfully he would never see her again. That should have put him at ease, but for some reason it didn't.

Wyoming discovered the store pretentious and well stocked. There were several customers being assisted by the two clerks, and while waiting to be helped Wyoming looked around the large store crowded with merchandise—everything from furniture, clothing, hardware, groceries, saddles and harnesses and farm implements.

Before long one of the clerks approached and Wyoming gave him his order. A half hour later he left the store with several bulky packages and rode back to the hotel where he dropped off the packages in his room and rode to the livery stables where he boarded Sparky, seeing that he was fed and rubbed down. Walking back to the hotel he stopped at a barbershop on the corner of Lincoln Street where he paid for a shave and haircut.

"Dog-gone," he soliloquized upon leaving the barber shop. The image of the girl's big eyes as she had stared at him still haunted him, and again he tried to recall their color. They could have been green but he wasn't certain, only that they were large and dark. And once more a feeling of regret came over him, a mood that did not soon dissipate.

CHAPTER FOUR

W hen Wyoming woke the next morning the sun was shining through the lacy curtains above his head with surprising brightness. The night before he had ordered up a bath and had spent nearly an hour soaking in the tub, falling asleep twice. Clean and smelling of lavender soap he had crawled into bed falling to sleep almost immediately not waking until morning.

Rolling out of bed he peered out the window at the already busy plaza across the street. He pulled on his new overalls and bending over the washbasin, washed sleep from his eyes, and combing his hair, quickly finished dressing. Tying a brand new checkered scarf about his neck, he cast one last glance in the mirror at the tall lithe young man reflected back at him clad in a new plaid long-sleeved shirt and denim overalls; at a sun-bronzed face clean as a babe's, eyes of intense, vivid blue, and dark brown hair neatly trimmed. About his waist however, was buckled a well-used leather belt containing a row of shiny brass cartridges, and holstering an ivory-handled blue-steel Colt slung low on his right hip. New decorated high-heeled, high-top boots that fit his feet snugly completed his outfit. The large rowels of his spurs drug the floor emitting a musical jingle as he walked. He settled his old sombrero on his head and left the room making his way along the hall looking forward to meeting his friend, Hank Ward.

Wyoming entered the lobby and immediately spied Ward standing at the door to the dining room apparently waiting for him to arrive.

"Mawnin', Wyoming," the rancher called, "Wal, now, yu shore cleaned up nice. Yu look rite decent," Ward grinned coming up to him. "Yu mind if we have guests fer breakfast? I kind of invited Dixon and his wife te join us."

"No, I reckon not," Wyoming replied slowly.

Following a step behind the rancher Wyoming spied the southerner Dixon and his wife at the far side of the lobby and he had a suspicion as to what this was all about. No matter, he thought, for he had no intentions of sticking around regardless of what kind of hunch his friend Ward had. Dixon rose from his seat as the two approached.

"Mawnin', Dixon—Ma'am," Ward said, greeting the couple. "Dixon, I reckon yu remember my friend here, Wyoming McCord."

"McCord! Of course. The range rider who did us all the good turn last night. You've changed your appearance some," he said looking Wyoming up and down admiringly. "Mother this is the cowboy I told you about last night."

"I'm shore pleased to meet you, Mrs. Dixon," Wyoming said, taking off his sombrero and bowing gallantly.

"Likewise, Mr. McCord. I'm certainly grateful for what you did, as I know Henry is," she said smiling up at him.

"Shore, it was nothing, ma'am."

"I was told you would say that." She glanced from Wyoming to Mr. Ward. "He's so young," she said, a note of incredulity in her voice.

"Age don't mean a lot here on the range," Ward spoke up.

"I'm beginning to realize that," she replied.

"Have a seat, Wyoming," Ward said indicating a chair across from the Dixons.

Wyoming peered across the space at Ward. He had an uneasy feeling about where this conversation was headed, and reminded himself that as much as he respected and liked the old rancher, he would ride out of here come Monday morning.

"Mr. Ward, Mr. Thomas at the bank said that by all means I could trust you. He sort of implied something shady about my deal with Mr. Hester, though he wouldn't explain," Dixon said. "You know I actually committed to this ranch deal by correspondence. It all appeared to be just what I wanted so I decided to close the deal."

"I told Henry that he should have seen what he bargained for before paying," reproved Mrs. Dixon.

"Well, I knew you womenfolk wouldn't want me buying it unless you saw it, so I took the bull by the horns," Dixon responded. "But Mr. Ward, you've got me up a tree with this talk about me needing a hard-shooting range-rider. Along with the ranch buildings, Ed Hester sold me approximately twenty thousand head of stock, including horses, mules, steers; cows—he couldn't give me an exact estimate. And also in the bargain, four cowpunchers, and said he'd arrange for three or four more and a good foreman. I told him the price was a little high and he wanted to know what I would pay and when I told him he accepted. Now, are you saying you don't trust Hester?"

"Well, Dixon, yu've got te learn that we Westerners are close-mouthed. We almost never talk to strangers about other Westerners. It's not conducive to long life. But in yur case I'm going te waive that…Yu've bought a ranch, all right, but yu'll find probably less than half twenty-thousand head of stock, maybe only a third—"

"Mercy, are you saying that Mr. Hester has cheated us?" Mrs. Dixon exclaimed.

"Well, ma'am that's what I'm sayin'. That's just part of the game when tenderfeet buy Western stock."

"Oh, dear," she sighed.

"What are we to do?" Dixon asked.

"I reckon it's too late now. Yu'll just have te swallow it. Thing is, the worst is yet te come, cause it's a safe bet yu're goin' te be cleaned out of most if not all of the stock they sold yu."

"Cleaned out! Steal, you mean?" Dixon ejaculated.

"Yep. It'll be rustled off. There's always been some stock stole. Every rancher will tell yu that. But rustlin' now is a business. The demand fer cattle's big. There's always ready money te be had."

"Goodness, you certainly paint a bleak picture, Mr. Ward," Dixon said.

"I reckoned yu'd see it that way, but I just want te start yu right. He peered at Wyoming. "That's why I suggested yu hire Wyoming here."

"Hold on folks," Wyoming said breaking his silence. "I shore don't want to get your expectations up. My friend Mr. Ward here has shore build me up, but I reckon I can't stick around here," he said glancing at Ward. "You see I was occupied a short while back in a little gun play up in Colorado and—"

"Oh, dear," exclaimed Mrs. Dixon. "Gun play? You mean a gun fight; you shot someone?"

"Yes, ma'am. But they shore deserved it."

"What do you mean, 'deserved it'?" Dixon questioned.

"Well, the fact is they was involved in a dirty low-down scheme to steal my pard and his new wife's ranch. They had the sheriff bought off…so I figured there wasn't any other way but to call them out."

"You say *them*. How many were there?"

"Three."

"And you shot them all?"

"Nope, only two, the sheriff backed out and left Higgins and his gun-slinging pard to face the music."

"You murdered them!" Mrs. Dixon gasped.

Wyoming's jaw tightened and his face paled slightly. "Murdered?" he choked. "No, ma'am. It was a—"

"Mrs. Dixon," Ward interjected, "We Western folk don't associate shootin' a man when each has an even chance te draw their guns, as murderin'."

"All this talk of killing. Are you no different than this desperado I've heard so much talk of, this—this Billy something or other?"

"Billy the Kid," Ward interposed. "No ma'am, in my book Billy the Kid was a true desperado. Wyoming here admittedly has a quick hand with a gun, and he shore saved my life up near Spanish Peaks two summers ago, but I reckon you wouldn't put him in a class with a criminal like Billy the Kid."

"I'll be!" Dixon exclaimed, glancing at his wife who could only stare. "These Westerners talk of shooting and killing as we do of—of planting cotton. Well, I can't back out now," he said peering hard at Wyoming. "Mr. Ward thinks you're the man I need to get to the bottom of this rustling; someone I can trust, and I'm willing to go along with Mr. Ward's hunch as he calls it. I sure would like you to reconsider."

"Why don't you think it over, son," Ward said. "Give us yur answer in the morning."

"All right, that's fair." Wyoming said, even though he was already certain what his answer would be. "I'll sleep on it."

Wyoming stood, and excusing himself, made his way out of the room. He sallied forth into the sunlight troubled in thought. He did not know whether he was trying to escape from himself or find himself. It had been all very well feeling sorry for Dixon to say he would think it over, but now that he was out in the open he found it easier to push those feelings away. He did not notice the heat as he strode down the street toward the livery stables. In the cool interior of the stables he paused. He sat down on a bench and took off his sombrero and wiped his face with his bandana. He became aware of his labored breathing. He weighed the danger of sticking around, seeing this thing through. He knew he could be of value to Dixon. He knew this Hester's plan; he knew about Jimmy Anderson. He had never seen his face, but that didn't matter. He also knew it would be reckless, even foolish for him to stay. No, he mustn't give in to that sense of chivalry that had been his bane in the past. He would ride out of here as he planned. But then the lovely image of the girl in the department store flashed before his eyes. He had dreamed about that kiss. He shook his head clearing his thoughts. In Arizona he could start with a clean slate. That settled he saddled Sparky and mounting reined him in the direction of the fairgrounds, looking forward to seeing the sights.

Arriving there he was greeted by a hustle and bustle of activity. Crowds of people, girls in gay apparel, cowboys in full regalia, Indians in picturesque attire, and horses and prize cattle seemed to be everywhere, which explained why there were fewer people on the streets of town. Somewhere a brass band was playing a lively tune scarcely heard over the shouts and chatter of voices, and the neighing and bawling of animals. From the numerous and varied food booths the heady aroma of sundry dishes permeated the late morning air.

Glancing about Wyoming espied a gaily-decorated booth advertising lunch, and since he had left without eating breakfast, he rode up to the booth and dismounted. Straddling the bench in front of the booth he pushed back his sombrero with his thumb.

"Howdy there, Miss," he said to the girl behind the counter whose back was to him. The girl turned. He was not prepared for the vision that met his eye—the girl from the store—bewitching in a trim blue dress. She wasn't wearing a bonnet and her curls blazed golden in the sunlight. Her eyes encountered his. Standing only feet away he could now plainly see the color of her eyes. They were green, a deep jade green. Wyoming had looked over his gun at many pairs of challenging eyes, but never at two, which so made chaos of his faculties.

"What would you like?" she asked. If she recognized him as the dusty individual of last evening, she gave no indication.

"I'll have one of your sandwiches, and a bottle of pop," he finally said distractedly, gazing at her lips. They were sweet and full and red, and just now curved into a little perplexed smile. So much for never seeing her again. Maybe fate had a hand in this he pondered.

"We don't sell pop," she replied.

"Make it ginger ale then," he grinned making an attempt to regain his jaunty self.

"No ginger ale," she said, slowly shaking her head.

"Pink lemonade?"

"No," she said, "We sell only sandwiches and coffee and cake. Can't you read?" she asked, pointing upward with a slim finger to the sign above his head. There was something in the inflection of her voice that made him wonder if she were laughing at him.

"Read!" he exclaimed in an injured tone. "Shore I can read. I went to school for eight years. That's about four more than any cowpuncher I ever met."

"Indeed!" she returned, demurely.

He stepped back and looked up at the sign draped across the front of the booth.

"Dog-gone," he drawled shaking his head in pretended consternation, "I reckon I'll just have coffee with that sandwich."

With an amused expression on her face she sat a steaming mug of coffee before him and a sandwich wrapped in brown paper.

"How much?" he asked.

"Twenty-five cents."

He laid a silver coin on the counter. Maybe she wouldn't recognize him. It had been a crazy thing to do, kissing her. She was nothing like any rancher's daughter he had ever met; a lady for certain.

"Thank you," she said, peering at him peculiarly as though she was on the verge of remembering something. A gay young couple came up to the booth and after a moment's hesitation she went to wait on them. The young man looked proud in a store-bought suit, and his pretty companion, wearing a stylish yellow print dress, couldn't keep her eyes off him. With sandwiches and drinks in hand the two went to sit on a bench under a nearby tree.

Wyoming sipped his coffee watching the girl behind the counter his keen eye began to note that a string of cowboys kept coming and going past the booth for the obvious reason of catching a glimpse of the girl, and by the look on her face, that nonchalance which a woman feigns when she suspects she is being regarded with admiring eyes, she was well aware of their antics, as she was of Wyoming's intent gaze.

Other customers came and the girl stayed quite busy, and for a long while he sat there watching her and every passing moment added to a realization of charm. What was happening to him, he pondered. Whatever it was, it was a lot, he decided. It was as though he had been struck by lightning. Who was she? He had never in his life met such a girl. She couldn't be married. Too young and—he didn't know what! But the thought that she might be, made his heart momentarily sink. He stole a glance at her left hand for a ring, something he had failed to do yesterday in his excitement. Her ring finger was bare! He was struck again by her small, shapely hands. They were not red or rough like those of most ranchers' daughters. There came a break in customers and Wyoming found himself alone at the counter. The girl walked over holding the steaming coffee pot.

"More coffee?" she asked obviously aware of his scrutiny.

"Yes, ma'am, I shore would," he drawled keeping his eyes on her face as she filled his mug. "And I reckon I'll have a slice of that cake."

She proceeded to cut a slice and handed it to him. Reaching to take it he accidentally touched her bare hand with his. The soft contact shot a thrilling current through him. He lost his hold on the plate and both it and the cake fell into the dirt.

"Gosh, Miss, I—I'm shore terrible sorry!" he said contritely. "I'm not usually so clumsy."

She tilted her head, peered doubtfully at him, then her eyes suddenly widened in recognition and a blush filled her cheeks.

"Now I recognize you! How dare you—" she sputtered and before he could react she slapped him hard.

"Dog-gone," he muttered, rubbing his cheek. "I reckon that means you're not going to dance with me."

"What!" she snapped perplexed.

"The rodeo dance tonight. I don't reckon you'll dance with me?"

She stared at him as though she couldn't believe her ears. Then her lips began to quirk at the corners. She quickly turned away before he could see the impetuous smile that shaped her mouth. It had been a very pleasant kiss.

"I'll cut you another slice of cake," she said.

A moment later she turned back toward him with another slice of cake. She hesitated.

"I'll just set it on the counter."

"Hmm. There's a chance then…that you might dance with me?" he asked giving her his best smile.

"I'll think about it," she said lips twitching in an effort not to laugh as she began to wipe down the counter.

"I bet every cowpoke at this rodeo has a dance with you though," he declared.

"Not every cowpoke," she replied offhandedly continuing to clean the countertop.

"No fooling! Wait! This is serious stuff. You mean not all your dances are taken?"

She laughed outright, nodding.

"Well, *would* you dance with me tonight?" he asked without any pretence.

"Yes," she grinned, giving up any impression of annoyance.

"How many times?"

She gave an unladylike snort. "You should be happy I'm even talking to you," she said.

At that moment several couples came up to the booth, all seeming to be talking at once. She went to wait on the new arrivals. Wyoming backed away as they crowded around and walked to where his horse stood hipshot. He slipped one arm over Sparky's neck watching the girl busy serving the laughing group of young people. It didn't matter that she hadn't answered his late question. She hadn't slapped him again and she had agreed to dance with him, he grinned jauntily. Catching up the reins of his horse he stepped into the saddle. The girl glanced at him and her dark eyes met his across the space and he could have sworn there was an amused expression on her face. He looked back over his shoulder after a short distance and she was still watching him.

CHAPTER FIVE

T he cowboy rode away between the row of booths in the direction of the corrals. Annabelle stood watching him until he disappeared from sight. He had a pleasant face…and my goodness that kiss! There had been something familiar about him she realized when he first approached her booth, but not surprisingly she hadn't recognized him as that unshaven cowboy in dusty overalls and worn boots who had shocked her with his stolen kiss. Not until his hand had touched hers when she handed him his cake. It had sent a shiver up her arm, much like the quiver that raced down her backbone when his lips had touched hers. Maybe that had been the reason she hadn't recognized him. The kiss had been an unexpected shock catching her totally unawares. And even as she had stared at him all she could think of was how his lips had felt on hers. It had been a surprisingly stimulating experience.

He certainly looked different this morning though, clean-shaven and decked out in new overalls and shirt. That big gun on his hip however was the same. She should have known him by that. Who was he? He hadn't told her his name…but then she hadn't told him hers either. And she had promised him a dance—perhaps more than one, she smiled, as she thrillingly resigned herself to the unknown pleased now that she had volunteered to help operate the charity booth for the church.

Before long the remaining customers departed and she set about cleaning and putting everything right. Although she had no way to tell the hour she guessed it was nearing time the rodeo would be starting. That thought had no more crossed her mind when her father arrived.

"Well, daughter, everything closed at one. The *rodeo* has started and we're already late. Hurry now and close up, but don't forget the cash, we'll turn that over to Father Cordova."

They hurried into the crowded stand, where her mother and sisters waited having kept seats for them. Settling upon the bench Annabelle gazed excitedly around. She had never been to a *rodeo* before. As her gaze roamed over the crowd a tall figure caught her eye. He stood talking with the rancher Hank Ward whom she had been introduced to two days before. They had just entered the area at the base of the stand. Annabelle felt herself tremble.

Wyoming gave his horse to a boy at the stalls and went round to the stands. A long shed, open in front faced the arena directly next to the circular fence. Horses and cowboys stood about mostly in small groups, smoking, talking, laughing. He wondered if one of them was Jimmy Anderson, and his keen eye swept over the group. But then he reminded himself that he wouldn't know Anderson if he saw him. He had only heard his voice, and so after reaching the stock pens, he turned back toward the stands. The *rodeo* had begun, which accounted for the deserted appearance of the midway and the grounds adjacent.

Wyoming heard someone shout his name and looking around espied his friend the rancher Hank Ward approaching.

"Howdy Mr. Ward," he said.

"Decided to watch the excitement, huh," Ward grinned. "Say I'm meetin' with Dixon and his family up in the stand. Why don't yu join us. They're right good seats."

"Shore, I'd be obliged."

Wyoming followed Ward making their way up through the crowded stand. His eyes caught sight of Mr. Dixon and his wife when he was only a few feet from them. He smiled and nodded. It was then he noticed the three girls seated one after another next to Mr. Dixon.

Annabelle watched Ward and the cowboy weave their way through the thong an unbidden flush filling her cheeks. She could tell he hadn't noticed her yet and wondered what his reaction would be when he did so, and at the same time considered why that mattered to her. Her father nodded to Hank Ward.

"Mr. Ward, I wasn't sure you'd find us in this crowd."

Ward laughed. "I brought along our friend," he said indicating Wyoming with a jerk of his chin.

"Howdy, Mr. Dixon, Mrs. Dixon" Wyoming drawled.

"Why, howdy yourself, Wyoming," her father replied.

Annabelle hadn't taken her eyes from Ward's companion. 'Wyoming; what an odd name,' she thought. Yet somehow it fit him. Her father reached to shake the cowboy's hand turning as he did so to peer at her.

"McCord, I'd like you to meet our daughters, Annabelle, Angelique and Allison. Girls this is Wyoming McCord."

"I'm shore pleased to meet you ladies," Wyoming said, quickly doffing his sombrero and bowing gallantly.

"How do you do, sir," Annabelle returned, with just a hint of mischief in her jade green eyes hoping her glowing cheeks weren't too noticeable.

Lord Almighty! He had kissed Dixon's daughter; flirted outrageously with her at the food booth! Had she told him? No, she couldn't have, not with the friendly way Dixon was looking at him. He forced his eyes to move to the girl on Annabelle's right.

Dixon's middle daughter, the one who had accompanied Annabelle at the department store, smiled as she gazed up at him from under the wide brim of her stylish bonnet with innocent eyes that could conceal anything. She knew! He could see it in those same jade green eyes.

The youngest daughter, the one he had seen before at the café with her parents, peered up at him unabashedly as only a nine year old could. She had dark hair, obviously taking after her mother, and matching jade green eyes that appeared to be a family trait.

"Girls, this is the cowboy I told you about just last evening; the one who saved your old dad from losing a pile of money to that cardsharp. Have a seat Wyoming," Dixon said. "Scoot over Annabelle, make room for Wyoming."

Wyoming glanced at her as she tucked her skirt about her knees making room for him.

"Are you going to?" she whispered eyes on the field below.

"What?" he whispered back.

"Accept daddy's job offer."

He looked askance at her. She appeared engrossed in the activity below. He opened his mouth to reply but then closed it realizing that Arizona was no longer a consideration. Fate had dealt him a hand and there was no use denying it. He divined now that he had always been destined to come to this wild range. All the reasons he should keep on the run no longer seemed to matter. He had been struck through the heart. What would happen to Dixon…to Annabelle, her sisters, if he rode away? The rustlers would prevail—her father would be ruined and the family irreparably hurt in the process. He couldn't, wouldn't let that happen. It was not a decision to be made—no, only a realization and acceptance. The decision was made the instant the question was presented. But this wasn't the time to make that known to her.

The calf-roping event was underway, but the feel of Annabelle's hip against his was unnerving. He was only vaguely aware of rider after rider as they roped and swiftly tied their calf.

"Bulldoggin' steers is next," Ward said consulting his program.

"Goodness! Do they chase the steers with bulldogs?" spoke up Allison in bewilderment.

"Har! Har!" Ward laughed slapping his knee. "That shore is a good one."

Wyoming couldn't help grinning in spite of himself.

"Why is everyone laughing?" Allison demanded, "I've never been to a *rodeo* before."

"I plumb forgot," Ward returned apologetically, still chuckling under his breath.

"Watch, Miss Allison," Wyoming said solicitously leaning forward to look at her as he pointed to the field below.

A wicked wide-horned steer broke out of a chute and came tearing down the field followed by a mounted cowboy. After a short chase the rider leaped from his horse onto the neck of the steer, and swinging down by the horns, he tumbled it head over heels.

"Oh!" all three girls gasped in unison.

When the dust cleared there sat the cowboy on the head of the steer holding it down.

"Wal, girls, what do you think of that cowboy?" Ward wanted to know.

"I think he's crazy," returned Allison feelingly.

"This *bulldoggin'*, as you call it, is too brutal. Where is the sense of it?" Angelique said.

"Angelique is right," agreed her mother. "Whoever heard of such a thing?"

"I reckon there ain't no sense in it," the cattleman replied, "But it shore takes a slick rider to do it."

"A cowboy at the booth today bragged to me that he didn't have an unbroken bone in his body," Annabelle said. "Now I can see why."

The events followed one after another. The bucking broncos were next. Out of the chute came a black mustang with rolling white eyes. His rider a lithe young cowboy in a colorful shirt and a bright red scarf spurred him hard. The mustang bound high in the air coming down stiff-legged, only to spring up again twisting violently sideways hoofs almost perpendicular to the ground.

"Would you look at that boy ride!" Dixon exclaimed.

Wyoming eyed the rider. He had to admit Ward was right; the boy was a superb horseman. He lost his sombrero and his hair flamed red in the sunlight, but when that whirling, dusty, snorting, and yelling mêlée ended the young cowboy was still in the saddle.

"Oh, wasn't he just grand!" Annabelle cried.

"Shore, I reckon," Wyoming grunted, torn between admiration and jealousy.

The next rider had his horse fall back on him, rolling clear over but he came up still in the saddle. At this the crowd roared. Following this event came the bull riding. This last found Annabelle yelling in unison with everyone, and at one point in her excitement when a rider was thrown and nearly gored by the bull, a wild-eyed Brahma, she clenched Wyoming's arm so tightly he nearly called out. She didn't immediately release her grip and Wyoming gloried in the warm feel of her hand on his arm.

"Well, girls how did you like your first *rodeo*?" Ward asked after the last event.

"Fabulous!" Allison cried bouncing up and down on the wood bench.

"Rather brutish—and idiotic," Angelique sniffed her tone an articulation of boredom. "Outlandish gawks, all hats and boots trying to kill, or at the very least, maim themselves."

"Har! Har!" Ward guffawed.

"Well, I thought it was rather—thrilling," Annabelle said, darting a look at Wyoming.

"I say, Mr. Ward, this *rodeo* is well and good for the men," Mrs. Dixon conceded smiling charmingly, "but it's the dance where the weaker sex shines."

"I shore do believe yu're right, Mrs. Dixon," laughingly agreed the cattleman.

"Indeed, and I suppose we had better get back to the hotel. It's near dinner time and we don't want to be late for the dance," Dixon commented as they made their way with the rest of the crowd down out of the stands.

"Dada, do I have to stay in the stuffy old hotel room all by myself tonight while Anna and Angie get to dance?" Allison demanded.

"You won't be alone, child. Mrs. Lindsay will be with you, and besides a grown-up dance is no place for a nine year old," her father replied. "You'll get your chance when you turn of age."

"Humph," the girl snorted, but said nothing more being astute enough to know that it was a winless argument.

"Mr. Dixon," he called.

The man turned halting as did the others; the two older girls gazing at him curiously.

"Could I speak with you…sort of private like?" Wyoming asked. He avoided looking at Annabelle.

Dixon walked to where Wyoming stood out of earshot of the others.

"Is that job offer still open?" Wyoming asked.

"It is for a fact," Dixon said peering intently at him.

"Then I'd like to take you up on it."

"You're kind of a sudden fellow. Decided not to sleep on it, huh? What changed your mind?"

Wyoming hesitated. The answer to that was actually quite simple. He glanced at Annabelle.

"I reckon Ward was right," he said looking Dixon in the eye. "I can help you. But don't get too comfy," he said forcefully. This would be one of the toughest propositions he had ever faced. "This rustling outfit is well organized and it'll be hard and dangerous to take on. Most if not all of Dixon's new riders will remain on Hester's side of the fence. I won't be able to tell who they are until they prove themselves one way or another. It'll shore result in gunplay."

"I see," Dixon said glancing toward his wife and daughters. "We're in the west now, Mr. McCord. I'm ready to face up to whatever is to come. I'll tell you straight, I was up a stump when you left us this morning. I wasn't sure what I was going to do." He reached to shake Wyoming's hand. "Glad to have you. You know, I moved my family out here from over in Louisiana scarce more than a month ago on doctor's orders—say will you be needing a cash advance?" queried Dixon.

"Well, with the winnings of last night I'm not quite broke," Wyoming replied.

"Ah, yes," Dixon grinned. "Well, speaking of that what sort of wages are you expecting?"

"I reckon we can discuss the particulars tomorrow," Wyoming said clasping Dixon's hand.

"We'll be staying over 'til Sunday so as to attend church services then head out to the ranch. Ride back with us if you like. Can't wait to get out there and look things over," Dixon said. "I've decided to rename the ranch the Triangle A."

"Hmm; Triangle A?"

"Yes, after the girls. I've already registered the brand on Mr. Ward's advice."

"Yes, sir," Wyoming replied just now appreciating that Dixon's three daughter's names all started with an A. "That's shore sensible."

"Alright then," Dixon grinned, "I'll see you at the dance."

Wyoming watched them depart in the direction of the corrals, the three girls walking arm in arm with each other. Then he continued on toward the stalls where he had left Sparky firm in his decision. Stepping into the saddle he started off. On the way to the hotel he stopped at Carter's Department Store and a short while later left in possession of a new dark suit and crisp white shirt and black string tie. Now that he had a good stake and a job he didn't have to pinch his pennies so tight. He decided it might be a good idea to set up a bank account. He didn't like carrying that much cash around with him.

Wyoming took particular care with dressing himself on this evening, aware of an undue regard for his appearance. He shaved and washed and donned his new suit. He buckled on his gun belt and stared with satisfaction at himself in the mirror. The coat hid the holstered Colt effectively. Then he was off feeling eager and somewhat amused at himself.

CHAPTER SIX

Wyoming, dressed in his new dark suit and boots, absent his spurs, strode out into the late evening. There were buggies and wagons parked all along the street on both sides of the wide thoroughfare, as well as numerous horses standing hipshot at hitching rails when Wyoming arrived before the dance hall. He made his way up a wide stairway to the top floor. Here he had to run a gauntlet of laughing and smiling faces in order to get into the hall.

It was a big hall festooned with festive decorations of red, white and blue bunting and colored lights. The shiny floor was vacant at the moment. Along the fringes young people sat or stood in gay conversation, and many had the lithe build of cowboys. At the far end of the hall there was a wide stage on which the musicians sat tuning their instruments. It was pleasant inside the hall as arched doorways led out upon a veranda that overlooked the street, allowing the cool evening breeze to flow freely. Wyoming's quick eye took in all these details, as well as the fact that the majority of those present were cowboys, and young men about town, all accompanied by the girls of their choice. There were also a number of Mexicans; dusky-eyed *señoritas* in colorful gowns, and slender almond-skinned young men, sons of landowners, attired in fancy embroidered suits with flared lace-filled bottoms.

It had been a while since he had been to a dance. The last one he recalled was at Casper two years ago, the final night of the rodeo. But he wasn't a slouch he reckoned, thanks to Peggy Hart. He remembered the look on her face, her words that first time he had danced with her...

"Wyoming, you're holding me too close."

"I am?"

"Yes, you are. You don't have to bear-hug a girl, so as she can't breathe."

"Sorry," he mumbled easing the pressure of his arm, he remembered, with some reluctance.

"There, that's much better," she said smiling up at him. "You know Wyoming; you're very nimble on your feet for a cowboy. You'd be a good dancer if you didn't try so hard. Just relax, flow with the music—don't look at your feet! Yes, very good."

The memories were bitter sweet. He had been to her no more than a brother and at the time it had been a sour pill for him to swallow. He knew now his love for Peggy Hart had only been growing pangs.

"Here, cowboy," a stocky man wearing a star on his vest called, interrupted his reverie as he laid a hand on Wyoming's shoulder. "All side arms got to be checked here at the door."

With undisguised reluctance, Wyoming unbuckled his gun belt and handed it to the deputy.

"You can pick this up on your way out," he informed Wyoming giving him a round metal-rimmed token with a number imprinted on it. An identical one he tied to Wyoming's gun belt.

Wyoming watched to see where his gun belt was hung on a wall next to the door along with several others. Wyoming moved around the hall eyeing the guests. He didn't see the Dixons and settled in to wait their arrival. He spotted Hank Ward as he entered the hall a woman his age on his arm. Wyoming guessed she was his wife. She was buxom and comely, fair and some years younger than the rancher. A pretty blond girl and a tall young man accompanied Dixon and his wife. Wyoming sauntered that way.

"Howdy Mr. Ward," he greeted. He knew the old rancher's keen eyes had noted his approach.

"Wyoming, come te do a little dancin' huh?" he grinned. "Ma, this is Wyoming McCord. Yu've heard me speak of him more than once."

"Yes, I have. I'm very pleased to meet you, Wyoming."

"Likewise, Ma'am," Wyoming said making a gallant bow.

"Wyoming this heah is Jack, my oldest, and my girl Alice. Jack, Alice, Wyoming McCord. He saved yu're paw's hide up in Colorado two years ago."

Young in years, Jack Ward looked and breathed the very spirit of the range. He was tall, lean, lithe, with a handsome face dark from sun and wind and still gray eyes. Yellow hair curled about his ears. Alice was perhaps sixteen, slim and fair with pale blond hair, and not by any means lacking in good looks, with the same gray eyes that appeared to run in the family. She wore a pale green muslin gown.

"Glad te meet yu, Wyoming. Paw's shore speaks highly of yu," the young man said, reaching out his hand. His rough calloused palm and strong fingers closed like steel on Wyoming's.

"Hello," Alice smiled.

The orchestra struck up a tune at that moment and Alice glanced shyly at Wyoming.

"Miss Alice may I have this dance?" Wyoming said.

She nodded and held out her hand and he clasped it and swept her out upon the floor. They had no more than circled the floor when his vigilant gaze caught sight of the Dixons as they entered the hall. The two older girls followed behind their parents. They had all changed to formal attire, and Wyoming watching expectantly to see Annabelle was still unprepared for the vision of loveliness that met his gaze when he caught sight of her in a white gown with flounces of exquisite lace. Her beautiful arms and shoulders were bare, and there was a smile of excitement on her face and a dancing emerald lightning in her eyes. Her golden curls caught and held the light. She was an apparition and a reality that sent the blood thrilling in Wyoming's heart.

Annabelle saw him the moment she entered the hall. He wore a black suit and looked tall and slim, not at all like the dusty cowboy who had kissed her the day before...and he was dancing with a girl in a pale green gown. She looked quickly away. As soon as the dance ended and before she could think she was surrounded by several young men each clamoring to claim her for a dance and she lost sight of him. Her first dance was with a slim blond curly-haired rider who was light on his feet and was fun.

It developed that intermissions were frequent, but brief. When the music burst forth again another partner claimed Annabelle. But even in the whirling throng she did not lose sight of the tall rider she had promised dances. Now and then as she glided by she saw him leaning against the wall and on each occasion she met his gaze. It followed her everywhere. He didn't ask any of the other girls to dance, after that first girl she saw him with when she first entered nor did he mingle with the crowd. She was aware that he was noticed by many of the young ladies who whispered to one another, and by some of the cowboys who eyed him keenly. The meaning of the feminine glances sent his way was not lost on Annabelle.

The next dance she was approached by a tall elegantly dressed rancher. She knew who he was; Ed Hester, the man who had sold the ranch to her father. And she didn't trust him nor did she care to dance with him, but it would have caused a scene if she had refused and so she allowed him to lead her out upon the floor annoyed that Wyoming McCord had yet to approach her for one of the dances she had promised him.

Watching Annabelle as she entered with her family Wyoming was aware that she saw him at once. It was that slight hesitation as her gaze passed over him that his keen eyes picked up. Mrs. Dixon joined several other ladies in the far corner of the floor. When the dance ended he escorted Alice to where her mother stood with several other older ladies and thanked her. She smiled prettily. The music struck up and almost immediately several young men approached Alice. Wyoming was aware of a like number of young men surrounding the two Dixon girls. A cowboy of medium height with flaming red hair and bearing the lithe hallmark of a rider led the younger daughter Angelique, a rosy flush in her cheeks, out onto the floor. The cowboy was wearing a fancy patterned shirt, new overalls and expensive Mexican boots. A colorful bandana was tied about his throat. His elaborate garb set him apart. Wyoming remembered him from the rodeo; the cowboy who had won the saddle-bronc riding competition. A tall man in a fashionable suit captured Annabelle's hand and whirled her out upon the floor. Wyoming watched the two. He didn't like how close the man held Annabelle.

"Wyoming," someone said and he turned to see Mr. Dixon.

"Howdy boss," Wyoming smiled.

"Well, I hardly recognized you in that fancy suit," Dixon remarked. "Dang if you don't look like a regular high stepper," he laughed.

"Thanks, sir. I figured I ought to dress up some for this dance."

Dixon nodded. The two men stood watching the dancers whirl by, Wyoming's eyes again seeking out Annabelle. She passed by in the arms of her partner her golden curls gleaming in the candle light, a fixed smile on her lips. The waltz drew to a close and the man led Annabelle to where he and Dixon stood. Wyoming's keen eyes surveyed him. He made a superb figure, lithe and graceful, a forceful, doubtful character. He was about thirty years old Wyoming guessed, though his lean face indicated long years of experience.

"Mr. Dixon," the man said, his hand resting lightly upon Annabelle's back. "Your daughter is a lovely dancer."

"Hester," Dixon acknowledged.

'Ah, so this was Ed Hester,' Wyoming mused. Suddenly glancing over Hester's shoulder he caught sight of a familiar face. He was broad shouldered, bronzed of face, with a barrel chest. Bull Burton! With a start Wyoming recognized him. Burton hadn't been with Higgins when Wyoming called the man out that day in front of the Buckhorn Saloon. But fate had intervened again. Instinctively Wyoming's hand reached to undo the button of his coat before he remembered his Colt was hanging on the wall by the door.

"I'll be returnin' to my ranch tomorrow," Hester said, "but I've arranged for a reliable foreman like I said I would." He turned to barrel-chested man behind him. "Dixon, this here is Bull Burton. His real name's Jake, but he's most known by Bull."

"Well, Mr. Hester that won't be necessary," Dixon acknowledged rather formally. "On Mr. Ward's recommendation I've already hired a hard-shooting range rider to manage my outfit."

"Ward? Hank Ward?"

"Yes. I'm sure you know him. He's a neighbor and we've found him to be very helpful."

This comment was manifestly not so pleasantly received by Hester. The man kept his smile, a purely calculated one, Wyoming noted, yet so subtle that had he not been peculiarly stimulated by curiosity about this man Wyoming would not have recognized it.

"Hmm," Hester murmured. "Well, I don't know who this feller is that Ward recommended, but I reckon my man is 'bout the only one that can handle that fire-eatin' outfit of riders I sold you with the stock. Maybe you best reconsider."

"No need to reconsider," broke in Wyoming, his voice remarkably piercing and arresting.

Burton whirled with a violent start. He bent slightly staring hard, then straightened.

"What'd you say?" he demanded.

"You heard me, Bull."

"Who are you?" Hester interjected menacingly.

"Well, now," Dixon spoke up. "Meet my new foreman, Wyoming McCord."

"Boss, so help me Gawd, it's that Wyoming rider that plugged Higgins and Blake," Burton rasped in a hoarse whisper and his hand moved as if to snatch at a gun that was not on him, but it froze in midair, and he stared ashen-faced. Then he made a passionate gesture as it apparently dawned on him that Wyoming was unarmed as well, and his face lost much of its pallid cast. Wyoming cursed under his breath angry that he had given up his gun, something he vowed never to do again.

"Boss, if this here feller is ridin' fer Dixon, then I quit," snapped Burton.

"Wyoming, huh?" Hester mused and his opaque formidable eyes held steady on Wyoming. They were cold, complex, cunning. "Well, Dixon, this'll break up yore outfit. You'll be left flat. Without Bull here te ramrod 'em I reckon the outfit will stick with me."

"So be it," Dixon said bravely. "I've a hunch I'll be better off without your foreman."

"You'll have a fine time ranchin' it with no outfit," Burton cut in. "Rustlers made off with two thousand head of your cattle just a week ago. Let's see how your hard-ridin' Wyoming here drives them back. Haw! Haw!"

"Shut up, Bull!" Hester snarled. He turned to Annabelle. "Miss Dixon," he smiled and whirling about stalked away. Burton hastily followed.

Wyoming watched them depart. Bull Burton gave him little concern. He was an obvious braggart, but Hester was a different story. The man was cold and cunning and would be dangerous in a fight.

Dixon glanced at Wyoming, "The fats in the fire now. Don't let me down, son."

Before he could reply someone addressed him; a softly accented voice he immediately recognized.

"Mr. McCord, I do believe this is the dance I saved for you."

Wyoming turned to see Annabelle standing at his elbow her jade green eyes peering roguishly up at him.

"Miss Dixon," he said making no effort to hide his pleased surprise.

"I see Hester sought yu out," Hank Ward said, pausing beside Dixon as Wyoming led Annabelle out onto the floor.

"Yes. He wanted to let me know he was sending out a foreman."

"Yeah? What did yu tell him?"

"I told him there was no need that I'd already hired a hard shooting range rider."

"Har! Good fer yu," the old rancher chuckled. "Dixon the west don't know what it's in fer," Ward remarked peering out at the dancers circling the large room. "Them handsome healthy girls of yurn are goin' to take this territory by storm. Wal, I reckon they'll be two strappin' riders somewhere out there that don't know the great good luck that's in store fer them."

Wyoming had wanted to hold her in his arms since the moment he first saw her. Slipping his arm around her waist he swung her gracefully out on the crowded floor.

Annabelle gazed up at him. His presence did not quite make her oblivious to his strong arm, nor was she surprised that he could dance so well. He moved like a natural athlete, with the same easy grace he sat upon his horse. She was glad she wouldn't have to help him learn his steps.

Wyoming soon discovered that Annabelle was like a fairy on her feet, which made his own steps seem effortless. Her head came to just below his shoulder, and she barely escaped contact with it.

"I was shore afraid you had forgotten to save me a dance," he said, using all his will power not to crush her against him.

"Shhh, don't talk," she returned.

He smiled, but obeyed. He was vaguely aware of the swaying, gliding, circling dancers, the low murmur of voices mingled with sliding feet and the overriding strain of the orchestra, captivated by the sheen of candle light on her bare shoulders and the warmth of her hand in his. The dance, which seemed as fleeting to him as a moment ended with them at the far end of the hall near one of the openings onto the veranda. She lifted the small ornamented fan suspended by a small cord around her left wrist and with a flick of her hand spread it and began to fan herself.

"I declare it's warm in here," she said, "Would you take me out on the balcony?"

"Why, shore," he replied haltingly, scarce able to conceal his amazement and joy.

She walked ahead of him out through one of the arches onto the porch high up over the street. Moonlight flooded the balcony. Couples were leaning over the wooden railing talking and laughing. One of the couples he recognized; Annabelle's sister Angelique and the red-haired cowboy she had danced with earlier, the same one from the rodeo.

Wyoming had been hopeful he would find the place unoccupied. Annabelle walked to the far corner of the porch away from her sister and the others where she turned and leaned her back against the support post. The porch caught the gleam of moonlight, but left her face partially in shadow. Her eyes, almost black in the dusky light, peered questioningly up at him.

"What did all that mean?" she asked.

"All of what?" he asked innocently.

"You know what I mean. All that with Mr. Hester and that other man," she said with a frustrated little sigh.

"It was only an incident of range life, and shore it turned out favorably."

"Only because neither one of you had guns," she said.

"I reckon that's so," he acknowledged thoughtfully.

"That man Burton, he was no stranger to you, was he?"

It was a moment before he answered.

"I reckon we've met before."

"And there is bad blood between you?"

She peered down at the street at the row of buggies and horses filling both sides of the thoroughfare.

"There is, that's a fact."

She turned to regard him, once again leaving her face partially in shadow as she leaned back against the post, hands clasped behind her back.

"Mr. McCord, I may be a girl, and only nineteen at that, but I have ears and I've listened to Mr. Ward and daddy talk. That Mr. Hester has swindled daddy, and—and now daddy probably has no riders at all—and those rustlers are going to steal all that remains of the cattle he bought, isn't that so?"

"I reckon that's true," he admitted slowly.

"And that's why Mr. Ward told daddy to hire you, because you are—are fast with a gun. Mr. Ward says you'd be a whole outfit in yourself. He said you are different; that there are bad gunmen and good gunmen. That Mr. Burton is one kind and—and you are the other. Daddy is the most wonderful man in the world. He's trusting and kind and—and likes most everyone, but I've never seen him taken with anyone as he is with you. He needs someone he can trust if he's to not lose the ranch and with it his health—"

Wyoming leaned closer trying to see more clearly the lovely face, the deep eyes that flamed at him, only to lose himself there in that shimmering abyss. He wanted to kiss her upturned mouth again. He shook himself.

"Miss Dixon," he returned, swiftly, to get by the danger. "If you're through interrogating me, I've something to say. I shore was intending to ride out of here come Monday—until I saw you. And, well, now, I'd shore like a chance to prove I could deserve you—your friendship."

"I see, Mr. McCord—"

"Wyoming."

"I beg your pardon?"

"Just call me Wyoming," he drawled.

"Alright…Wyoming, I respect you for your admission, but—can daddy truly rely on you?"

"I don't reckon there's any reason he can't," he drawled checked in his romantic imaginings by her cynical question. "And I'll tell you this, Miss Dixon, before long there's shore going to be guns and blood out at the Triangle A."

Annabelle's cheeks paled.

"What you and your dad need is a man who can ride this range—a handy man with guns," he drawled. "And he just happened to have dropped in."

CHAPTER SEVEN

W yoming saddled Sparky and slung his saddlebags behind the cantle, securing them there as he did his bedroll and slicker. He stepped into the saddle and reined Sparky out through the wide doors of the livery stables. It was Sunday morning and the town appeared deserted as far as the main street was concerned. The Dixons were presently attending services at the large Catholic Church at the end of San Francisco Street. Although the Dixons had stayed at the dance well past midnight he had only danced that one dance with Annabelle. Instead, he watched as she danced the night away with one partner after another, seeing her laughing up into their faces with unaffected gaiety as they beamed back at her. She glowed with life, with delight and mischief, with the joy of living, and of dancing. Her smile took on a fresh warmth with each partner. Ah, to be the recipient of such a smile…

"Well, Sparky, old horse, I reckon if I ain't burning them, I'm shore leaving my bridges behind me," he remarked, patting the sorrel's glossy neck.

Wyoming reined up; waiting for the Mexican he had hired to drive the heavy wagon out through the doors onto the street.

"Chico," he called to the swarthy-faced Mexican sitting on the driver's seat wearing a huge sombrero with a tall pointed crown, "Head on over to Carter's store. He'll be there to open up so we can load up the supplies we need."

"*Si, Señor,*" the Mexican said, smiling broadly, showing white teeth as he chucked the horses into motion. Wyoming liked the man's humble, honest face.

Wyoming had made a list of the foodstuffs and other essentials he suspected they would need. Not knowing what they would find at the ranch, he didn't want to come up short. Once the items were packed in the wagon, Chico drove to the hotel. Wyoming followed on horseback. They were to meet the Dixons at the hotel for the ride to the ranch, which Wyoming was told, was ten miles or so southeast near the piñon-covered foothills of the *Sangre de Cristo* Mountains. The Dixons drove up in a double-seated buckboard pulled by a fine-looking team of bays shortly after Wyoming and Chico's arrival at the hotel. Dixon was driving; his wife seated beside him. Annabelle and Angelique sat on the rear seat an older lady in her forties between them. The youngest girl sat between her parents. All were still in their stylish gowns.

"Howdy, folks," Wyoming grinned. He casually included everyone in his slow glance, winding up on Annabelle.

After a brief nod she averted her gaze. She was still annoyed at him from last night. He had only danced that one dance with her... and he never made an attempt to kiss her again. Well, she supposed she hadn't given him much of a chance after his last comment to her out on the balcony. That talk about guns and blood had shaken her.

"Good morning," Dixon greeted glancing from Wyoming to the wagon and back again. "Looks as though you've got everything ready to go," he said, nodding approvingly. "Time to get underway then. No use hanging around here spending money for hotel bills. I'll get someone to bring out our trunks and boxes and bags. Is there room in the wagon?"

"I figured you'd have luggage so I left some space. How many trunks you got?" Wyoming asked.

"Fifteen, and twenty boxes and bags."

"Whew!" Wyoming breathed shaking his head. "That'll never fit in one wagon. Not with the rest of the supplies. We'll need another wagon and driver. I'll ride back down to the livery stables and rent another wagon."

"Fine. Annabelle give Wyoming some cash. How much do you think you'll need?" he asked glancing at Wyoming.

"Anna is our treasurer, Mr. McCord," Allison declared gaily. "Dada never handles money so you best look out for your wages."

"Allison! That's unkind! I'm not that bad!" Annabelle denied flushing.

"Thanks, Miss Allison. I'll shore keep that in mind," Wyoming grinned as Annabelle unfastened the clasp on a leather bag and pulled out a bulky envelope. "I reckon twenty dollars should cover it, Miss Dixon," he said and watched her count out the bills.

"While you're handling that, I best go check out of the hotel and get somebody to pack out our trunks."

"Should we change our dresses for the drive?" Mrs. Dixon asked.

"It might get a little hot and dusty," Wyoming said.

"Then we should change," Mrs. Dixon returned emphatically.

Wyoming stepped from the saddle to lend a hand to the women as they climbed from the buckboard.

"Incidentally, Wyoming, this is Mrs. Lindsay," Dixon said as Wyoming helped the older women down from the buckboard. "Mrs.

Lindsay has been our housekeeper since Angelique was just an infant. She's agreed to come help us set up our new house."

Mrs. Lindsay was a slender woman with sharp brown eyes and a quick smile.

"I'm shore pleased to meet you Mrs. Lindsay," Wyoming drawled.

The women crossed the board sidewalk to disappear through the wide lobby doors. With a last glance at Wyoming, Dixon followed.

When Wyoming returned nearly an hour later he found Dixon waiting on the hotel porch. Chico and the new driver had just finished the loading when Mrs. Lindsay and the girls and their mother joined them. They were dressed in plain cotton gowns and wore wide-brimmed straw bonnets. Mrs. Lindsay carried a picnic basket over one arm as did the youngest girl who bound eagerly up onto the front seat between her parents. Annabelle and Angelique settled beside Mrs. Lindsey on the rear seat.

It was past midmorning when they got underway, Wyoming rode in the lead with Mr. Dixon and his family following in the buckboard out of town heading southeast on the well-traveled road. The Mexican teamsters in the two heavy wagons brought up the rear.

For Wyoming it felt good to be astride Sparky on a real journey with real work at the end, and he was able for the moment to set aside the rustler threat that shadowed him like a dark cloud. After a mile or so the road circled a bit to the east then back south leading up a slope through pine and juniper. When they reached the summit, the sky for a time became overcast with heavy gray clouds clinging to the mountain ridges, darkening the day. However, as the morning went on the sky cleared. The road at this juncture narrowed to only a wagon trail winding down through stands of hickory pine and big-tooth maple with a few bright-red autumn leaves clinging to their branches. Deer and coyotes and even elk fell under Wyoming's keen watchful eye. Once he espied a group of dark riders, far off, topping a ridge. By mid-afternoon they were a good ten miles out by Wyoming's estimation. Reaching the crest of a wooded hill Wyoming spied a tree-bordered stream a mile or so down the long gradual downgrade. The afternoon sun glistened off ripples as the stream wound through grassy banks bordered by thick piñon forests. He reined Sparky about and rode back to meet the trailing buckboard and wagons, which were lagging farther and farther behind. Coming insight of the buckboard he surmised immediately that things were not right. Dixon, pale of face, leaned his head upon his wife's shoulder.

"Mr. McCord," Mrs. Dixon called, a worried expression on her face, "I'm afraid Henry has worn himself out. He hasn't the strength to handle the horses any longer. And I'm afraid neither I nor the girls have ever driven a team."

Wyoming quickly dismounted.

"I'll hitch Sparky to the rear of the buckboard and take over driving. We're not so far yet to go I don't reckon," Wyoming said.

Mrs. Dixon nodded, much relieved, and she and Wyoming helped Dixon to the rear seat where he lay with his head in his wife's lap, his breathing labored. Annabelle, holding up her skirts to reveal tiny black slippers and trim white-stockinged ankles, climbed over the backrest onto the front seat. Angelique followed scooting to the far side of the bench seat. Annabelle took Allison upon her lap. Taking the reins Wyoming chucked the horses into motion. He glanced down at Allison.

"Are you all right?" he asked seeing the anxious expression on her face.

"Is dada going to be all right," she whispered.

"Of course, Al," Annabelle whispered.

"But mother is crying," she hissed worriedly.

"You know how mother is. Daddy will be fine," Annabelle assured her though the look she gave Wyoming over the girl's head was one of less certainty.

As they drove along Jackrabbits and wild turkeys abound, and wild ducks skittered off the shoals to wing in rapid flight up the stream. The wagon trail angled due south and Wyoming saw in the far distance what must be the ranch.

The ascent here was gradual, and the breath of pine and juniper blew strong on the warm breeze. They entered an open park, level with patches of brown mats of needles under the green pines that stood far apart. There were several cabins, and what looked like a bunkhouse, a barn and stables and corral, and pastures beyond the barn. Most of the buildings were weathered and gray with darker hue on the split shingle roofs. The largest building, which Wyoming saw was the main ranch house, had wide eaves and sturdy gray chimneys, and glass windows. It was shaped in an ell, with one gabled end facing the yard. A long porch ran the remainder of its front reached by two wood steps. The house appeared to be well made, sited under the overhanging green of a tall pine that seemed to tower over it protectively. As he drove the buckboard into the yard the thought crossed Wyoming's mind that he had seen a sight of ranches, but this was one of the finest he had ever set eyes on. A hound began to bay, deep and hollow apparently announcing their arrival.

The door of the bunkhouse opened, and a man stepped out on the porch. He was ruddy complexioned with thick dark eyebrows, brawny shoulders and unkempt hair low on his thick neck. He stood watching the little caravan pull up to the main house with expressionless eyes. Wyoming pulled the buckboard to a stop and climbing down helped the others.

"I'll get my wind in a bit," Dixon said to Wyoming, and leaning on his wife's arm walked to the porch where he sat down on a rocking chair there. Annabelle stood by the rear of the buckboard watching curiously as Wyoming walked over to the bunkhouse.

"Wal, now. What have we here?" queried the ruddy faced rider. His sombrero was pulled low and Wyoming could catch only a gleam of intense eyes.

"Howdy," Wyoming greeted the man, pushing back his sombrero with his thumb. "I reckon I'm in the right place if this is the Triangle A," he drawled.

"You reckoned wrong mister," the cowboy replied. "Never heard of no Triangle A."

"Well, I reckon you have now. My boss, Mr. Dixon yonder, is the new owner of this place," Wyoming drawled, "and that's what he's decided to call it, the Triangle A."

"Dixon? Shore, why didn't yu say so first off. Fact is we been kinda on the lookout fer the new owner," the man returned walking to the edge of the porch. Three other riders stepped unhurriedly out onto the porch. Wyoming recognized one of them; the cowboy from the rodeo. Close up in the bright light of day Wyoming saw that he was no more than twenty. His sombrero was pushed back off his forehead exposing flaming red hair. His bright blue eyes took in Wyoming with mocking contempt. His companion was almost identical in appearance, long-limbed and slim-hipped, though slightly older. The last rider was Mexican. Swarthy of face, he had a thick black mustache which extended below his lips, and black slits for eyes. Wyoming noted that all were armed.

"Howdy. You fellers got handles?" Wyoming said, his keen gaze taking in the three.

"Ackers," the first man replied, "Jed Ackers. This here is Jimmy Anderson an' Ned Walters. Thet greaser there is Jimenez. Who air yu?"

"I'm Wyoming McCord, foreman for Mr. Dixon"

"Where's Bull?" the man challenged.

"He ain't here," Wyoming said.

"Why not? Hester said he'd be takin' charge."

"Well, he ain't here 'cause I'm riding for Dixon and this ranch won't be big enough for the both of us," Wyoming declared.

"What'd yu say yur name was?" Ackers queried slowly as the other three came up to stand slightly behind him.

"Wyoming McCord."

"McCord, huh?" Ackers replied ponderingly.

"That's right," Wyoming countered, eyes shifting momentarily to Anderson. *So this is the cowboy Carmelita was stuck on. And it looks as if he's taken a fancy to Annabelle's sister. Well, I shore don't want him hanging on, and none of the others either,* he considered rapidly making up his mind. "And if you're pards with Bull Burton I reckon you'll not be doing any riding for this outfit either."

"I reckon thet cuts it," Ackers said, "If Bull's not givin' orders, I'm though with this outfit! Walters, Anderson yu and Jimenez fetch yur hawses and mine. We're packin' te leave this rut-hole outfit." He eyed Wyoming. "I reckon we got wages comin'."

"Shore, I'll see to that," Wyoming replied easily. "My calculations are you got one month coming each. In the meantime pack your gear."

He walked over to where Dixon and the others waited.

"Miss Dixon I'd like some cash if you have it to pay off four punchers that I let go."

"Oh. Why, certainly," Annabelle replied as she hefted the bag from the buckboard and opened it. She looked at Wyoming questioningly.

"Make it a month for each rider at thirty-five a month," Wyoming instructed, and watched her count out the money.

"Thanks, Miss Dixon," Wyoming said taking the bills. He strode back to where the men waited with saddled horses.

"Here's what's due you," Wyoming said handing over the cash. "Now you and your pards, get off this ranch," Wyoming ordered.

"We're goin'," Ackers retorted darkly mounting his horse and wheeling it about. Anderson, Walters and the Mexican Jimenez swung in behind him.

When Anderson came abreast of the buckboard where Angelique sat he reined his horse to a stop.

"Hello bright eyes," he grinned easily. "Fancy meetin' yu here."

"Hello, Jimmy," she smiled. "I—I didn't know you worked for my father," she said shyly.

"Used to," he replied pulling out the makings and slowly rolling a cigarette. He casually struck a match with his thumbnail and lit the cigarette. He puffed out a cloud of smoke then peered lazily down at Angelique. "Thet gun totin' foreman of yur paw's just sacked me."

Her eyes rounded in surprise. "But—" she began, and then shot an angry look at Wyoming before turning to her father.

Dixon tilted his head peered questioningly at Wyoming who gazed silently back at him his expression plain. Dixon either trusted his judgment or not. If not, then Wyoming had no business here. Dixon was quick to recognize that fact.

"Come mother, let's have a look at our new home," he said.

"I'll see yu around bright eyes," Anderson said, and spurred off, his three companions at his heels.

Wyoming watched the dark figures vanish down under the trees.

"Well," Dixon said, taking off his hat and wiping his face with a kerchief, "I take it we have no riders?"

"I reckon that's so," Wyoming mused.

"Why did you let—let Jimmy go?" Angelique demanded. "You just met him. How—"

"Well, Miss Angelique I reckon he wasn't a good fit for this ranch."

With lips compressed she climbed down from the buckboard and stomped up onto the porch. Wyoming watched her, jaw tight. Besides being a first-rate horseman, Jimmy Anderson was also a lady killer.

"What are we going to do with no riders?" Dixon asked.

"Hire some more; ones we can trust. I'll talk to Mr. Ward." He looked up at the Mexican hand still seated on the wagon's high seat. "Chico we best start unloading the wagons."

"*Si, Señor* Wyoming," he replied cheerfully leaping to the ground, the other driver joined him.

"Mr. Ward mentioned that no one has been living in the house for some time. I suppose it'll need a good cleaning," Mrs. Dixon said, shaking her head worriedly as she stepped cautiously up on the porch where Angelique stood back stiff. She waited as her husband fumbled to remove a key from his vest pocket with which he unlocked the door. He stepped inside and Mrs. Dixon, Angelique and Allison followed. Mrs. Lindsey brought up the rear.

"Why did you fire those riders?" Annabelle asked coming up beside him, irritation evident in her voice.

"Well, Miss Dixon, they were rustling your dad's cattle," Wyoming replied.

"Good Lord!" she exclaimed. "How can you be so sure? That Jimmy Anderson…Angelique thinks he's nice, and he acts so—so pleasant, and friendly—"

"Shore, I reckon he does," Wyoming retorted his gray eyes, with their unfathomable clearness, making Annabelle uneasy. "And I suppose you even have a good word for Ed Hester."

Wyoming's dry tone added to Annabelle's discomfort. Her cheeks flushed, and that annoyed her even more.

"Believe me, Miss Dixon," Wyoming continued, "I know. And I reckon we've not seen the last of them."

She stared at him a moment longer, then turned and hurried up the steps and disappeared inside the house.

While the two Mexicans untied the ropes securing the two wagonloads, Wyoming mounted the porch and stepped inside the front door, which stood open. Mrs. Dixon was standing in the center of the large parlor. She looked every bit that of abject disillusionment. Wyoming glanced about. A dilapidated couch with several springs showing sat beneath the window to the right of the door. Two equally decrepit-appearing stuffed chairs were against the opposite wall, one on each side of a rickety side table. In that corner the wallpaper had peeled back exposing the bare plaster. What appeared to be a moth-eaten rug covered much of the floor space. There were no other items in the room.

"Would you just look at this mess," Mrs. Dixon moaned. "And the other rooms are just as deplorable. Filthy, cobwebs everywhere and hardly any furniture at all, and what there is—is totally unusable. The kitchen appears to be the only room that's half decent. It must have been used a lot."

Dixon came into the room at that juncture. He appeared to have his color back. From his expression it didn't appear he shared his wife's antipathy.

"Wyoming, it's a fine sturdy house, dirty and grimy but full of promise at that," he exclaimed, "I sure was concerned about what we'd find. We'll have to do a lot of cleaning and sprucing up, and bring in all new furniture, but we can turn it into a home."

"I reckon that's good," Wyoming said. "I'll make a list of paint and such things we'll need to make the place shore enough comfortable and fit. And Mrs. Dixon, I'll take you back to town tomorrow so you can pick out just what furniture and other items you want."

That appeared to brighten Mrs. Dixon's outlook.

"How many rooms in this place anyhow?" Wyoming asked stepping into the hall. He saw four doors leading off the hall, two to the right and two to the left.

"Well, there's this parlor, a setting room, and four bedrooms, though it appears one was used as an office," Dixon replied. "Then there's the kitchen. It's big enough to serve as a dining room as well. All the rooms have stoves, which is a good thing, and the kitchen range is large and looks in fairly good condition."

Wyoming walked down the hall and peered in a doorway. Annabelle stood staring, almost absently, out through the dirty glass panes of a window on the opposite side of the room upon which hung faded and torn lace curtains. An old desk sat in one corner. There was no other furniture in the room. She glanced back over her shoulder as Wyoming stepped into the room.

"Daddy said us girls could choose whatever room we wanted for our bedroom, and I chose this one," she said.

"Well, I reckon you shore got a good view," he remarked coming up beside her to peer out the window.

"I suppose," she murmured turning away from the window. She glanced despondently around the room. "Where are we to sleep tonight?" she sighed. "There are only two beds in the whole house and from the looks of them I would rather sleep on the floor."

"I reckon that's the case, unless your dad wants to go back to town and get your old room back at the hotel."

"I don't think that's very practical."

"I reckon not. Where are your sisters going to sleep?"

"Angelique and Allison picked the room across the hall, but I think we'd like to stay together, at least for the night—us girls, I mean."

"Then I'll fix up a pallet of thick blankets here on the floor for the three of you," he said.

"Thank you. Where will you sleep?"

"In the bunkhouse I reckon."

"Oh? Couldn't you be a little closer, like in the parlor, until we're settled? After all, daddy's not well, and there's only us women."

"You'll all be safe in here I reckon, but if it'll make you feel better, I'll throw down my bedroll there in the parlor," Wyoming replied, feeling suddenly like Sir Galahad vowing to protect the Holy Grail.

CHAPTER EIGHT

C arrying saddle and pack the short distance to one of the cabins he had observed on arrival he tossed them on the porch. A big gray hound crawled out from the space under the cabin's porch and ambled over to him. He patted the dog's head, which seemed to satisfy the animal. Undoing his chaps he tossed them over his saddle. He looked up at the cabin. It appeared well constructed as he had noticed were the other buildings. He pushed open the door and stepped inside where he stood surveying the room, noticing several initials curved into the logs beside the sturdy wood bunk, and the charcoal drawings of brands on the stone fireplace above which hung bleached antlers. A table that could serve as a desk sat opposite the bunk. On the table sat a lantern with smoke-blackened glass globe. It appeared to still contain some kerosene. After a moment he walked back out on the porch and carried his saddle and pack inside. It was a nice well-built cabin, nothing fancy, but it would do him fine.

Leaving Sparky standing reins down in front of the cabin, Wyoming set out to check the other buildings. One he surmised was the cook shack. Pushing open the door he saw a very messy kitchen. Flies buzzed about the cluttered and grubby cabinets. A large cooking range sat against the opposing wall stacked with several blackened pots. A stovepipe, once black but now heat-sheared and rusty, extended upward and out through the side of the building. Racks and shelves containing various cans and sundry other foodstuffs covered an adjacent wall. Immediately to the right an open door led into a long narrow room. Adam peered through the door. A wooden table with sturdy wood benches on each side, which would surely accommodate a dozen or more riders, ran nearly the length of the room. He shook his head disgusted. It was going to take a lot of cleaning to get this place back in shape.

Wyoming started off toward the barn and stables leading Sparky. There were rows of stalls halfway along on each side of the wide walkway of the stables. In the barn he saw hay and fodder, but not an overly amount, he thought, what with the cold weather soon to come. He noticed a bin with corn that appeared to be from last year. He saw wagons and harnesses that looked well used. The barn reeked with the heady odor of hay and manure. Strolling out the wide back doors, still leading Sparky he saw a dozen or more horses milling about in the corral. A long fenced lane ran down to pastures. He saw more horses and heard cows mooing from the direction of several small buildings nestled among a grove of aspen about seventy-five yards down the gradual incline. Curious, he stepped astride Sparky and rode over to have a look. A short amiable looking Mexican stood before a chicken coop silently watching him approach.

"Howdy," Wyoming called.

The Mexican nodded, but said nothing. Between his limited Spanish and the man's limited English, Wyoming was able to determine that the Mexican, whose name was Ramon, came with the ranch. Riding back to the stables after securing a pail of milk and a chicken the Mexican had killed and cleaned, he removed Sparky's saddle and turned him into one of the empty stalls. He poured a pail-full of grain into the bin and tossed in a pitchfork of hay, after which he filled the water trough from a rain barrel outside the wide doors.

He started for the house, the dog following at his heels sniffing at the dead chicken wrapped in a bloody newspaper. As he walked along he considered this Jed Ackers and his outfit. There was no doubt in his mind he would hear from them again…and not too long in the waiting. He stepped up on the porch his spurs emitting a musical jingle. Entering the kitchen he found Annabelle, Angelique and her mother going through boxes of the foodstuff they had packed in. He glanced about the kitchen. A large cooking range sat against one interior wall. Opposite the stove was a well-used dry sink with a tall blind door cupboard top with three drawers and three side doors that must have made its way west on some long ago wagon train. In the center of the spacious room was a large table.

"Say, Mrs. Dixon, I've been having a look-see around, and I discovered there's a Mexican down yonder back of the barn a ways that raises vegetables, chickens, and pigs. The man's name is Ramon and he's got more'n a half-dozen milk cows. And shore enough; he's in Mr. Dixon's employ, so we can live off the fat of the land you might say. Ramon killed and cleaned a chicken while I was there, so I lugged it up, along with a jug of milk," he grinned plopping the dead bird and the jug of milk on the table.

"Wyoming, that's wonderful news," Mrs. Dixon exclaimed. "Annabelle, mix up a batch of dough for biscuits—"

"And I'll prepare the chicken," Mrs. Lindsey said. "I know everyone is hungry."

"Something I can help with?" Wyoming asked.

"You can bring in some more wood and see to the fire," Mrs. Lindsey smiled.

"Angelique you start peeling potatoes," Mrs. Dixon instructed.

"Yes, mother," Angelique sighed searching in one of the cabinets for a paring knife.

"And where has Allison run off to anyhow?"

Allison picked that moment to bounce excitedly into the kitchen. "Guess what I found," she cried.

Mrs. Dixon glanced over her shoulder. "There you are. Where have you been?" she demanded.

"Outside. And I made a new friend—"

"A new friend?" her mother exclaimed alarmed.

"Yes, a big dog. He's kind of scrawny though."

"Yeah, I made his acquaintance," Wyoming grinned.

"You did? Do you know his name?"

"Nope. I reckon you'll just have to name him."

"Oh! Well, I'll call him Caesar. Do you think he'll mind, having a new name?"

"Silly," Angelique scoffed, "It's just a dog. Why would he care?"

"Dogs have feelings too," Allison protested.

"Caesar sounds like a fine name," Annabelle said.

"Just you be careful that dog doesn't give you fleas," Mrs. Dixon cautioned.

The sun was dipping below the tops of the tall pines when Mrs. Lindsey called everyone to supper.

"I sure hope I don't make a mess of ranching," Dixon said shaking his head worriedly as they gathered about the table. "Now that we're here, where do we begin?"

"With the house here," answered Wyoming. "There's shore lots to do. My idea is to hire some riders, which I'll set about doing tomorrow. They can help with cleaning and painting, and hauling in new furniture. After we get the house all spruced up I'll do some looking around and try to get a lay of your ranch, maybe get an idea of just how many cattle you've got."

Sometime later, Wyoming made his way down to the cabin that he had decided to make his abode. Once inside he practiced drawing his pistol for more than half an hour, something he had neglected to do the last few days. Satisfied, he holstered his pistol and got his bedroll. On the way back to the house he checked on the two Mexicans who had settled for the night in the bunk house. Once back at the house, he spread his bedroll under the window in the parlor. Stretching out after removing only his boots and gun belt he laid there peering out the curtainless window at a black sky alive with a million twinkling lights.

In one of the bedrooms not far away the three girls undressed amid whispers and laughs and crawled under the blankets. On her side Annabelle wearily stretched out with a sigh. Allison snuggled close and lovingly.

"I like Wyoming," she whispered, "Don't you?"

"Of course," she whispered back.

"Hush you two and go to sleep," Angelique rejoined languorously.

Annabelle lay awake, gratefully aware of Allison's warm cheek and trusting little hand in hers. She stared out through the curtainless window at the starlit sky. She did like Wyoming she admitted and felt her cheek warm as she thought of his stolen kiss—and that he hadn't tried to steal another. She would let him, of course, but she would never tell him that she sighed as her thoughts trailed off and she dropped into the land of her dreams.

During the night Wyoming woke to what sounded like coughing from one of the bedrooms. It was a deep hacking sound, which went on for some time. He knew it was Mr. Dixon. Wyoming was finally able to get back to sleep, but was up at the first touch of gray in the window. Pulling on his boots, he buckled on his gun belt and went into the kitchen.

"An indoor pump, what do you know?" Wyoming marveled applying his hand to the handle and after one or two pumps saw water gush out into the basin.

He washed his hands and face and dried them on a towel hanging on a rack above the basin after which he let himself out. A short distance beyond the cabin he had picked for his abode was another, which appeared slightly larger. He walked over to it and pushing open the door peered into the dim interior. A thick layer of dust lay over the floor, but otherwise the cabin was empty. The big room had two windows and the floor and walls seemed solid and in good shape. What the cabin had been used for in the past he had no idea, but gazing about he had an inspiration. He went back outside and stood peering up at the house recalling Hank Ward's comments the morning of the rodeo.

"Wal, son that old ranch will shore te be jumpin'," Ward had said grinning broadly. "Shore, them cowboys all got a look at them Dixon lasses. Once word gets out they'll be riders from all over callin' at the Triangle A."

Wyoming started off toward the stables running Ward's words over in his mind as he walked along. He knew cowboys and knew Ward was right. And, blast it all, it seemed Angelique had already set her sights on a young man—who just happened to be a rustler! Sure enough there was going to be hell to pay. Reaching the stalls he saddled Sparky and rode over to Ramon's place. He returned sometime later with a slab of bacon, fresh eggs and another jug of milk.

He found Mrs. Lindsey in the kitchen. She had already started a fire in the big kitchen range and the pungent smell of burning wood hung in the air. He saw that she had also put a coffee pot on to boil."Good morning," she said glancing over her shoulder at him as he came into the room.

"Morning. Say, I been out getting some groceries," he said, depositing the items he fetched from the Mexican on the table.

"Mr. McCord, aren't you a miracle worker!" Annabelle said entering the kitchen at that moment. "Bacon and eggs…and milk!"

She wore a colorful gingham apron over a bright yellow gown, which did nothing to conceal her shapeliness. Her sleeves were rolled up above the elbows of her slender round tan arms, and her golden curls were pulled back on her head and tied with a ribbon. Allison skipped in behind Annabelle.

"Is there any chicken left over?" she asked.

"You want chicken for breakfast?" Annabelle cried.

"No, it's for Caesar."

"There's a few pieces left," Mrs. Lindsey smiled. "In the box there."

"Thank you," Allison said hurrying over to the large wooden box on the cabinet.

"I heard coughing during the night. Your dad's not feeling any better?" Wyoming asked.

"It doesn't seem so," Annabelle replied quietly. "Daddy had another bad spell and momma's staying with him. I don't think either one got much sleep last night," she said worriedly.

"I'm shore sorry to hear that," he said.

"Yesterday and last night is the first real bad spell he's had since we got here to New Mexico. I was beginning to hope this high altitude was really helping."

"Give it some time," Wyoming encouraged. "I've seen some fellows twice as bad off as your dad come out cured and strong. That was up in Wyoming, which is shore not as wonderful as this Northern New Mexico."

"I hope you're right," she said.

"Shore I am. Tell your dad to rest a lot but get outdoors and breathe this sage and mountain air as much as he can."

She gave him a strange look; appreciative, amazed, encouraged, he couldn't tell which, but it left him with a feeling of high spirits.

"Thank you," she murmured. "I'll tell him what you said."

"I was planning on getting Chico and his cousin to drive the wagons into town and pick up paint and some other things this morning. We'll need both wagons to carry everything. I don't reckon your mother will feel like coming along with us to pick out furniture?"

"We talked about that this morning and momma gave me a list. I'll go instead of her—"

"I want to go!" Allison cried, "Please, may I?"

"If momma says," Annabelle answered. "But do we have to ride in one of those wagons? They look so rough and bouncy."

"Then we'll take the buckboard and let Chico and his cousin drive the wagons."

"That'll be nice. I didn't look forward to riding in that big old wagon."

He leaned back in his chair watching her as Allison hurried to ask her mother if she could ride into town with Annabelle and Wyoming.

Mrs. Lindsay went about fixing breakfast, softly humming a tune all the while, and soon the delicious smell of baking biscuits, percolating coffee and sizzling bacon satiated the room.

"I'll go wake Angelique and see if momma and dad feel like eating," Annabelle said.

But before she could do so her parents came into the kitchen dressed for the day.

"I couldn't stay in that rickety bed any longer. It's sure hard on my back. Can't wait to get a new bed and mattress. Course I could smell those biscuits and frying bacon," her father said. He looked washed-out and drained though his voice was strong.

"Don't tell me Angelique is still abed," Mrs. Dixon exclaimed.

"Let her sleep, mother," Dixon said. "It's been a tiring last few days."

"You're just going to encourage that lazy girl," replied Mrs. Dixon. "At her age she should be up and about."

"Mr. Dixon, you know we're going to have to paint every room in this house, and do a lot of scrubbing," Wyoming spoke up. "It shore won't be healthy trying to sleep in here all while that's going on. So I was thinking, why don't all of you stay in them two cabins across from the bunkhouse? It wouldn't take much to clean them and we could fix them up with furniture; beds and such. You and Mrs.

Dixon could take the smaller one and the girls and Mrs. Lindsey the other. Then when work on the house is done, we'll move all of you back in here."

"I thought you were going to stay in the small cabin," Dixon said.

"I will after you folks resettle in the house. Until then I can sleep in the bunkhouse."

"Wyoming, that's a splendid idea," Dixon said, and Mrs. Dixon nodded approvingly. "When you go into town today Annabelle can pull some additional cash out of the bank so as to pay for everything."

CHAPTER NINE

Wyoming looked forward to the ride into town in the buckboard with Annabelle seated beside him. Allison sat in the rear one arm around the hound whispering in his ear. At this altitude the air was brisk, but the sun was still warm on his back. Big-tooth maple trees, with gold and russet leaves tinged with green lined the riverbank. Wild turkeys and deer scarcely made an effort to move into the green brush. There was a dreamy hum of murmuring water mingled with the sough of wind in the great silver spruces and pines. Annabelle was quiet as they rode out of the yard under the cool shade of the tall pines, and Wyoming wondered what she was thinking for she seemed deep in thought; or perhaps, he considered, she was just engrossed in the sights. When they reached the point where the road turned alongside the river, she turned to peer at him.

"Mr. McCord—"

"Didn't I ask you to call me Wyoming? A pretty girl calling me Mister shore makes me feel ancient," he drawled.

"Is that so?"

"Yep."

"Alright, Wyoming, if you insist. So, may I ask you a question?"

"Shore, ask away."

"This ranching business; just how does one make a living at it?"

He was somewhat taken aback by her question, which seemed extremely naïve to him. He glanced sharply at her.

"I mean," she continued, "at our—old home at La Grande Pointe along Bayou Teche—that's in Louisiana," she explained glancing up at him as though that was important to know, "Daddy grew cotton and sugar—Oh, we had hundreds and hundreds of acres—and lots of workers…but then M'sieur Rousseau—" she bit her lower lip suddenly catching herself.

She was silent for a long moment. He glanced at her and he realized that she hadn't meant to make such a confession. He wondered what she had been about to say, and who was this M'sieur Rousseau? She took a deep breath.

"Daddy's health turned poor and, well, there were some financial problems too," she sighed. "The doctors said he should move to a higher, dryer altitude, so he sold everything, and he bought this ranch, sight unseen—"

"That's what I heard. Probably not a wise thing to do, but I'm shore glad he did."

"Yes, exactly," she said, failing to notice his insinuation, or choosing to ignore it. "Daddy has no idea how to raise cattle—"

"Well, now. I wouldn't be so shore about that. Your dad shore has his share of brains; else he couldn't have done so well in the cotton trade."

"That's debatable," she replied forlornly. "Buying the ranch, then the long journey across Texas—weeks in a cramped railway car, and then living in a hotel, all the waiting—daddy hasn't been one to manage money well and mother refuses to. That's why I became the family treasurer. Daddy is very proud. He would not admit he has made…well, used bad judgment… Mis—Wyoming," she corrected, "can this ranching business work?"

"I should smile it can work, and it shore will. This is fine grazing land," he said glancing out over the open countryside, rolling and vast and dotted ending in the deep purple distance. "Its shore fit for cattle. Now, I know it's too early to know just how many head your dad has, but let's take a ridiculous estimate, say you got two thousand cows left after what the rustlers have driven off so far. I shore hate to brag, but there's nothing I can't do with a rope. I bet I could find a thousand calves out in them canyons that you've never dreamed of. That number with the branding of mavericks will—"

"Mavericks?"

"Shore. A maverick's a calf that's lost its mother, so to speak. All ranchers brand mavericks more or less."

"And that's not rustling?" she asked, skeptically.

"Heck no! Shore not like brand-burning. You see out on the range with mixed herds from different ranches there can't be no positive identification of whose calf it is unless the calf accompanies a branded cow, so if a calf or a yearling or even a two year old hasn't got the mark of one outfit, it'll shore get that of another, eventually. Now, what was I saying? Take that two thousand, well; we could double that this coming year. That means say, forty-five hundred. Following year six thousand head. Third year—well, I reckon you get the picture. With branding and calving, and with two-year-olds selling at twelve dollars a head—in three years you'd be worth over a hundred thousand dollars—"

"One hundred and forty-four thousand!" she exclaimed turning on the seat to stare at him.

"Yep. That's what I figured. But I don't want to get your hopes up sky high—"

"Oh, but you have!"

She said nothing for a moment.

"How do you propose to do all this branding, with no riders?"

"I reckon I can pick up a rider or two; punchers we can trust. With a hardworking crew we could cover a lot of ground—as long as the rustlers leave us alone."

She said nothing more leaning back against the backrest hands clasped in her lap, her gaze following the gradual ascent to where the slopes rose in long slants, like ribs of a washboard, ending in a craggy mountain ridge. He glanced over at her out of the corner of his eye, at her pink lips, lips he wanted badly to kiss again. What would she do if he just leaned over and… She turned to peer at him at that moment. Her cheeks turned a rosy tint and she quickly glanced back over her shoulder at her sister, and he wondered if she had read his thoughts and was reminding him that they had company.

"Alie, that filthy dog is going to ruin your dress," she scolded.

"He's not filthy! I gave him a bath just yesterday," her sister retorted.

It was past noon and the sun was well over the mountain ridge when Wyoming reined the buckboard up in front of the bank. The wagons continued on down the street to Carter's Department Store. Wyoming helped Annabelle down from the seat and reached for Allison.

"What about Caesar," she asked. "Will he be all right in the buckboard?"

"Shore, come on," he said holding her hand as she jumped to the ground.

"Stay, Caesar!" she commanded.

The dog stretched out on the floor of the buckboard with a loud grunt.

"Good boy," Allison pronounced going ahead of Wyoming and Annabelle into the bank.

Allison flopped on a bench against the far wall and Wyoming sat beside her as Annabelle approached one of the vacant teller windows. Shortly Annabelle joined them clutching her pocket book under one arm obviously nervous about such a responsibility. Leaving the bank Annabelle stayed close to Wyoming's side as the three walked out to the buckboard. Allison hopped into the buckboard and knelt down beside Caesar.

"Did you miss me, boy?" she cooed.

"Allison. I told you, you're going to ruin your dress!" Annabelle admonished.

"I heard you already," the girl snorted dismissing her sister's concern. "And besides, the dress is old anyhow."

Wyoming drove down to the store where the wagons waited out in front. The department store, he remembered, had about everything, furniture, kitchenware, bedding, linen, rugs, paint, all that they would need. Wyoming left Annabelle and Allison to choose what furniture, bedding and other items they had decided on while he arranged for paint and cleaning supplies and a few new tools that were in short supply at the ranch.

Finishing his business he walked several blocks west toward the rail yards where the blacksmith shop stood. There he picked up the stamped branding irons that Dixon had ordered two weeks prior. They were made in one piece so the brand can be stamped on the animal in one operation. The design on the end of the iron rod was in the shape of a triangle in the center of which was the letter *A*. Wyoming paid the smithy; a short stout Mexican with a long drooping black mustache and went in search of Annabelle and Allison. As he walked along Wyoming glanced down at the irons in his hand. He preferred to carry a running iron, a straight bar with a hook on the business end since it was much lighter and a rider could run any type brand with it. Of course that presented a problem and could arouse suspicion since some crafty individuals could use the running iron in the practice of branding cattle that didn't belong to them.

Allison was sucking on a peppermint stick waiting while Annabelle worked on completing her list of items for the house when Wyoming got back to the store. He stood back watching Annabelle. She appeared quite serious and intent, her red lips set determinedly. She had removed her bonnet hanging it over one arm by its ribbon. Her soft golden curls were drawn back and tied with a narrow blue ribbon in a sort of ponytail. She looked extremely fetching and he had an urge to kiss her. She glanced up and saw him watching her. She looked quizzically at him, then blushed, and he realized he must have been staring fixedly at her.

"Wyoming, I'm almost done," she said still peering at him self-consciously. "Did you get everything on your list?"

"Yep," he nodded.

"I'm disappointed in the beds," she ventured. "I wanted wood frame, but all they have in stock are these made of iron and brass tubing. Fortunately they have new box spring mattresses. They do have everything else though, dressers, chests of drawers, chairs, tables, rugs—Oh, can we get it all in the two wagons?" she asked apprehensively.

All the while Wyoming and the two Mexicans loaded the various pieces of furniture and other items into the wagon, Annabelle waited in the buckboard with Allison who sat in the back trying to keep Caesar from snatching her candy. Finally the loading was all done and all was ready for the return trip.

"We're all loaded and ready to go," Wyoming said peering up at Annabelle. "But I reckon we ought to get a bite to eat before we start back."

She nodded. "Yes, we ought."

"There's a little café a few blocks over."

Wyoming climbed in the buckboard and set off down the street, the wagons following. At the corner he turned and continued another block to the little café where he had eaten that first evening in town.

"You fellers stay with the wagons. I'll send some food out," he called to Chico and his cousin.

"*Si, Señor,*" Chico grinned.

They found an empty table near the front. Allison slid into the seat next to the window and Annabelle sat beside her. A young Mexican girl was busy waiting on tables and Wyoming gave her only half a glance until a rough voice drew his attention.

"Look where yu're goin' little *Señorita,*" complained a hard voice. "I got a bunion on thet foot."

"I am sorry, *Señor,*" the girl murmured.

Wyoming glanced over his shoulder just as the girl turned toward him. Their eyes met at the same instant.

"*Señor* Wyoming!" she cried, and with a rush of tiny slippered feet, threw herself into his arms.

"Carmelita!" he managed as her slender tan arms wrapped about his neck. Carmelita leaned her head back, her arms still about him, peering up at him with big expressive brown eyes.

"*Señor* Wyoming, you did not go away?"

"I reckon not," he replied as over her shoulder he saw Annabelle's large staring eyes. Allison was grinning. "Are you working in this here café?"

"*Si. Papá* said I must help with the money, and *Señor* Wiley, he give me a job in the café. How do I look?" she beamed stepping back and holding out the skirt of her dainty white dress as she gazed at him with large dusky-hued eyes surrounded by long dark lashes.

"Why, I reckon you look right—handsome," he fumbled.

Her lustrous raven black hair was pulled back from her forehead with a colorful ribbon, and her eyes of velvet blackness peered openly at him. And he realized that there was not going to be any way to avoid having to explain how he was acquainted with the little Mexican waitress. Carmelita had already seen to that.

"Miss Annabelle, Allison, this here is Carmelita," he began, annoyed to feel the blood heat his face. "Carmelita's dad is a good friend; in fact he saved my life once some time back. Carmelita, this here is my boss' daughters…Miss Annabelle, and Miss Allison" he continued.

"*Mucho gusto*—it is very nice to meet you," Carmelita murmured, smiling at Allison, but then her eyes touched upon Annabelle. She turned to Wyoming, "She is very pretty, *Señor* Wyoming," she whispered, and her eyes were like ebony gulfs of changing brilliance, dark piercing as the points of daggers.

A bell rang at that instant and a voice yelled from the kitchen, "Carmelita!"

"I must go," she said hurriedly, her dusky eyes hooded. "The cook calls for me."

Wyoming took the empty chair across from Annabelle and Allison.

"Well, I reckon you shore left that little detail out of your story," Annabelle taunted coolly mimicking his manner of speech.

"Carmelita? I reckon I plumb forgot about her."

"Ah-huh," Annabelle replied barely refraining from rolling her eyes.

At that moment Carmelita appeared at the table. "Now, what would you like?" she inquired musically her luminous brown eyes upon Wyoming.

Allison quickly made her order. Annabelle pointed to an item on the menu without speaking.

"Well, I reckon I'll have your steak and some coffee," Wyoming said, "and could you fetch something to my ranch hands waiting in the wagons out front?"

Carmelita flashed him a smile and flounced off with a swish of her skirts.

"How did her father save your life?" Allison asked eyes round.

"Yes, tell us," Annabelle said overly sweet knowing she was acting like an infant, jealous that someone else was attempting to play with her new favorite toy, but for some reason she couldn't help it and that only made her feel more pitiful.

"Well," Wyoming began ignoring her sarcasm. "It all came about after that little incident up in Colorado that I told you about. I was shot up some and was kind of out of my head when I stumbled upon this little sheepherder's place. Carmelita's dad was the one who took me in and doctored me back to health. I reckon I wouldn't have made it but for her paw."

Carmelita arrived at the table carrying a tray laden with their food. Annabelle peered up at her, rich color in her cheeks.

"Wyoming just told us how your father saved his life," Allison beamed.

Carmelita flashed a look of pure innocence as she placed the dishes on the table.

"Oh, but *Señor* Wyoming did not tell you how he saved Carmelita from that *malhecho*, that ugly man, who try to kidnap Carmelita?"

The Mexican girl now held the stage. Both Allison and Annabelle slowly shook their heads.

"*Señor* Wyoming, shame for you," Carmelita scolded, deep-brown eyes upon him. She turned excitedly to Annabelle. "Then Carmelita must tell you," she said with a proud gay laugh. "I thought *Señor* Wyoming was a *bandito* when he came first to the house all bloody. He have this big gun he carry," she said archly with a roguish glance at Wyoming. "One morning—it was after *Señor* Wyoming was strong to get out of bed; two men came to our *casa*. I see one of the men before and he frighten me; the look in his eye. He say he want to tell me something…but when I come close he grab me up on his horse to carry me away," she said, eyes aglow, "but *Señor* Wyoming, he stop him, and when this man he try pull out his *pistola*, *Señor* Wyoming, he shoot him dead—"

"Oh," Annabelle exclaimed, and Wyoming saw her shiver as though a sudden chill had swept over her.

"Carmelita!" yelled the voice from the kitchen and the girl rolled her eyes and with a hapless smile hurried off.

"Well, I reckon I figured to leave that part out, so as not to disturb your sensibilities," he drawled. "I reckon that Hobard was shore going to pack her off to the mountains as I reckon he and many hombres like him have done before with girls. I did what any civilized feller would've done," he said glancing at Annabelle. She gazed at him, her jade green eyes unreadable.

They did not exchange half a dozen words after that throughout the meal, to which Wyoming did justice that would assuredly have flattered the cook. Annabelle, however, only toyed with her food, her eyes frequently resting upon Carmelita as she scurried about waiting tables looking cool and fresh even with the fast pace of her job.

The meal finished, Allison hurried out to the buckboard and climbed in. Kneeling beside the hound she unfolded her napkin to reveal the large bone left from Wyoming's steak. "Here you are Caesar," she cooed.

Wyoming helped Annabelle into the buckboard. The two Mexican teamsters lounged on the wagon seats done eating the food Carmelita had carried out. Climbing up on the driver's seat Wyoming chucked the horses into motion. When the buckboard started up the road on the gradual rise out of town Annabelle scooted over next to him.

"Let me drive the horses—Please?" she importuned. "I think I ought to learn how."

The feel of Annabelle's hip against his was particularly unnerving.

"You're in the wrong seat," Wyoming said as he passed the reins to her, "but here you are. Take two lines in each hand, arms bent at the elbows with the lines stretched tight."

She emitted a gasp as the horses, sensing the unfamiliar tension on the lines, picked up their pace.

"Keep your elbows in front of your body," Wyoming said one hand on her arm the other inadvertently sliding about her waist, "so if you have to pull back hard to stop the horses, you can do it without leaning back."

"Am I doing it?" she exclaimed excitedly.

"You have 'em all on your own," he assured her. "Practice a kind of give and take on the reins as the horses respond to your cues, keeping a light contact on each mouth."

"Oh, it's too much to remember," she cried.

"You're doing fine. Here now, give 'em enough slack to travel with their heads at a natural level so they can breathe normally," he cautioned her. "Now, if you pull up a little slack on this rein that will pull one horse in the direction you want to go when you want to turn, or you can bend, and give slack on the other rein. That's right—No, not so hard!" he admonished.

She flinched at his rebuke, but set her teeth firmly holding the team steady.

"Good girl," he praised, and she looked up at him, smiled nervously.

"When you get better at it you can use your whip to reach up and tickle the outside horse on the barrel about where a rider's leg would put pressure on him to turn, if there was a rider on him," he said.

Her lovely face was flushed with excitement by the time they reached the point where the road turned alongside the little stream; the horses moving at a steady trot. They passed now over rolling hills out upon open gray prairie sloping up toward the vague dark mountains. He marveled at her strong brown hands on the reins.

"Oh, this is fun," she said.

"Well, I reckon you're shore handling them like an old timer," he said.

"I am, aren't I?" she giggled turning her head to look at him.

He couldn't help himself. He leaned toward her. Her gaze fell to his lips, and he heard her quick intake of breath before his lips touched hers. Annabelle closed her eyes as a shivering tingle ran down her spine. This was what she had wanted, she realized dazedly as he continued to kiss her. A sudden bump and jerk of the buckboard forced them apart. Startled Wyoming looked to see the buckboard careening off the road down a shallow incline. He grabbed the reins from her shaking hands and pulled the buckboard to a halt. Dust swirled up around them. He looked over at Annabelle sitting ramrod straight hands clinched in her lap.

"Holy smokes," he mumbled huskily not looking at her.

"Anne," Allison piped up, "I think you better have more lessons."

The corners of Annabelle's lips quirked, and then she chuckled outright.

"Goodness, I believe you're right," she retorted cheeks taking on a pinkish tint.

Looking totally ingenuous Wyoming drove the buckboard back up on the road and continued on without another word.

Wyoming let Annabelle and Allison off at the house and drove the buckboard down to the large cabin following the wagons. They set about unloading the items. In no time Wyoming worked up a sweat lugging the heavy pieces of furniture into the cabin. Mrs. Dixon and Mrs. Lindsey walked down from the house to oversee the placement of beds and chest of drawers and other items that would be needed until the house was ready. Once the cabins were arranged to the women's satisfaction, Chico unharnessed the teams from one of the wagons, and fed and watered the horses. Chico's cousin started back to town with the rented wagon.

Wyoming walked over to the bunkhouse where he had moved his things. The sun was low over the trees with broken clouds above. He stood watching, his mood strangely jubilant, until the blazing sun slid below the tip of the tall pines. Then he went inside tossing his sombrero on the table and sat upon one of the bunks farthest from the door, one that appeared nobody had used in the past.

CHAPTER TEN

T he next morning work started on the ranch house. For the next four days the women were busy with washing windows, scrubbing and mopping floors. Chico, under Mrs. Lindsey's supervision, was put to hanging new wallpaper in all the rooms, an employment to which he undertook with surprising competency. Wyoming set his hand at painting woodwork and repairing broken and chipped plaster and replacing cracked windowpanes. By the end of the week the renovation of the house was complete and that Monday evening the Dixon's moved back into the house.

The following morning Wyoming was up early and headed up to the house. The sun was peeking over the trees when he stepped up on the porch and knocked on the kitchen door. It opened immediately and he surmised Annabelle had seen him through the window. She looked bewitching in a trim blue dress.

"Is your dad up?" he asked taking off his sombrero.

"Someone asking for me?" Dixon's voice came from down the hall followed by his entrance into the room.

"Morning boss," Wyoming greeted. "Just come up to tell you I'm taking a little ride out. I want to get a line on what cattle you've got. I figure to be back tomorrow evening, or maybe the next."

"I see. Well, I'm sure anxious to know what you find out," Dixon replied.

"Me too, boss." He turned to Annabelle. "Miss Dixon, I was wondering if you wouldn't mind fixing me up some grub to take with me?"

"Of course," she replied washing her hands in the pan at the dry sink. "But you'll eat breakfast before you go."

"Why shore, that'll be fine," he said, and set down at the table across from Dixon. Annabelle sat a steaming cup of coffee before the two of them. As he sipped the hot drink, Wyoming was unable to keep his eyes from seeking her out as she busied herself at the stove beside Mrs. Lindsey, and he was sure of only one thing—that she was decidedly pleasant to look at.

"It's an awful big and rough country," Dixon said, "you'll find your way all right?"

"Shore, boss. It won't take me long to get a line on this here range."

While Wyoming ate, Annabelle had her back to him fixing food for him to take along. Presently she turned to hand him a package wrapped in brown paper.

"Thanks," he said.

"You're welcome," she replied. She peered up at him as though she was about to say something, but after a brief hesitation, turned back to the stove, and bidding goodbye, he went out.

Wyoming rode west along the arroyo then headed a creek that ran about ten miles farther down. After two miles or so he came upon a worn path which he followed leading up under the tall spreading silver branches of towering pines and spruces. An early frost had turned the aspens gold, and their leaves quivered delicately and silently in the soft breeze. The wondrous hue blazed against sky and forest. A hawk sailed across the blue opening above. As he progressed the forest grew thick and darker, and the fragrance of pine and spruce filled the air. Through the break in the foliage he was afforded a grand vista and he drew rein. Staring out through the pines into the far distance he saw a colorful valley that spread out to merge into purple range. In the foreground a mass of slowly bobbing white dotted the grassy plain, and it occurred to him he was looking at the grass-benched slope near the sheepherder Dominquez' ranch. He thought of Carmelita and the promise she had made to have nothing more to do with Anderson. He sat there a long moment peering at the milling sheep far in the distance, before starting on. He came to a shallow, roaring stream. His horse drank the water, foaming white and amber around his knees, and then with splash and thump he forded it over the slippery rocks. As he cracked out upon the narrow trail a covey of grouse whirred up into the low branches of the spruce-trees.

"Tame as chickens, and they shore are pretty," he mused.

Shortly Wyoming struck the south end of a deep wild Canyon. Riding up through the canyon he found it to be some of the roughest country he had ever seen, and the most beautiful. The canyon headed up high in the timber and ran down deep and rough. But he saw lots of water and grass and cattle, some wearing the Bar E—Erickson's old brand as well as numerous unbranded calves and yearlings. Rustlers hadn't worked these canyons; pickings were too easy below. There would be plenty of work for a half dozen riders, Wyoming figured.

He spied lots of deer and turkey, and once he caught a glimpse of a huge black bear ambling up a rugged slope. He kept going working his way along. By mid-afternoon he was far up the canyon. He ran across two or three bulls at different times that eyed him bald-facedly demonstrating little or no fear. Cattle trails threaded the maze of narrow deer trails zigzagging through the brush up the slopes. The wind coming down through the canyon was cool and tangy with the scent of pine. He found himself ruminating over the ride in the buckboard remembering the feel of Annabelle's hip against his as he sat with his arm about her waist, and so he rode along thinking over the maddening situation. He was affected with a strange, fierce spirit to protect Annabelle and the Dixon family in their unfortunate circumstances.

He began to work his way down the canyon and came upon another grassy glade where a thin ribbon of water ran down a squat gully, forming shallow pools here and there. It was getting late and he was hungry. He decided this was as good a place as any to make camp. He led Sparky to one of the water pools, slipped saddle and bridle, and hobbled the horse. Although with plenty of water and grass Wyoming figured the horse probably wouldn't wander far even without the hobbles, but in this rough canyon he decided not to take chances. He built a small fire and put a coffee pot on to boil, then sat down on the bank and opened the package of food Annabelle had put up for him. He was surprised at the generous contents and wondered where his eyes had been while the girl had packed all this food for him. There was bread, cheese and several thick cuts of meat, a slice of cake and wrapped separately and almost missed by him...a lump of sugar.

"I'll be dog-gone," he muttered, the girl continued to confound him. He had never met anyone like her before.

When he had finished eating he drug his saddle up for a backrest, and stretched out before the fire. He sat there watching the glow of the embers and the ruddy flames. At this altitude, and at this time of year, once the sun went down it turned cooler and so after a moment he untied his bedroll and spread it out. He slipped under the blankets after removing gun belt and boots and hanging his sombrero on his saddle. Within moments he was asleep. He came awake during the night and replenished the fire, which had nearly gone out and went back to sleep. Gray cold dawn greeted him when he woke. He rolled out of his blankets and plucking his sombrero on his head, pulled on his boots and buckled on his gun belt, after which he untied his denim jacket from his pack and put it on. The early morning air held a chill.

He got water from one of the small pools, and put the coffee pot back on to boil. He then slipped a grain bag over Sparky's head and returned to the fire where he ate one of the sandwiches Annabelle had made for him, washing it down with hot coffee sweetened with a lump of sugar.

The sun had not yet cleared the mountain ridge when Wyoming set off. He rode some distance along the canyon, which was an opening of a valley leading upwards toward the high mountain ridge. Cattle dotted the landscape. By the time he reached the wide draw the mountains had lost their gray mantle and taken on the color of the sunrise. It wasn't long before he came upon tracks, and turning on them rode north. It was cool in the trees, among lofty pines and spruces. The forest began to change; the lofty pines and spruces were thinning out interspersed now by maple and oaks. Manzanita appeared, and tufts of grass in open spots. Wyoming had difficulty in keeping the charm of the forest from breaking his vigilance. Coming out of the cedars he saw a ranch house in the open grassy plain below sheltered by several tall aspens. It was a sturdy house of pine logs built with a porch or open runway between two identical log structures. A large garden plot set off a ways from the cabin, and there was a corral containing two horses and a mule, and a fair sized barn behind the cabin. Wyoming saw a boy leading a horse then a man at work under an open shed beside the barn. Wyoming approached the place slowly and was still some distance away when he helloed. The boy halted and stared. The man came out from under the shed roof but didn't advance. The boy led the horse over to where the man waited.

Wyoming rode into the yard. The man was about middle-aged; tall slim with a weather-beaten face. The boy was perhaps twelve, dressed in bibbed overalls that, like the man's, had seen many washings. Wyoming's keen eye caught sight of the butt stock of a rifle poking from behind a post near where the man stood.

"Howdy," Wyoming greeted.

The man nodded, but said nothing.

"I'm kinda new to this range," Wyoming said, "Guess I'm turned around some. I was looking for Hank Ward's place."

"Yu passed it aboot ten mile back, up over that ridge yonder," the man returned.

The door to one of the twin cabins opened and Wyoming saw a slender woman in a gray dress. She was about the same age as the man. A child maybe three or four peered wide-eyed from around the side of her skirts.

"My name's McCord. I ride for a feller by the name of Dixon. He bought the old Erickson spread."

"I knowed Erickson," the man said, and Wyoming decided he was not unfriendly, just cautious.

"You've been here a spell, then."

"Yep, near sixteen year. Name's Sid Roberts. This here's my boy, Hal. My oldest boy Dan is out checking our stock 'cross thet far ridge."

"How many cattle you have?" Wyoming queried, because he knew that was a natural question.

"Got aboot a thousand head."

"Losing much stock?"

"Some," the man admitted. "But not enough te rave aboot, though I reckon there's more rustlin' than for some years past."

"Price of cows up to twelve dollars. I reckon that's enticement enough for rustlers."

"Yep."

"Been raisin' turnips an' potaters an' some corn," the boy spoke up, and the man glanced down at him and smiled.

"I noticed," Wyoming said. "It's a right nice garden. Well, I reckon I ought to mosey. Nice talking to you," Wyoming said, and with a wave rode out of the yard.

Wyoming had recalled seeing cattle with a Bar R brand and figured they must belong to Roberts. He rode upwards toward the high mountain ridge. Cattle dotted the landscape. Near the summit he reined Sparky to an abrupt halt. His searching eyes had suddenly spied movement halfway down the slope perhaps two miles away. He made out two horsemen. They approached at a brisk trot winding in and out of the sage and juniper that dappled the rise. Seeing the two riders didn't necessarily mean anything, he realized. One would expect to see cowboys going about their business, honest business, but nonetheless he reined Sparky back up in the cedars out of sight and continued to watch them intently, his interest growing. There was nothing really distinctive about either rider. Both wore dark jackets and black sombreros and rode bay horses that blended well with the surroundings. He wished he had binoculars. That would be the next thing he bought, he vowed.

He stepped from his horse and wrapping the reins over a branch, hunkered down behind a rock outcropping to wait and watch. They came on unhurriedly keeping their horses at an easy trot. There was something familiar about one of the riders. Wyoming cursed under his breath, again wishing he had binoculars. Closer they came until they halted and appeared to be talking earnestly about something. One took off his sombrero and ran his fingers through his flaming red hair. Wyoming gave an almost inaudible grunt. There was no doubt of this rider's identity...Jimmy Anderson.

A short time later the two separated, Anderson riding off up among lofty pines and spruces. The other rider rode west along the draw and disappeared from sight. Wyoming waited. What was

Anderson up to? Wyoming returned to where he had tied his horse, and mounting started off. His thoughts came and went as he rode along. He knew Anderson was crooked. It would bear looking into.

It wasn't long before he came upon the tracks of Anderson, and turning on them rode north. Presently he saw where the rider had turned west on a gradual descent. He must have traveled several miles before coming out upon a ridge and saw a small cabin. He came upon it abruptly and quickly jerked Sparky back out of sight from where he surveyed the small log structure and surroundings. A corral next to the cabin contained half a dozen horses. One looked like the horse Anderson had been riding. In a larger fenced area some distance from the cabin were several hundred head of cattle. He wanted to get a closer look at the cattle in the fenced pasture, but without having to approach or be seen by those in the cabin.

Keeping in the tree line he worked his way west coming at length upon an arroyo, which ran north and south. He could see it would bring him close to the backside of the pasture. He slid down the steep bank of the shallow ravine and made his way along the sandy bush-lined course. Opposite the pasture he came upon a place where the dirt had caved away from the bank that allowed him an easy way up out of the arroyo. Keeping in among a growth of cedar trees, he was able get a good look at the cattle bunched in the fenced pasture. He was most curious as to whose brand they were wearing. From what he could make out the brands were burned in a crude Box B. He had no doubt they were brand-burnet with a running iron. Reining about, he skirted the arroyo making his way back again among the pine and cedars. He didn't want to push his luck. So far it didn't appear anyone had noticed him. He wanted to keep it that way. Once in the trees he angled north deep in thought. Erickson's old brand had been a Bar E. How easy was that to change? he mused grimly. He'd make it a point to find out who owned that cabin though he had a stinking hunch he already knew.

He kept to the lower slope of a ridge for some time winding through patches of aspen and pine before ascending the height. The sun was dropping below the mountain rim and twilight's shadows were already settling in the canyons. On top it was still bright and a cool wind met him. From this height Wyoming was afforded a magnificent view. A mile or so down the gray-green slope of pine and cedar stood a grand house; half-ringed by tall aspen their golden leaves fluttering in the breeze.

"I reckon that must be Ward's place," Wyoming mused reining to a halt.

Westward rolled the range, swelling, billowy, dotted by cattle. To the east, veiled in the growing evening shadows, rose the low foothills, which in turn mounted step by step to the purple-sloped *Sangre de Cristo* Mountains. Wyoming started down the slant winding through thickets of willow and mountain maple that clustered alongside a creek. Once across the creek he broke into a canter. He was still yards from the house when the door opened and a man stepped out on the porch that ran the length of the front of the building. Wyoming recognized Hank Ward.

"Wyoming McCord," Ward shouted while he was still some distance.

"Howdy, Mr. Ward," Wyoming returned reining Sparky up before the porch.

"This is shore a surprise. All's well?"

"Yep, just getting a lay of the range, and thought I'd drop by."

"Wal, get down an' come in."

"You shore got a fine looking place here," Wyoming said as he swung to the ground.

"Wal, there's shore been some ups an' downs, but I reckon I'm doin' all right," grinned the old rancher as Wyoming stepped up on the porch to shake his hand. "Come on inside an' meet the rest of the family."

Wyoming walked into the warmth of the house to Mrs. Ward crossing the floor to meet him.

"Morning Mrs. Ward," he greeted.

"Hello Wyoming," she smiled.

"Buck, come on in heah," he yelled, and a boy of perhaps ten appeared from another room. "This heah is Buck, my youngest. Yu've met Jack at the dance, he's down in the tack room. Let's walk on down."

Mrs. Ward excused herself and Ward and Wyoming left striding down the slight incline to the row of buildings opposite the barn Buck trailing behind.

Ward pushed open the door of the tack room and peered inside.

"Jack's not heah," he muttered, "Must have gone over te the stables."

Wyoming followed him. Entering the stables with its long row of stalls Ward called out spying his son, "Heah's Jack."

"Howdy, Wyoming," Jack said peering from under a dusty black sombrero. A holstered gun rode high on his right hip, visible above his leather chaps. "I'll be with yu in a bit, soon as I feed this little mare."

Leaning on the gate to the stall Wyoming examined the mare with a keen eye. She was black as pitch, not very tall; her withers came not quite to his shoulders. She had a long mane and tail, a graceful body, fine strong limbs and a spirited head. Wyoming reached over the gate and laid a hand on the glossy arched neck. He knew horseflesh and this little mare was one fine animal.

"That's a swell looking mare," Wyoming mused.

"Interested? She's shore fer sale," Hank Ward said.

"Might be," Wyoming shrugged. Why, you selling?" he said stroking the mare's nose.

"Wal, this little mare belonged to Chet Armstrong's little gurl from up on the breaks. Sue was her name. I've known Chet since he came te these parts. The gurl died 'bout this time last year; come down with a fever of some sort and never got better. Chet couldn't bear to look at the hawse an' was fixin' to put her down; brought back too many memories, he said. I just couldn't see thet, it'd shore have been a waste, so I bought her."

"What's her name?"

"Ye see that little white dot there on her neck close to her mane? Well, that's the only white on her anywheres. That's what she's called, *Dottie*."

"I reckon that shore fits," Wyoming remarked.

A girl of sixteen appeared in the doorway.

"Paw, Ma said to tell you supper's on the table." Alice glanced shyly at Wyoming as she spoke. "Hello," she said, smiling and blushing at the same time.

"Howdy Alice," he smiled.

"Wal, Wyoming I reckon yu'll stay fer supper," Ward insisted.

"Why shore, if I'm not putting you out."

"Not a'tall. And yu got a long way te ride, yu're welcome te stay the night."

They returned to the house, the girl walking ahead of them. Wyoming followed the others into the kitchen, spurs jingling. The long table was amply spread, steaming and savory.

"Set down, Wyoming, an' pitch in," Ward announced as he took his place at the head of the table.

Mrs. Ward sat at the foot and Wyoming found himself seated next to Alice, who served him most attentively smiling shyly all the while. Jack and the youngest boy Buck sat opposite.

"So, what conclusion did yu come te on yu're inspection of the countryside?" Ward asked.

"Saw lots of cattle, some wearing the E Bar; wilder than deer, cows, yearlings and calves, for all I could tell unbranded; mavericks, as well as some old mossy-horns."

"Yu shore seen a lot in one ride. Where'd yu come across all thet?"

"In that big canyon east of Dixon's spread."

"Ahuh, thet'd be Piñon Canyon. Wild as all get out, an' rougher than hell on hawse an' rider. Ain't many punchers hazard up there."

"That's shore a fact," Wyoming agreed. "But I reckon with a couple riders I could brand five or ten mavericks a day. And that's sort of what I wanted to talk to you about. I'm looking for one or two good riders."

"What about the ones Hester left Dixon?"

"They quit on me—or, I reckon I should say, I kind of encouraged them to look somewhere else for work."

"Haw! Yu're meanin' Ackers an' his two pards, Walters and thet greaser Jimenez. Shore better off without 'em. Yu know, Wyoming,

Jeb Ackers ain't nobody to trifle with. There's rumor that Ackers used to ride with Billy the Kid down in Lincoln County back in '78 and '79 along with a couple of fellers named Brewer and Scurlock, all of whom are dead now. Billy was killed somewhere down around Tularosa."

"I've heard of this Billy the Kid," Wyoming replied, "And it wasn't much good. But you can bet I shore won't take this Ackers and his bunch lightly." He met Ward's eye. "Say I met a feller by the name of Sid Roberts and his boy Hal back some ten miles southeast. Nice little spread."

"Yep, Sid's an' old timer; good honest feller," Ward nodded.

"That's what I figured," Wyoming said.

"His oldest boy, Dan's been moseyin' around rite frequent of late. I reckon just te chat," Ward said with a shrewd glance at Alice who appeared not to have heard, though her cheeks took on a decidedly red tint.

"I been doing a little thinkin' about what yu said, Wyoming about needin' one or two riders," Ward said and glanced at his son. "Jack, what yu think about Billy Reed?"

"Yu mean loanin' him out to Wyoming heah?"

"Yep, exactly." Ward looked at Wyoming. "Billy's a good sound cowboy; not taken to drink or cards. He'll put in a good day's work fer yu. Wish I could help yu more, but I'm goin' need all my punchers."

"I shore appreciate that, Mr. Ward. With your man and my Mexican, I reckon we can brand a good many cows before the snow flies."

"Wyoming is figurin' on workin' Piñon Canyon," Ward said addressing his son Jack. "Says there's lots of cattle up in there."

"I always figured there was," Jack returned. "But it shore is rough country. Maybe too hard a nut to crack to make it worthwhile."

"You shore could be right, Jack," Wyoming granted. "But every maverick we put a brand on we're twelve dollars richer."

"Ho, I reckon thet's so," Ward chuckled. "If them rustlers don't get te them first."

"Speaking of rustlers," Wyoming said, and proceeded to tell of seeing the two riders, how he followed one of them, though he didn't mention Anderson by name, coming upon the cabin back among the trees, and the herd of cattle. "I got close enough to them cows to see they was wearing a Box B brand."

"Hmm," Ward murmured casting a keen look at his son Jack. "I reckon we're familiar with that brand."

"That's one of Bull Burton's brands," Jack Ward said.

"Ah," Wyoming grunted. "I kind of figured as much."

"Him and Ed Hester air shore in cahoots I reckon. Run several brands," Jack added.

The eastern slope of the valley was a vast sweep of sage and hill and grassy bench and aspen, on fire with the colors made molten by the last flashing of the sun. Great black slopes of forest gave sharp contrast, and led up to the red-walled ramparts of the mountain range. Night settled down over the quiet foothills, the sun having disappeared by the time supper was concluded.

"Reckon yu ought te stay the night," Ward said. "yu'll shore lose yur way in the dark."

"I'll take you up on that, Wyoming drawled. Not relishing a night ride in unfamiliar country.

The room was finely furnished, bearing the distinct feel of a feminine hand. The thought struck him that he had been given Alice's room. Wyoming waited as she turned back the blankets with deft, sure little hands.

"Say am I taking your room?" he asked.

She nodded.

"Where'll you sleep?"

"In Buck's room," she giggled. He'll double up with Jack."

She walked to the door.

"There's plenty blankets," she said with a shy glance. "I think you'll be warm enough."

"I'm shore I will," he said. "Thank you, Alice."

She blushed. "Good night, Wyoming."

As soon as the girl left the room, Wyoming undressed and stretched out in the bed. He wondered if Annabelle would give any thought to his staying out another night. Perhaps she would think something bad happened to him. That thought made him smile. Whereupon he closed his eyes and slept.

CHAPTER ELEVEN

T he August sun, losing some of its heat if not its brilliance, was dropping low in the west over the black New Mexico range. Purple haze began to thicken in the timbered notches. Gray foothills, round and billowy, rolled down from the higher country. They were smooth, sweeping, with long velvety slopes and isolated patches of aspens that blazed gold. The sage slopes below seemed rosy velvet; the golden aspens on the farther reaches were on fire at the tips; the foothills rolled clear and mellow and rich in the light; the gulf of distance on to the great black range was veiled in mountain purple; and the dim peaks beyond the range stood up, sunset-flushed and grand.

Wyoming McCord rode along the slope, with gaze on the sweep and range and color of the mountain fastness. Trailing close behind was a tall stooped-shouldered rider somewhere in his early forty's. Billy Reed was an old-timer to this New Mexico range, as well as an old hand with cattle—lean, supple, a powerful fellow, with a rough, bronze face, hard as a rock, and steady, bright eyes. Wyoming took a liking to him immediately.

The sunset had just reached the wonderful height of its color and transformation when Wyoming and Billy Reed reined up in front of the stables. They turned their horses over to Chico and walked up to the house. Wyoming knocked and then opened the door and walked in to find the Dixons all seated at the table eating supper.

"Why hello," Dixon said, "Did you just ride in? Who's that with you?"

"Howdy folks," Wyoming replied, and turned to Reed who had followed him into the room. "This here is Billy Reed. He's going to ride for us. Billy, meet the Dixons late of Louisiana."

"Hod do," Reed drawled as a half dozen curious pairs of eyes peered up at him. He removed his sombrero, holding it in both hands.

"Well now," Dixon said getting to his feet and reaching to shake the weathered rider's hand. "You are certainly welcome."

"Indeed," Mrs. Dixon said. "Henry, you should introduce everyone."

"Yes, yes, of course. Reed this is Mrs. Dixon and these are our daughters, Annabelle, Angelique and Allison…and Mrs. Lindsey, our housekeeper."

"Ma'am," Reed bowed to Mrs. Dixon. His clear blue eyes appeared to twinkle as he looked from one upturned smiling girl's face to another.

"I'm shore glad to meet you gurls," he drawled, "And I reckon you shore are the dog-gonedest purtiest gurls I ever saw."

Allison giggled.

"Watch out girls," Mr. Dixon laughed. "Our new rider has the devil's own tongue."

Reed grinned clearly enjoying the attention.

"Are you two hungry?" Mrs. Dixon asked.

"I should smile," Wyoming drawled.

"Than set down," she ordered. "Angelique, fetch a chair from the other room for Mr. Reed."

Both men hung their sombreros on the pegs beside the door. When they sat down, Mrs. Lindsey placed a mug of coffee before each one. Wyoming talked as he ate, explaining his plan to work Piñon Canyon, branding as many cattle as they could before snow and winter prevented further work. By spring they would hopefully be in a position for a round up and would certainly have a good idea of how much stock Dixon had. As he talked he was aware that Annabelle was listening attentively as she helped Mrs. Lindsey clear away the supper dishes.

Finished eating, Wyoming led Reed to the bunkhouse where the lean rider threw down his bedroll and pack next to a bunk. Wyoming bade him good night and walked over to his cabin where he removed his chaps and after washing off the trail dust, undressed and climbed into his bunk.

The next morning Wyoming led Billy Reed out to the large corral behind the stables where about a dozen horses milled about. They were mostly bays and sorrels, but Wyoming saw two or three paint horses and a dun or two. Reed draped his arms over the top rail as Wyoming rested one foot on the lower rail of the fence where they surveyed the horses.

"They're not a bad looking bunch," Wyoming remarked.

"Yep, except fer thet glass-eyed sorrel yonder," Reed said.

Wyoming peered at the blue-eyed sorrel. He knew the old tale that said blue-eyed horses didn't see well or were night blind, but as far as he could ever tell most saw as well as any other horse.

"Are those all the horses we own?" a feminine voice asked and Wyoming glanced quickly around to see Annabelle and Angelique approaching. The huge hound Caesar trailed along at Allison's side.

"I reckon these are it," Wyoming said addressing Annabelle.

"They look wild," Angelique remarked staring at the milling horses. "Are any of them safe to ride?"

"Shore," Wyoming answered. "They're been rode a lot so they'll be safe I reckon. Have you girls done any riding at all?"

"Of course," Angelique sniffed. "We had fine thoroughbreds at our plantation back home."

"Well, have a look see," Wyoming drawled. "Any of them mustangs catch your eye?"

Angelique scampered up to the top bar of the corral fence like a squirrel. There she perched, her expression serious as she surveyed the dozen horses crowding the corral.

"That pinto. Could I have him?" she demanded.

"Shore," Wyoming drawled. "Billy, saddle that little paint for Miss Angie."

With an almost lazy flick of his wrist Billy Reed tossed a loop over the paint's head.

"How about you, Miss Annabelle?" Wyoming asked watching her lean over the top fence rail to stroke the neck of a fine looking buckskin.

"This one" she said.

"Don't forget me," Allison chirped up.

Wyoming looked down at the girl. "I reckon them horses are too much for you, Miss Allison. Maybe your dad will let you have a pony to start off with. How's that?"

The girl's lips turned down, but nodded as she stared at the horses.

The next morning Wyoming weaved his way down through the willow thickets and growths of mountain maple alongside the dry creek and rode up to Ward's ranch house. Crossing the yard he spied Hank Ward and his son Jack at the corrals and reined Sparky in that direction. It hadn't taken much to convince Mr. Dixon that the little black mare would be a good horse for Allison.

"Howdy," Wyoming said leaning his forearm on the saddle horn and pushing back his sombrero.

"Howdy yourself, Wyoming. What brings yu this way so soon?" Hank Ward replied.

"I reckon I come to talk to you about a horse; that little black mare Dottie in particular."

"I figured yu'd be back askin' aboot her," he chuckled, "Come on."

Wyoming dismounted and tossing the bridle ambled alongside father and son into the barn where they stood elbows resting on the top of the stall and peered over at the little black mare.

"You say she once belonged to a little girl?" Wyoming said. "How old was she?"

"Yep, if I recollect, aboot ten or eleven."

"What're you asking?"

"Thirty bucks; forty, an' I'll throw in a fine Mexican saddle, double-cinch, silver-mounted with tapaderos, blankets—and spurs to boot. How aboot thet?"

"It's a deal," Wyoming agreed pulling out his billfold and counting out the money. For this little mare he was paying with his own cash. Leading the black mare out of the barn Wyoming spied Alice.

"Morning, Wyoming. I thought I recognized that big sorrel," she smiled; hands clasped behind her back.

"Morning, Miss Alice," Wyoming drawled.

"You've bought Dottie," she said seeing the silver mounted Mexican saddle cinched to the little black mare.

"Yep. I figured she'd do nicely for the youngest Dixon girl; Allison's nine."

"Oh, I'm glad. I've met Anna and Angelique, but I haven't met Allison though. I know she'll fall in love with Dottie."

"Say, how about you ride over with me?" Wyoming said as the thought struck him. I reckon the girls would enjoy your company."

"Oh!" she exclaimed gray eyes dancing, "Can I paw?"

"Shore," her father agreed. "Dixon's gals are most likely lonesome fer female company their age. It'll do both them an' yu good, I reckon."

"Thanks paw," she said and hurried off presumably to saddle her horse.

Allison was the first to come skipping eagerly out to meet Wyoming leading the little black mare all decked out with the silver mounted Mexican saddle. He led the horse over to the corral as Alice followed. By the time they reached the corral Annabelle and Angelique had joined Allison. Stepping easily from the saddle Wyoming tossed Sparky's bridle and turned to the three curious girls.

"Howdy," Alice said shyly as the three sisters excitedly welcomed their visitor.

Wyoming laid a hand on the little black mare's sleek neck.

"Miss Allison," he called to the little girl. "Here you are."

"W—what," the girl gasped staring open-mouthed.

"This little mare; she's yours," Wyoming said.

"Mine?" she whispered looking from Wyoming to the mare and back again. "Wyoming...do you mean it?"

"Shore do," he grinned. "Her name is Dottie. See that little white dot on her neck; the only white spot on her. That's how she got her name."

Allison took a hesitant step forward, reached and touched her hand to the mare's soft muzzle. The mare nuzzled her hand and then her cheek eliciting a giggle from the girl. Annabelle smiled with undisguised happiness at her sister before gazing at Wyoming. She blinked rapidly her eyes misting.

"By jiggers, she's picked you shore enough," Wyoming said, dropping to one knee beside Allison. "Dottie used to belong to a little girl just about your age. She had her since she was a filly—"

"Then why did she sell her to you?"

"She didn't. The little girl's name was Sue. She died last year. She loved Dottie very much and Dottie shore loved her too, and was shore lonesome without her. So, she asked me to find her another nice little girl who would care for her."

"She did? She talked to you?" Allison asked narrowing her eyes skeptically.

"Shore, horses talk to me all the time," Wyoming said in mock affront, hand over his heart.

"You're teasing me, Wyoming, but, oh, thank you," she whispered throwing her arms about his neck. "And I'll take special care of Dottie so she won't ever be lonesome again."

Wyoming glanced up meeting Annabelle's gaze. She was staring at him a strange light in her Jade green eyes.

Alice and Angelique, being the same age seemed to take to one another immediately, and the two spent the afternoon together deep in conversation. Agreeing to spend the night, Alice shared Angelique's room and Allison found herself sleeping with Annabelle as the two older girls stayed up late talking.

CHAPTER TWELVE

When Annabelle awoke the sun had just peeked above the distant pine covered ridge beyond the ranch house. She leaped out of the empty bed with an excitement that was new and strange. Allison, always an early riser, was probably seeing to her little mare, or else pestering Angie and Alice. Donning overalls, shirt and boots, an outfit she had purchased in town but had yet to wear, and snatching up her sombrero and gloves, she sallied forth from her room. She peeked in Allison's and Angelique's room only to discover it empty.

"Oh, heck," she muttered under her breath. They were all probably down at the barn. She had hoped to be out ahead of her sisters and their visitor. She wanted a little privacy when she first got on her newly acquired horse. Oh, she had ridden before, but it had been a good ten years ago when she had been Allison's age, and never one of these western *mustangs* as Wyoming called them. So, if she was courting disaster she didn't want any witnesses.

When she entered the kitchen Mrs. Lindsey was in the process of removing a tray of fresh-baked biscuits from the oven.

"Gee, those smell good," she sighed. "May I snitch one?"

"Of course, child," Mrs. Lindsey said. "But don't you want an egg to go with it?"

"Just a biscuit and coffee will be fine."

As the older woman placed a steaming biscuit on a plate, Annabelle poured herself a cup of coffee then sat down at the table.

"Where is everybody?" she asked taking a sip from her mug.

"I haven't seen your folks yet this morning, but Angie and Ally and their friend Alice were here earlier and ate breakfast. They rode out together about ten minutes ago. They said they were going to ride over to Alice's place but would be back before dark."

"I surely hope so," Annabelle said aloud. She smiled to herself, however, taking another sip of coffee. Good, there wouldn't be any spectators.

Finishing with her meager breakfast, Annabelle excused herself and headed for the barn. She knew Wyoming, Reed and Chico had ridden out earlier, so she would be all alone. As she stepped into the cool interior of the barn it suddenly occurred to her that she would have to saddle the little buckskin herself. Well, she could do that. After a few fumbling attempts she managed to fasten the bridle and led the horse out of his stall and over to the tack room across the open area between stalls. The saddle she discovered was much heavier than the English model she had used before. After spreading a colorful blanket on the horse's back she heaved the saddle up on the horse with an unladylike grunt and tightened the cinch.

"Well done," she panted proudly congratulating herself.

She took the bridle and led the buckskin out of the barn and over to a secluded spot shaded by tall pines where she felt safe from prying eyes. She managed to mount the little mustang after one or two fumbling attempts and rode him about in a circle. She nudged him into a trot and then into a canter. Feeling much more confident she pulled the horse to a stop and slid off in one step as she had seen Wyoming do. That was easy she decided. She felt elated. Clasping the saddle horn she started to swing back up on the buckskin but to her horror the saddle slid off dumping her on the ground. For a moment she couldn't understand what had happened as she stared up at the horse above her. The animal swung his head about and peered down at her and she just knew he was grinning. It suddenly dawned on her as she stared at the saddle dangling beneath the buckskin's belly that she must not have pulled the cinch tight enough.

"Are yu hurt?"

Mortified, she looked back over her shoulder to see Ed Hester mounted on a tall bay horse. She scrambled to her feet brushing at the seat of her overalls.

"I'm fine," she muttered cheeks burning as she watched him step easily from the saddle and approach.

"Looks like yur cinch came loose," he said and she was certain he was doing his best not to smirk.

"How long have you been there?" she demanded.

"Just rode up," he replied with an easy-going smile as he sat about straightening her saddle and after giving a swift kick to the horse's belly with the instep of his booted foot, proceeded to tighten the cinch.

"You know some hawses are shore shrewd. They have a way of swellin' their bellies with air and you think you got the cinch good and tight but when they let out the breath they've been holdin' the cinch's too loose and…wal, yu get the idea."

"I see," she growled glaring at the little mustang.

"There," Hester said giving the latigo a last hard tug, "That ought to hold yu."

"Thank you," she said stiffly.

"Looks like yu were headed out for a ride. Yu don't mind if I join yu?"

Oh dear. What was she to say?

"Of course,' she said smiling to hide her unease.

They rode out side by side on a path past the Mexican Ramon's little adobe house with its small barn and fenced pasture and puttering chickens in the yard. Purple haze was beginning to soften in the timbered notches. Foothills, round and billowy, rolled down from the higher country lightened with the advance of the morning sun. Annabelle held her tongue as they rode along and the silence lengthened. Finally Annabelle glanced at the rancher beside her.

"What has brought about your visit, Mr. Hester?" she asked.

"Why, I reckon I was feelin' a mite concerned about how yu folks was fairin'." he answered easily.

She looked sharply at him. He seemed sincere. "Oh?" she replied.

"Shore, I kinda feel responsible—"

"Responsible? Whatever for?"

"Why, I sold yur paw this ranch in good faith an' I'm some worried yur paw's makin' a greenhorn mistake hiring' this feller as his foreman—"

"Wyoming McCord? Why is that?" Annabelle asked.

"Wal, fer one thing, what do yu know about him?"

What *did* she know about Wyoming? He was sudden, and even a little reckless; after all he'd unexpectedly kissed her that day in the department store—never mind that it had been a very pleasant kiss. And he readily admitted to his skill with a gun, having shot any number of men. But another matter, somewhat perplexing yet significant was Wyoming's gift of the little black mare to her sister Allison. That wasn't something one would expect from a hardened gunfighter.

"Do you know Mr. McCord?"

"Not personally," Hester drawled. "I first laid eyes on him at the rodeo dance, but I reckon he's got a reputation for bein' quick with a gun. My man Bull had a run in with him up in Colorado sometime back. He killed a rancher an' his foreman; never gave them a chance to draw."

A killer! Oh, she didn't want to believe that! But still…Wyoming had admitted the incident. Had he told her the whole truth?

They went slowly down the gentle slope, stepping over a few small logs fallen across the way. Here and there along the slope, where big tooth maple and a few aspen groves clustered, Annabelle spotted cattle in the open spaces between. Hester pointed out that they belonged to her father. He kept up an easy running monologue, but she only half listened.

Annabelle's quick eye caught sight of a sorrel horse on top of the ridge, silhouetted against the green. She recognized the slim, erect rider immediately, and realized that he must have seen them beforehand for with mane and tail flying he sent the sorrel plunging down the slope. She reined her little mustang to a halt watching him with a growing sense of uncertainty, tension indicated in her stiff posture and rigidity. He reached the level, and with an almost lazy grace stepped out of the saddle and tossed the bridle. With that same easiness of stride he stepped to the side and halted, standing slightly sidewise. His stance was significant even to Annabelle and there was no mistaking the look in those eyes. She shot a hurried glance at Hester. That worthy had halted beside her.

"I reckon you're not choosy about the company you keep, Miss Dixon," Wyoming drawled eyes never leaving Hester though he addressed her.

"Have a gander, Miss Dixon," Hester said coolly resting his forearm on his saddle horn ignoring Wyoming. "Do you doubt my words? The man lives by the gun."

"Wy—Mr. McCord what are you doing?" she cried, unable to escape the sudden heat engendered in her veins. She was angry; angry mainly at herself. She knew she shouldn't have allowed Hester to come along with her, and she also knew she shouldn't have let his disparaging words about Wyoming affect her as they had.

"Mr. Hester asked to accompany me for a ride, and…he has been a perfect gentleman," she managed.

"Well, I reckon your little ride's over," Wyoming replied.

That was too much! Now she was furious…insulted even. She wasn't a child to be ordered about and she would let him know it.

"Mr. McCord! This is my father's ranch and I shall ride with whomever—"

"Don't press it on my account Miss Dixon," Hester interrupted. "I'll stop by one of these days an' speak to yur paw, an' maybe we can go for a ride if yu're a mind."

Touching fingers to the brim of his sombrero, Hester whirled his horse about and spurred him up the slope.

"Well, was that really called for?" she demanded glaring at him.

"What?" Wyoming drawled, eyes glinting.

"You were trying to start a fight with Mr. Hester, weren't you?"

"What were you doing riding with him?" he countered.

"Why shouldn't I—?"

"Cause he's a slick lying rustler!" Wyoming spat. "And him and his pard Bull Burton stole half of your dad's cattle after selling them to your dad; and presently they're planning to rustle the rest—"

"How do you know?" she gasped, face paling. "Just because Mr. Ward said—"

"Shore, I reckon Hank Ward only suspects, but—I know!" he said tersely with an impatient sweep of his hand.

"You—know? How can you be sure?"

"Miss Dixon, I'm always shore before I shoot!" declared Wyoming. "It ain't enough to suspect. Out here you've got to know, and then you have to act quick. Bull Burton, Hester's henchman, is the crookest, slickest kind of cattleman. I ran into him up in Colorado, like I told you at the dance. I should have shot him long ago. Hester's one of these shady cattlemen who never stay long in one place. He bought this ranch following some shady dealings, and never did a lick of improving. He's now ranching over here near twenty miles on Miles Creek. I had a look-see at his place. Fine range, but no ranch. A log cabin and some corrals; and a bunch of brand-burnet cattle that used to belong to your dad—"

"Wh—what is brand-burnet, and what do you mean—used to belong to dada?"

He came to stand next to the shoulder of her little mustang and laying a hand on the horse's neck peered up at her. Heart racing at his closeness she stared down at his angry features. Slowly his hard gaze softened.

"I reckon I forget you're not western, and you can't know the hard facts of range life," he said voice gentling. He reached a hand up to her. "Get down and I'll show you what I mean 'bout brand-burnet cattle."

After a moment's hesitation, she placed her hand in his and swung down from the saddle. He didn't turn loose of her hand but led her a short distance away to a bare patch of ground. Kneeling he drew her down beside him and with the flat of one palm smoothed a place in the dirt.

"Say a legitimate brand like the Bar 'E' that your dad bought with the ranch—Erickson's old brand; well, with a running iron—you know what a running iron is?" She shook her head and he explained which elicited a quick nod of understanding. "So, you see it's easy to change that Bar 'E' to a Box 'B'...there, like that," he said finishing drawing in the dirt.

"Oh, I see," Annabelle said peering over his shoulder, her breath warm against his cheek. "They just change the 'E' to make it a 'B' and draw a box around it. How very clever. So that's how rustlers work."

"It's one of the ways."

"And that's what this Burton fellow is doing—He's stealing dada's cattle!"

"Now I reckon you get the idea," Wyoming said.

"You bet I have, and it's upset me!"

"And Hester's the brains behind it."

"Bull Burton. You knew him in the past...is that how you know about the rustling?" she asked.

"I reckon I ought to tell you something about myself," he said meeting her eyes. He decided for the time being to keep quiet about what he had overheard outside the window at Carmelita's between Jimmy Anderson and the rustler Hobard.

"I'm listening."

"Well, I was born and raised near Saratoga, Wyoming. My folks were from Indiana. They came west after the big war. I was orphaned at fourteen, which ended my schooling, and so I just grew up a cowboy riding for one outfit then another, which were good and bad for me. Shore, I have to admit, I became handy with a gun, but I swear I never shot a *hombre* that didn't need shooting—"

She uttered an audible gasp, but he continued as though he hadn't noticed her shocked reaction.

"What I'm getting at is I took up riding for a feller by the name of Childers; ran the Circle 'C' near Grand Junction, Colorado. I stayed there probably the longest of any punching job I ever had, about two years. It was fine range and things were good and thriving, until a feller by the name of Higgins and his pard Bull Burton decided he wanted that range for himself. He had the law bought off, and, part of his devious scheme was to waylay my pard's girl as well. So I called him and his little beady-eyed gunslinger henchman out. Worse luck Bull wasn't with them or he'd be pushing up daisies now."

"You killed them!"

"I should smile," he said grimly.

"In cold blood!" she exclaimed in horror.

"Cold blood! You think me a murderer?!" he demanded his whole frame tensing. "See here, lady I braced them fair! Something that shore had to be done in order to save Rick Childers' ranch...and his girl," he declared pale of face. "And I don't reckon I could stay on here if you believed I was a murderer."

Somehow it was infinitely worse having her think him a killer then it had been her mother. It was unjust. He could not change the west or help what had gravitated to him.

"You would leave—?"

"I shore reckon so, as much as I'd hate to, if you didn't believe in me," he replied, looking down at her.

"I—could believe. If you tell me there will be no sheriff trailing you to hang you—I will believe you."

"Well, Miss Dixon, I'm not so dang shore about that. But if there is, it'll shore be on a trumped up charge."

CHAPTER THIRTEEN

nnabelle came to peer out the window, again. It was perhaps the fourth time in the last hour. But still there was no sign of Angelique and Allison. They had been gone since early morning and it was now late afternoon. According to Mrs. Lindsey they had said they were riding over to the Running W—Hank Ward's ranch with Alice Ward. Annabelle turned from the window just as her mother entered the room. Her eyes met her daughter's.

"They are not back yet?" she asked frowning.

Annabelle shook her head.

"Oh, dear," Mrs. Dixon sighed. "We must send someone to look for them. They surely have gotten lost."

"I don't think that's the case," Annabelle replied soothingly. "They were with Alice Ward. She grew up here, she knows the country. I'm sure they'll be along shortly."

"I see riders," Mrs. Lindsey called staring out the window,

"It's them," Annabelle said hurrying to peer over the older woman's shoulder.

"Thank goodness," Mrs. Dixon exclaimed.

"Who is that man with them?" Mrs. Lindsey asked.

"Hmm," Annabelle said watching the tall slim rider step from the saddle. He was young perhaps no older than herself but with the lean build of a cowboy. She recognized him immediately. She had danced with him, twice, at the rodeo dance. Jack Ward, Alice's brother, and he was helping Angelique down from her horse while a laughing Allison leaped nimbly to the ground.

Alice and Jack stayed for dinner and Annabelle was afforded no opportunity to talk to her sister until much later after their visitors had departed and they were preparing for bed.

"What!?" Angelique cried in response to Annabelle's question. "No way! Just because I danced with him three times at the rodeo dance he thinks that now he has some claim on me."

"You don't like him?"

"Well, sure, I like him, but that doesn't mean anything. We've only just met; at the dance and then today. His sister Alice is sweet, though. We're going to be the greatest of friends."

"I like Alice too," Allison said entering the room at that moment, the big hound Caesar trotting at her heels.

"That dog is not staying in this room!" Angelique declared jabbing a finger at the dog.

"Why not?" Allison challenged.

"Because he's got fleas!"

"He does not! I gave him a bath just yesterday," Allison protested dropping to one knee and hugging the animal's neck.

"I don't care," Angelique retorted emphatically, hands on her hips. "He's not sleeping in here!"

"It's my room too! He'll sleep on the floor."

"Oh, no you don't! During the night he always finds his way up on the bed."

Allison turned round eyes up at Annabelle who held up a staying hand.

"Don't even ask," she said unsympathetically. "He sleeps out in the hall...or better yet out on the porch."

"That's not fair," Allison sniffed leading the dog out into the hall. "Sorry, Caesar, you'll have to sleep out here tonight. But don't worry I won't be far away."

Wyoming didn't say much during supper, nodding occasionally at some remark by the others. He was thinking about the incident this afternoon with Ed Hester. He glanced at Annabelle. She was smiling at some remark by Jack Ward who, Wyoming noticed, couldn't keep his eyes off Angelique. She, on the other hand, appeared rather bored. Well, Wyoming mused thoughtfully, he would just have to kill Hester and Bull Burton, deciding at that moment that this deed was decreed for him.

When Wyoming stepped up on the porch of his cabin much later he was still thinking of Hester and Bull Burton. A dark figure loomed out of the shadow. In a flash Wyoming's Colt leaped into his hand.

"Don't shoot, *Señor*, Wyoming! It's me, Chico."

"Damn it, Chico. Don't be slipping up on a feller like that. I nearly plugged you."

"*Perdón, Señor.* I wait here to talk to you."

"What is it?"

"Today the *Señora* Lindsey, she send me to Ramon's for *los huevos y la leche.* On the way by the *arroyo* I see somebody, over in the trees," he said. "I act like I no see, and when I come back he was still there. He stay there a long time. I think he watch the house."

"Hell you say," Wyoming exclaimed.

"*Si, Señor.* When I see he ride away I go look. I see he smoke many cigarettes—"

"Did you get a good look at him?"

"*No, Señor*, I no see his face very good," he shrugged. "He ride a brown horse with the white face."

"Hmm," Wyoming murmured. "I reckon that shore sets me to wondering. In the morning show me the place; I'd like to have a look around."

"*Si, Señor*, I show you."

Wyoming waited as the Mexican glided silently away disappearing into the dark shadows, and then he went inside his cabin. He didn't light the lamp, but instead set on his bunk in the dark going over in his mind what Chico had told him. Why would someone be watching the house? Hester—watching to catch Annabelle alone? Unlikely. Hester would have ridden in bold like, not hiding and spying. Obviously someone was spying on the ranch, though, and he didn't like it. He got up and barred the door, undressed and climbed into bed.

The next morning Wyoming and Chico rode over to the spot where the Mexican had seen the horseman the day before. The site was on a slight rise backed by the banks of a dry wash and boxed on three sides by a thick growth of cedars and sage. It was a good place of concealment for someone who wanted to remain out of sight from the ranch house. Wyoming saw where the rider had approached along the dry wash and ridden up the bank into the trees where he dismounted.

Wyoming stepped from the saddle and bent to study the tracks, which were plain to see in the soft earth. The man had squatted on his haunches while smoking several cigarettes. Wyoming peered at the boot tracks. Whoever was wearing those boots had a sizable worn spot on the ball of his left boot shaped like a half-moon. He imbedded the image into his memory.

"I reckon you ought to keep your eyes peeled from now on, Chico," Wyoming said

"*Si, Señor*, I keep my eyes peeled, you bet," Chico nodded.

When Wyoming rode up in front of his cabin he discovered Allison Dixon seated on the top porch step one arm around the hound Caesar's neck.

"Morning Ally," he said stepping from the saddle. He tilted his head as he peered at her. "That's an awful big frown you got there, kid. What's the matter?"

"Nothing," she declared staring at the ground.

"Nothing, huh? Well, it shore must be a terrible big nothing by the size of that frown."

She looked up at him, eyes serious, puckered brow deepening. "Well, first of all Angie wouldn't let Caesar sleep in our room last night; says he's got fleas."

"Ah-huh."

"He doesn't have fleas," she declared pinning him with a glare.

"Course not," he quickly denied. "And...?"

"And this morning she went off riding without me."

"She did, huh?" he said glancing around. "By herself?"

"Yes. She told momma that she was going to visit Alice. She could have taken me with her."

"Hmm, you're right, Ally. Reckon I ought to go after her. You want to ride along?"

"Yes!!!" she cried jumping to her feet.

"Well, let's go saddle Dottie and tell your mother."

Allison jabbered happily away as they rode, Caesar loping easily alongside her little black mare. Wyoming made noncommittal comments now and then, his attention on the imprint of fresh horse tracks showing clear in the soft dust; the tracks of Angelique's little paint horse. As far as he could tell she was headed in the direction of Ward's ranch. He didn't like the fact that she rode off alone, though he probably was making much out of nothing, but his mind kept going back to that mysterious rider who had been spying on the ranch house.

"What are you looking for, Wyoming?" Allison asked, suddenly realizing that he wasn't paying particular attention to her commentary. "You keep staring at the ground...oh; I see them; horse tracks. Are those Angie's? They are aren't they?"

"Yep," he grunted, reining Sparky to a halt and motioning her to pull up beside him. "And it shore looks like she met up with another rider. See there, Ally, them tracks? Peers like whoever it was they spent some time talking."

"You think it was Alice?"

"Ump-umm," he said shaking his head. "Look see, they rode off that a way up through the trees. If it was Alice she'd met up with, I reckon they would have rode on for her paw's place, or else turned back for home."

"Oh," she said staring wide-eyed at him.

"Come along, pard," he called and started off proceeding more cautiously.

If the long grass had not been wet he would have difficulty in trailing the two horses. Evidence seemed clear now that—probably Angelique's clandestine companion—was attempting to hide their tracks by keeping to the grassy levels and slopes which, after the sun had dried them, would not leave a trace. He doubted if the girl even noticed.

After a while Wyoming came across the spot where the two had stopped beside a big-tooth maple. He could see that they had spent some time there, one horse facing one direction and the other the opposite. Caesar, nose to the ground, sniffed eagerly about the site. Then uttering a baying howl bound off in the direction the two had ridden.

"Caesar! Come back here!" Allison yelled, but the dog paid no heed and was soon lost from sight racing up a rise along a willow-bordered brook.

"I reckon he's doing what he was bred for," Wyoming drawled reassuring the anxious girl.

They took up that trail, following after the dog. They had ridden perhaps a mile by Wyoming's estimation when Caesar came scampering into sight looking exceedingly proud. A hundred paces behind came Angelique. She carried her sombrero in one hand her golden curls tousled prettily, her cheeks a bright rosy hue.

"Who were you with?" Allison demanded watching her sister suspiciously.

"Did you send that silly dog to find me?" Angelique retorted. She avoided Wyoming's gaze as they headed back the way they had come.

"I didn't either! That's what Caesar's suppose to do. He's a tracker."

"He's a nuisance."

Wyoming said nothing falling thoughtfully in behind the girls who continued bickering back and forth about one thing or another the remainder of the way back to the ranch. He would talk to Annabelle later and find out what he could about Angelique's companion who she adroitly evaded mentioning.

Most of the next day was spent getting horses and outfit ready to work Piñon Canyon and Wyoming had little opportunity to meet Annabelle on the topic of Angelique. The following morning failed to present an opportunity and Wyoming and Billy Reed, along with Chico leading the loaded pack horse, headed out for Piñon Canyon. They proceeded up one of the draws that made up the wild canyon where water was plentiful in pools in the rocky streambeds. Cattle trails threaded the maze of juniper and piñon, and a number of cattle were seen, mostly cows and yearlings. Birds and small game were abundant. The canyon became wilder and rougher as they proceeded. Wyoming wasn't surprised at how wild the cattle were. They would come up on several head and as soon as they spied the riders the steers would sprint off, crashing through the brush.

Chico turned out to be a surprise breaking brush like the best of riders. Wyoming did not concern himself much about anything now except the amassing of a herd. There were times; however, when he had been so busy with the branding that he had completely forgotten that he had once planned to head to Arizona only a few short weeks ago.

One morning Wyoming found himself alone. As he climbed the yellow, brush-coated canyon side, working round above the valley, his mind was centered on the task at hand. He had come upon a surprising number of cattle. He decided to continue exploring the canyon instead of driving them down lower where Reed and Chico were working. Bench after bench Wyoming ascended, and the higher he got the denser and more numerous became the pine and cedar thickets as well as bunches of cattle. Presently a long black slope of spruce confronted him, with its edge like a dark wall. He entered the fragrant forest, where not a twig stirred nor a sound pervaded the silence. Upon the soft, matted earth the hoofs of his horse made no impression and scarcely a perceptible thud.

Wyoming headed to the right, avoiding rough, rocky defiles of weathered cliff and wind-fallen trees, aiming to find easier going up to the summit of the mountain bluff above. This was new range to him, consisting of moderate-sized spruce and a few straggling cedar. A brightening of the dark-green ahead showed him that he was approaching a large glade or open patch, where the sunlight fell strongly. He rode out upon this park and drew rein. From this height he had a spectacular view of the vast open range stretching out below.

Movement in the far distance caught his eye. Two riders. He recalled the two he had followed a week or so before. Never taking his eyes off the two he reached in his saddle bags and took out a pair of binoculars. He hadn't had these the other time. He focused the glasses on the riders. Although he could make out features fairly clearly he concluded both riders were strangers to him. It appeared to Wyoming that they might be waiting for someone.

Some time went by during which the riders sat smoking, and Wyoming was certain now they were waiting for someone. He watched them off and on through the binoculars, wondering at one point if he was being foolish spying on the riders when he had work to do. Perhaps a half hour elapsed before two other riders entered Wyoming's line of sight from the west. They came on unhurriedly keeping their horses at an easy trot. When they were within sight of the other two horsemen they drew rein and it was apparent they were in some sort of discussion.

"That little paint horse shore looks familiar," he muttered turning the binoculars on its rider.

Wyoming gave an audible grunt. The slender youthful figure sat straight in the saddle, face partly shielded by a tall-crowned sombrero, but there was no mistaking the splash of golden curls peeking from under the sombrero's wide brim. Angelique Dixon! He moved the glass to her companion but knew before the rider came into focus who he was.

"Be damn—Jimmy Anderson! And I'll bet my spurs he was the hombre she was with the other day when Ally and me trailed them."

After a while Anderson rode ahead joining the other two. Angelique stayed back several yards waiting.

CHAPTER FOURTEEN

I t took Wyoming nearly half an hour to descend the rough canyon. Straightway the situation confronted Wyoming and gripped his soul. He could feel himself changing inwardly, as if a gray, gloomy, sodden hand was now leading him into shadows. It was that cold, bleak feeling that always marked him when he knew there would be a chance he had to kill a man. He recognized this mood for what it was a foretaste of the black gloom that would follow his action. He didn't fight it for it brought that sureness of mind and steadiness of hand he would have need of when faced with that inevitable moment.

Reaching the mouth of the canyon he drew rein. By his estimation Angelique and Anderson, who had started back this way at a slow easy walk, would not have yet arrived at the curve of the canyon wall. The other two riders Anderson had met had departed in the opposite direction. Would he shoot Anderson there in front of the girl? No, he had to admit, not unless the man forced the issue.

He heard the sound of voices before they came into view. They rode side by side. He held her hand. Her cheeks were rosy. He was the first to notice him, and he jerked his hand from hers, his own moving as though he would snatch at his holstered Colt, but halted his hand hovering nervously in mid air. Angelique's eyes rounded as her gaze met his, this Wyoming perceived although his concentration remained on Anderson.

"Wyoming," she said coolly. "Are you following me again?"

"Ride over here," he ordered softly, eyes never leaving her companion.

"W-what?" she replied with a nervous laugh.

"Hold on, Mister," Anderson said voice husky. "I don't reckon this is any of yur affair."

"Miss Angelique Dixon; I'm waiting," Wyoming said in a strange almost inaudible voice.

It was that weakness of voice that arrested Angelique and sent a chill through her more than if he had shouted. She swallowed and with quickening breath nudged her horse forward. Wyoming's cold keen gaze bore into Anderson, and it seemed at that moment he made up his mind to some yet unresolved course.

"Let me see the bottom of your left boot," Wyoming said.

"What the—! Are yu serious?"

"*Dead* serious," Wyoming drawled.

Anderson kicked his left foot from the stirrup and held it out so Wyoming could see the sole. The fancy Mexican boot's sole was smooth and unworn. Anderson was not the same person who had been spying on the ranch house.

"Satisfied?" Anderson sneered.

"Ah-huh," Wyoming grunted. "But I reckon you ought to make yourself scarce."

Anderson gave Wyoming a piercing glance, as if recognizing in him now a character he had mistaken or had disallowed.

"Ride off the range, before you dangle at the end of a rope," Wyoming continued in his soft cool voice, as if he was advising a thoughtless young man.

Anderson's face blanched to the very lips. "The hell yu say," he burst out, eyes darting to Angelique, but his bravo was obviously intended for the girl's benefit rather than Wyoming's.

"Wyoming!" Angelique exclaimed.

Anderson's eyes then locked with Wyoming's for a long moment. Without a glance at the girl he jerked his mount about and spurred him into a gallop. Wyoming watched until he was out of sight.

"Why are you doing this?" she demanded. "Why don't you like Jimmy?"

"He's a bad hombre."

"You're just saying that! Tell me why you're so mean to him," she insisted slapping her little fist on her thigh causing her horse to fidget.

"He's a rustler!" he declared, "He stealing your dad's cows."

"I don't believe you! You're just making that up!" she remonstrated though the color had drained from her cheeks. "How do you know?"

"I reckon you're just going to have to take my word for it," he drawled leaning his forearm on his saddle horn.

"Well, I don't—take your word! You're just a bully! And you'll not stop me from seeing him!"

"I reckon I will—if he's dead."

Angelique gasped, for a moment quailed into sequacity by the chill timbre of his words. Then her eyes narrowed to shards.

"I hate you, Wyoming McCord!" she sobbed and wheeling her horse about spurred him into a reckless gallop in the direction of home.

"Well, I reckon you shore did a first rate job of that," he muttered.

Angelique rode away so angry she could hardly see straight. And to make matters worse she literally ran into another rider approaching from the opposite direction as she cantered around a bend in the trial. With a squeal she jerked back on the reins, but too late to forestall the collision. She found herself sailing over the neck of her little paint, turning a half summersault in the air before crashing unceremoniously on her posterior in the dirt.

"Ohhh!" she gasped when she could finally catch her breath. She had lost her sombrero and a mass of golden curls dangled over one jade green eye. She screwed her mouth to the side and with a puff of breath blew the hair out of her eyes, and looked up to see, Jack Ward.

Angelique groaned as she stared up at the rider high above her. She watched him swing from his horse, taking a deep breath and struggling to hold back the angry exclamation she was so strongly tempted to utter. Damn Wyoming McCord who had set her in the foul mood that had sent her racing hell-bent. And of all people to see her sprawled on her backside like a graceless amateur it had to be Jack Ward. Oh, how mortifying!

"Are yu hurt?" he asked reaching a hand to help her to her feet.

"Not in the least," she huffed taking his hand.

She stifled the urge to rub her throbbing bottom certain as could be that there would be an enormous bruise.

"Was there somebody chasing yu?" he asked glancing alertly back down the trail.

She stared at his undeniably handsome profile. She didn't want to be attracted to this man. Not when all she could think of was Jimmy Anderson and the way he made her feel, all warm and excited inside. She *would* see him again, *he* couldn't stop her!

"I reckon I will—if he's dead."

She frowned, shook her head, rearranging her thoughts. Surely Wyoming was bluffing, trying to intimidate her. But she remembered the look in his eyes…no, he hadn't been bluffing.

Jack turned his head, looked at her. Goodness, he had the deepest blue eyes. She was not drawn to him! It was Jimmy she wanted to be with. There was something wild, untamed about him that excited her, made her knees weak. No, it was a simple case that Jack was drawn to her, she wasn't, and never would be drawn to him. Still his deep blue gaze pulled her. She found herself unable to look at anything else and that left her momentarily uncertain and unsettled. She had to get away, be alone; clear her head. Think.

"Are yu on yur way home?" he asked. "I'll ride with yu."

"I know the way," she replied.

"I reckon yu do, but I'll come along anyhow."

He fell in beside her and they rode in silence for some moments.

"There's a dance in town this Saturday," he said. "Are yu going?

"Of course, I'm going," she declared gruffly.

She glanced at him ruefully when he made no immediate reply. She wasn't really angry at Jack Ward. It was Wyoming McCord she was furious with…and to a certain degree, Jimmy Anderson. She felt betrayed. Was he really a rustler, stealing her father's cattle?

The ranch house came into view.

"Then I reckon I'll see yu there," he said and with a wave of a gloved hand reined his horse about and set off in an easy lope back the way they had come.

The weather this morning was cooler, which made it easier on the horses but harder on the men. It was near the end of August and Wyoming estimated that they had burned the Triangle 'A' brand on two hundred calves and mavericks.

"Boys, I reckon we ought to work that side canyon in the morning before we head in to the ranch," Wyoming said as the three sat about the remnants of the campfire talking over the day's labor before heading to the bedrolls.

Morning found red cattle dashing pell-mell down the slope, raising dust, tearing the brush, rolling rocks, and letting out hoarse bawls. Wyoming followed on the heels of the yearlings crashing down out of a rough brushy draw. Spurring forward to turn back one of the cows who attempted to break free Billy Reed came up alongside Wyoming's horse. Suddenly Billy's horse stumbled and fell headlong. Wyoming pulled up sharply. Reed's horse struggled to get to its feet, muscle's quivering, eyes wide in near panic. By the time Wyoming dismounted and grabbed for its reins the horse had managed to gain its feet. But then it collapsed its front legs threshing violently and then was still. Reed, however, remained on his back, face ashen, clearly in pain. There was a splash of blood on Reed's leather chaps, but it was the opposite ankle that immediately drew Wyoming's attention. It was misshaped, twisted grotesquely, obviously shattered.

"Hold still, Billy, let me take a look," Wyoming said.

"What—the hell—happened?" Reed grunted a dazed look in his eyes.

Wyoming pulled out his jackknife and slowly, carefully cut away Reed's boot. The foot was badly smashed and had already turned a ghastly black-blue.

"Aw, hell, Wyoming, I reckon it's bad," Reed muttered through clenched teeth.

"Damn, Billy, it don't look good," Wyoming admitted grimly. He glanced at Reed's horse. It lay unmoving, a trickle of blood showed just behind and above the horse's off side elbow. Chico was kneeling beside the fallen horse.

"*Señor* Wyoming, *Señor* Billy, ees horse, she been shot," he said.

"Shot!" he called out in disbelief darting a look about. "Are you shore?"

He hadn't heard a gunshot, but then with the loud snap of cracking brush and the clatter of hoofs on stone he could have well missed the pop of a distant rife shot. Someone had taken a shot at him, and it was only by chance that Reed had spurred along side of him that his horse had taken the bullet instead of him.

"Chico, let's get Billy on your horse and get him down to the ranch," Wyoming called.

No time to worry about the shooter now. Between the two of them they managed to get Reed into the saddle. When they reached the ranch, Allison came out on the porch Caesar at her heels.

"Ally, call your dad," Wyoming said.

"They're not here. No body's here but me and Mrs. Lindsey. Tonight's the dance in town and they left hours ago. You're in trouble," she smirked.

"Dog-gone!" he exclaimed, "I plumb forgot about the dance."

"What happened? Is Billy hurt?" she asked worriedly peering at Reed bent far over the saddle.

"I should smile. Billy's bad hurt," Wyoming explained hurriedly. "Horse fell on his leg and broke it. I cut off his boot. His foot's all smashed. Chico, come on let's get Bill down to the bunk house. Then I reckon I best get into town and fetch the doctor."

Mrs. Lindsey came out on the porch wiping her hands on her apron, her face expressed her concern. She had heard Wyoming's comments and now stepped down from the porch and approached Reed. She glanced up at his face then reached a hand timidly to touch his leg.

"Oh, dear," she sighed.

CHAPTER FIFTEEN

Annabelle placed one slippered foot on the hub and swishing her skirt out of the way of the wheel stepped down from the buckboard. She adjusted her shawl about her shoulders exposed by the low-necked sleeveless evening gown she wore. The night air was chilled. She turned to watch as her father offered a hand to her mother. Annabelle was ready for bed. It had been an exhausting night, her toes still ached. She had danced every dance it seemed. Ed Hester had been there; Wyoming McCord had not, and that had aggravated her more as the night progressed. Secretly she had looked forward to dancing with Wyoming and in his absence she'd danced with Hester, more than a few times, along with about every cowboy for miles around. Hester though monopolized her, not that he was unpleasant; on the contrary he was very amicable, not at all what she had been led to believe by someone in particular, she sniffed.

On the long drive back from town she had planned just what she intended to say to Wyoming when she saw him. She would let him know by her very indifference just what she thought of his lack of consideration in not coming to the dance as he had promised he would. Oh, she would make him pay, that was for certain…as if that would matter. All he had on his mind these days it seems was cows.

Angelique climbed from the buckboard and walked straight into the house. Annabelle watched her curiously. She was so pretty, but she was afraid the girl had become a conscienceless flirt. Angelique had danced once or twice with Jack Ward, but otherwise ignored him, dancing and flirting with several other cowboys. One in particular, a handsome red-haired rider that she remembered was one of the cowboys Wyoming had let go upon their arrival to take over the ranch. Annabelle liked Jack and thought it very rude of her sister. Annabelle followed Angelique into the house and down the hall to her room where they found Allison asleep in the big bed, the hound Caesar curled at her feet.

"Would you look at that!" Angelique hissed making as though she would chase the dog off the bed. "Useless hound!"

"Oh, leave him, Angie. Come, you can sleep with me in my bed," Annabelle said.

"Oh, all right. I'm too tired to argue," Angelique replied yawning and followed her sister into her room across the hall.

"Gee, you sure had a good time this evening," Annabelle said as the two assisted each other in unfastening the hooks down the back of their gowns.

"It was wonderful fun," Angelique exclaimed, dreamily. "Except for that Jack Ward."

"I thought you were very rude to him—"

"Well, he deserved it."

"But didn't you say you liked him."

"Did I say that? Well, not anymore. He and Wyoming are just alike; bullies!"

"What do you mean?"

"Just that, they're bullies; telling me who I can talk to and—and ride with. Do you know what Wyoming said? That Jimmy was a rustler, stealing from dada, and I'd better keep away from him, or—or he would shoot him!"

"He didn't!"

"He most certainly did! Shoot that sweet handsome boy!"

But it was all going to be all right, Angelique smiled to herself. Jimmy had taken care of it he had assured her at the dance. Wyoming wouldn't keep her from meeting him any longer. They must have worked things out between them. She knew Wyoming would like Jimmy if he just got to know him. She was glad. Yes, it had been a wonderful night. Jimmy had kissed her—twice.

Annabelle turned her back so Angelique couldn't see the expression on her face. Wyoming had told her the same thing about Mr. Hester. That, she realized now, was what had made her so uneasy around Hester. There was something about the man that made her wonder if Wyoming spoke true.

"Thank heavens you're home, Mr. Dixon," Mrs. Lindsey's voice sounded in the hall catching Annabelle's attention.

"What is it?" her father demanded.

"Billy Reed that new rider—the doctor's seeing to him now."

"Well, your rider's foot is sure messed up, but I've seen worse," the man in the dark suit informed Annabelle's father as he stepped onto the bunkhouse porch. Annabelle and Angelique had followed their father.

"Well, that's good news, Doctor," Mr. Dixon said.

"He'll be in bed for a spell, but he should recover completely. He was sure worried he'd be a club foot, but not to worry," the doctor added.

The news about Reed's recovery was uplifting in one aspect, but not so for the fact that he would be of no use for possibly months. With only the two of them now, Wyoming mused, it seemed their branding would have to come to a halt. Wyoming glanced at Annabelle.

"Dog-gone," he said, shaking his head. "With no riders available I don't reckon we can do much more branding until spring with just the two of us. And with other ranchers set to hold round up, all them mavericks we could have burned our brand on will wind up wearing somebody else's iron."

While Mr. Dixon continued talking to the doctor, Annabelle and Angelique stepped into the bunkhouse. Billy Reed's bunk was at the far end. Wyoming walked and stood at the foot of his bed looking down at him. Annabelle squeezed Angelique's hand encouragingly and the two girls approached the invalid.

"Well, Billy, I reckon your day's shore brightening up. Look here who's come to call on you," Wyoming said.

"Hi, Billy," Angelique greeted solicitously. "Are you in lots of pain?"

"It's plumb awful bad, Missy," he whined his face a picture of misery. "I reckon I'm not long fer this world."

"Oh, you poor dear," Angelique sighed hands clasped to her breast in an exaggerated display of sorrow. "Do you want—need anything?"

"If yu'd kiss me, Miss Angie, I reckon I could die peaceful," he whimpered pitifully.

"A kiss?" she sighed gazing down at his tightly closed eyes and lips puckered and ready. "Oh, how could I refuse?" And she bent over him to plant a gentle kiss on his ruddy forehead.

"Huh?" he jerked.

"Billy," she said sweetly, "when you pass over to that great cowboy range in the sky...may I have your spurs?"

"Aw, Missy," he groaned, "You're shore a cruel, heartless woman."

"Self-preservation is the first law of life," Angelique laughed. "You range-riders will never get the best of me."

"Ump-umm, Missy, it's gonna happen, just you wait," he grinned good-naturedly.

The three exchanged playful banter for a little while longer after which, being assured Reed was resting comfortably, the two girls bid him goodnight. Wyoming, who had watched and listened, accompanied them out onto the porch.

"What happened," Annabelle asked eyes serious as she turned to peer up at Wyoming. "Chico hinted something about a gunshot."

Angelique halted halfway down the steps and whirled upon Annabelle. "A gunshot?" she gasped eyes round. Clearly that bit of intelligence was new to Angelique.

"Is that true?" Annabelle queried ignoring her sister's startled exclamation.

"I reckon that's a fact," Wyoming replied. "Somebody shot Billy's horse. That's what pitched him. His horse rolled on his ankle."

"Oh, why would someone shoot Billy's horse?" Annabelle demanded.

"Well, I reckon they was aiming at me, but Billy got in the way," Wyoming said.

Annabelle said nothing in response, only nodded and he watched the two girls make their way back to the house before setting off for his own cabin.

Angelique stared up at the darkened ceiling. Tired as she was, her mind remained active and she laid thinking, trying to remember exactly what Jimmy had said to her at the dance. He hadn't actually said that he and Wyoming had reconciled their differences…but that's what she had understood him to say. What if he had meant something entirely different, something sinister? She twisted restlessly.

"You can't sleep?" Annabelle asked softly.

"W-what? Oh, I was just thinking. What about you?"

"I was just thinking also."

"Oh?" Angelique said lying very still.

"Somebody tried to shoot Wyoming."

"You like him, don't you?"

"Yes."

"Well, that settles it," Angelique mumbled half under her breath.

"What did you say?" Annabelle asked.

"Hmm, nothing," her sister sighed turning over on her side. Something wasn't right. Would Jimmy lie to her? How well did she actually know Jimmy? Sure, he was cute and said nice things to her, but what if Wyoming was right? Oh, Jimmy couldn't be…stealing from her father and at the same time saying cooing words to her! Well, she intended to find out! She would put it to him directly. She didn't like beating around the bush, and they were to meet tomorrow. What better time.

A long moment later Annabelle heard Angelique's deep slumberous breathing. Unable to sleep, Annabelle slipped from the bed and walked on bare feet to stare out the window at the dark shadows seemingly lost in reverie. Across the yard the moonlit line had grown to a broad white band creeping down, imperceptibly diminishing the darkness beneath the tall pines. A breeze ruffled the curtains. An owl hooted in the gloom and insects sounded their low constant drone.

What's going to happen now? she wondered. She had fallen in love with the west and had surrendered to the bewildering assurance that it had claimed her. There was this passion she had conceived for horses and her resolve to learn to ride like those slim-hipped riders—yes, like Wyoming. She would fight against going back to Louisiana, even if her father was in favor of it, though thankfully that didn't seem the case. The New Mexico range was endless, the distances frightening, but there were neighbors. She liked the Wards, especially Alice, a wholesome, attractive girl.

But there was that disturbing presence of the bold Ed Hester, who hounded her at the dance, the dark worrisome state of affairs that someone had taken a gunshot at Wyoming, and lastly the perilous conquests of Angelique. She knew Angie had secretly been seeing Jimmy Anderson. Allison had told her how she and Wyoming had followed the two.

At length Annabelle turned from the window and slipped back into bed. Angelique was locked in slumber, but disturbed, unconsciously reverted to her old childish habit of snuggling close to Annabelle. Annabelle smiled in spite of herself and closed her eyes letting sleep overtake her.

CHAPTER SIXTEEN

T he hour was sunrise, with the golden rays streaking ahead of Angelique's little paint mustang down the rolling sage hills, all rosy and gray with rich, strange softness. Groves of aspens stood isolated from one another—here crowning a hill with blazing yellow, and there fringing the brow of another with gleaming gold, and lower down reflecting the sunlight with brilliant red and purple.

Angelique went to their meeting place in a clump of aspens with white trunks and yellow fluttering leaves. But there was no sign of him. She dismounted and let her horse graze. Settling beneath an aspen she leaned back resting her shoulders against its rough bark and waited. She needed to talk to Jimmy; she had to know for certain that he had nothing to do with Reed's injury. He would tell her the truth, she was sure of it. She was making much out of nothing.

An hour passed, then another as she sat listening to the sounds of life all about her; the caw of a jay and the fluttering flight of a butterfly dipping and flapping over some waving, slender, white-and-blue flowers. They smiled up wanly, like pale stars, out of the long grass that had a tinge of gold.

Presently, however, she got to her feet and brushing off her pants caught up the reins of her mustang and stepped easily into the saddle. If he wasn't coming here this morning, she would find him. She would start looking where they had met those two riders last week. She had noticed cattle that day, maybe she would find him working. Mind made up she started out. Down out of the cedars and pine and clumps of aspens she descended out upon the grassy belt of sage brush. She suddenly became aware of cattle bawling and smelled smoke. And another odor she recognized that of burned hair.

She came abruptly upon a small rudely constructed corral containing a dozen or so cows and calves. Her hurried gaze flitting over the cattle instinctively noted the nearest cow wore a brand, which looked like an 'E' with a line beneath it—Bar E she realized almost unconsciously. A small fire burned a short distance away and she saw a calf roped by its rear legs and head. Two cowboys had the animal stretched out in the dirt, and a third cowboy was in the process of burning a brand on the calf's side. A fourth rider sat his horse back a ways watching the procedure. He was ruddy complexioned with thick dark eyebrows, brawny shoulders and unkempt hair low on his thick neck. Angelique remembered seeing him before at the ranch the day they'd first arrived. His sombrero was pulled low and Angelique could catch only a gleam of intense eyes, eyes that sent a chill down her spine as they settled on her. The cowboy doing the branding glanced up at a gruff hail from the ruddy-face rider, and she recognized Jimmy Anderson. He darted a look in her direction and got easily to his feet. Shoving the iron into the hot coals he walked over to her. From where she sat she could now see that the brand he was burning on the cow appeared to be a Box B.

"Wal hello, sweetheart," he drawled, "what air yu doin' here?"

"What do you think?" she replied giving him a dazzling smile. "I rode up to our meeting place this morning, but you weren't there," she pouted prettily. "You said you would meet this morning."

"Yu did? Wal, gee, I plum forgot. Sorry, but I reckon a cowboy's got te make a livin'," he grinned laying a dirty gloved-hand on her knee.

"Doesn't that hurt that poor cow, burning its hide like that?" she asked frowning.

"Naw, they're just dumb critters."

"What is that brand you're burning on it? It looks like a Box B."

He darted a sideways glance at the ruddy-face rider, then stepped closer.

"Yu got sharp eyes, sweetheart. That's my boss, Bull Burton's brand," he said.

"Oh, I see, 'B' for Burton."

"It shore was grand of yu comin' by like this," he breathed, his hand warm on her thigh. "How about a kiss, darling?"

"Those others are watching," she retorted shyly.

"So, let 'em look."

She leaned toward him as though she would comply, but then straightened.

"I should say not! You smell like cows," she said wrinkling her nose.

"Yeah, I reckon I do," he laughed brashly squeezing her leg. "I'll meet yu this evening after I clean up. Shore we can make up fer lost time."

"Yes," she nodded with a wide smile.

She reined her horse around. She didn't look back as she spurred the mustang into a lope crossing the grassy bluff, and up the long yellow slope to where the pines towered aloft. Her heart was thudding in her chest. She had the nearly overwhelming urge to turn and look over her shoulder to make sure that ruddy-faced rider was not following, but she resisted the impulse. She would faint if he was. She felt sick; sick at what she had only feared before, she now knew was true. Annabelle had told her how rustlers changed the Bar E brand that was on the cattle her father bought with the Box B. Jimmy Anderson *was* a rustler!

Tears blurred her vision and she blinked her eyes rapidly. She had trouble seeing. As she rode, blind to her surroundings, her queasiness began to lessen as anger slowly took its place. She had been such a fool. Suddenly the thud of horse's hoofs coming up behind her vibrated in her differing and arousing emotions. She darted a harried glance back over her shoulder, but through the mist of tears she could make out only the shadowy figure of a horse and rider bearing down on her. Oh, God, he was after her—the ruddy-faced rider! Panic drove her now. She set spurs to her horse flattening herself over the mustang's neck letting him have his head. The wind caught at her and whipped her sombrero from her head. Another frantic look over her shoulder and she saw that the rider was gaining. As she stared the rider leaned far from his saddle and at a full gallop reached a long arm to snatch her sombrero from the ground in a strong grip as he rode past it. She twisted forward straightened in the saddle and exhaled a sigh of mingled relief and frustration. Her pursuer wasn't the ruddy-faced rider.

"Damn," she cursed. How irritating! Of all the people to catch her in such a disheveled mood it had to be, Jack Ward.

In a moment he came up beside her and she reined her mustang to a halt.

"Dog-gone, didn't yu hear me yellin'?"

She shook her head. "I thought you were someone else," she retorted. She glanced down at her sombrero clutched in his hand. "May I have my hat back?"

He took his time brushing it off and reshaping the flattened crown before handing it to her.

"Thank you," she sniffed.

"What're yu doin' ridin' so far from home all alone?" he queried.

That was too much. The back of her throat felt raw as she fought the tears that threatened to spring once more to her eyes.

"I'll ride where I want to, Jack Ward," she replied and made to ride away but he reached out a hand and clasped her reins staying her action. She dipped her head refusing to allow him to see her distress.

"What's wrong?" he demanded.

"It's none of your concern," she said quite piercingly giving license to her anger.

"I reckon I'm makin' it mine," he declared.

"Well, you can't—because I won't permit you! Now let go of my horse!"

"Ump-umm," he said. "I reckon somebody's got to talk straight to yu. Yu're set on playin' with fire young lady. That puncher Anderson is bad news."

"I don't need you to tell me that," she cried slashing at his hand with her short leather quirt. "I said let go my bridle!"

An ugly red welt sprang up on the back of his hand and her eyes widened in sudden contrition as she saw his face lose its bronze hue.

He slowly turned loose of her bridle. Horrified at what she had done she stared scarlet of face. But it was too late.

Eyes shuddered, lips thinned with suppressed passion, Jack's hand snaked out grasping Angelique around her waist and dragging her off her horse virtually onto his lap. Her mustang shied away jerking the reins from her slack grip and bound off until the dragging reins snagged him to a halt. She struggled, kicking out with her feet in a vain attempt to free herself from his steely hold.

"Let me go, you brute!" she cried.

He held her in front of him with his left arm around her and her head against his shoulder. He gazed down at her suddenly pale face. She was watching him with a look no man could have interpreted.

"I hate—you," she panted.

"Did yu let him kiss yu?" he demanded hoarsely.

"That's none of your business—"

Her protest was abruptly cut off as his mouth came down over hers. She tried to pull away but his hold was unrelenting. She thrashed fiercely bucking and twisting, but his kiss only deepened. Her head trapped as it were against his shoulder rendered her helpless. She uttered a soft moan and then suddenly went slack sinking heavily against him. One tiny gloved hand which had been forcefully clinching his arm gradually crept upward to his shoulder where it rested impotently. Slowly, as though stunned by what he had done, he drew back.

"I'll kill—you!" she whispered huskily.

"I reckon, I'm goin' to hell anyhow," he groaned, and kissed her again.

Wyoming walked from his cabin to the bunkhouse. Stepping up on the porch he could hear Reed and Chico's querulous voices. He went inside not knowing what to expect. Billy Reed looked up from the game of checkers he was playing with Chico.

"Morning," Wyoming replied eyeing the two.

"*Buenos dias, Señor* Wyoming," Chico grinned.

"Mornin' boss," Reed acknowledged.

"Dog-gone, Chico can't yu see a jump when yu got one? Jump why don't yu," Reed said.

Chico stared at the board, and then moved one of his pieces. Reed promptly jumped three of Chico's chips.

"Crown my man!" he laughed gleefully.

"¡*Carramba*!" Chico exclaimed, looking up at Wyoming. "*Señor* Wyoming that is four games that I no get a king!"

"Wal, Chico, yu gots te use yur noggin' fer sumthin''sides a rack fer yur sombrero," Reed chuckled.

"Stupid *gringo* game," Chico said disgustedly.

The tread of light footsteps on the porch drew Wyoming's attention and he glanced up to see a face surrounded by soft golden curls peek around the corner of the door frame. Angelique took a cautious step into the bunkhouse and halted her jade green eyes, almost black in the dim light, met and held his.

"Wyoming?" she called hesitantly. "May I speak with you?"

"Why shore, Miss Angie," returned Wyoming.

She retreated back outside and when Wyoming stepped out onto the porch she was standing at the edge by the steps peering out toward the timbered slope. He came up beside her and waited holding his tongue. A long moment passed before he sensed out of the corner of his eye her darting an uncertain glance at him. He didn't look her way.

"You were right," she said in almost a whisper.

He looked fully at her then. Her eyes were puffy and red as though she had been crying. She didn't look away, but bravely held his gaze.

"You were right—about Jimmy," she confided. "And I'm still sick to my stomach."

"Ah, you poor kid," he grunted awkwardly.

"I came upon him and three others branding one of dada's cows, changing the Bar E to a Box B—"

"Rustlers!"

"Yes," she asserted. "But I acted stupid and pretended not to understand. I acted like I thought they were just branding their own stock."

"Dog-gone kid, I reckon you shore got a head on your shoulders!" Wyoming ejaculated staring at her in undisguised admiration.

She gave him a shy smile, but then sobered. "But Wyoming," she faltered. "I was so scared. One of the men was that ruddy-face puncher that you fired that first day—"

"Ackers?"

"I guess. I don't know his name. But the way he looked at me—" She shuddered. "I thought he was going to come after me—oh!"

"Ah-huh," he muttered under his breath.

"And—and, I can't get this morning out of my thoughts," she whispered.

"Miss Angie, you're all upset," said Wyoming, moved by her words and convulsed pale face. "But I reckon Ackers' on borrowed time as it is."

"Oh, what are you going to do?" she asked wheeling upon him eyes alight.

"Well, Miss Angie, I reckon you needn't worry none about that," he replied.

"But I shall! I—"

"Well, I'd like to call Ackers and them others out and have it over with—"

"No—no!" she cried.

"Are you concerned about your Jimmy?" he queried tersely.

"He's not *my* Jimmy!" she spat. "I was thinking about how that would distress Anna—"

"It would? How so?"

"Never mind," she said with a dismissive wave of her hand.

"Ah-huh. Well, I was planning on branding as many cows as possible before the snow flies. I reckon that would shore put a burr under them rustlers' hide and make it a mite tougher for them to do their rustling, but seeing how there's only me, a Mexican and a cripple," he shrugged. "Some things will have to wait a spell, unless I can hire some more riders; then again, I reckon one would do the trick."

Angelique nodded and without further comment turned and Wyoming silently watched her as she made her way up to the house. Angelique went straight to her bedroom. Overwhelmed by her own complicated emotions, she suddenly broke down and began to sob as though her heart was breaking.

CHAPTER SEVENTEEN

Wyoming woke the next morning with a tiredness he hadn't known in some time. Resolutely he swung his legs over the side of his bed and stood. He went about washing and dressing desperate to smother the melancholy under which he had labored for weeks. What he wanted to do was to be his old self; that would have taken him hell bent to a showdown with Ackers and his bunch, but that could never be, he speculated dispassionately. He stepped out on the porch. The ranch was picturesquely located in a grove of pine and scattered aspens, through the middle of which ran a brook. Beyond was the pasture leading past the Mexican Ramon's place and out to the open range. It was indeed a ranch to delight the heart, wholly aside from the three charming Dixon sisters, one in particular who had utterly beguiled him.

Speaking of which he looked up to see Annabelle and Angelique approaching rather resolutely arms locked together their lovely faces set determinedly. He straightened bracing himself for whatever uncertainty that was about to descend upon him. He backed up as they ascended the steps still arm in arm. His gaze went from one to the other finally settling on Annabelle. She was dressed in something white that revealed her beautiful form. A rich color tinged with gold had displaced the former paleness of her face. Her wonderful jade green eyes, intent and grave, regarded him.

"We've come to talk to you," she said unwaveringly.

"Oh, yeah?" he replied beset by an army of emotions.

"Yeah," Angelique mimicked.

"Well, have at it," he said somewhat recovering his poise.

"You'd better sit down," Annabelle advised.

"Aw!" he expelled heavily. "I can smell trouble a mile away, and shore it on me."

"No such thing," Annabelle protested.

"Well, out with it, anyhow."

"Are you going to sit down?" Angelique asked sweetly.

"I reckon I shore better," he said settling in the lone chair and indicated the bench pushed up against the wall. "You joining me?"

"Nope, we'll stand," the girls said in unison.

"We've been thinking," Annabelle said. "And we've come up with a plan—"

"Hmm," he grunted. "And just what does this plan involve?"

"We'll—Angie and I, we'll take Mr. Reed's place."

Wyoming stared at her. She peered back at him, lips set determinedly. "See here, Mr. Wyoming McCord, you filled my head with dreams the other day. You said there were cattle out there just waiting to be branded; that we'd be rich—"

"Shore, I reckon that's no lie, but—"

"And you told me that if you could brand a lot of cows," Angelique interjected, "that would keep the rustlers in check—"

"Ump-umn!" he denied. "I said it would slow them down."

"Same thing," she said taking a deep breath. "Wyoming, dada's near broke. He was counting on selling some of the cattle. This will kill him."

"Miss Anna, Angie, I don't reckon you two know what you're asking! Nope it can't be done."

"I'm sure you're right," Annabelle sighed. "I know I'm ignorant of how to chase cattle or anything—goodness, I don't even know the first thing, and that scares me, but I'll not have dada lose this ranch."

"Well, I'm not scared," Angelique interrupted. "I know how to ride. I'll show you!"

"And furthermore," Annabelle said, "you could teach us. I'm quite capable of learning, and I'm tougher than you think—and don't give me that look."

"What look?" he said, staring. "You're both serious ain't you?"

"Of course, we're serious. We've made up our mind."

"Well, I haven't! And neither one of you are punching cows! That's final!"

"Like hob it is!" Annabelle retorted. "You're not our boss. I remind you that you work for us!"

"Nix, I work for your dad."

"Exactly. And he's given his consent—"

"Ha! Your dad's an old southern gentleman. He'd never do such a foolhardy thing."

"Then you'd best go and ask him," Annabelle replied smugly.

"That's just what I'll do." And he stormed off with long strides toward the house.

Wyoming found Dixon seated in a rocking chair on the porch drinking coffee. Wyoming stepped up on the porch ready to do battle. Dixon glanced up at him.

"I say Wyoming you look a little putout," he acknowledged his tone easy.

"Boss, do I have to go along with this foolishness?"

"Ah, I see you've talked to the girls."

"Yep," he rejoined. "It's not heard of, boss, women brush riding! And I told them it wasn't going to happen in no uncertain terms, but they said you okayed it."

"Well, Wyoming, I don't suppose you have to agree with the idea, but it sure would make life easier on me," Dixon sighed.

"Boss, you can't be serious. Cow punching is a dirty, messy and dangerous job—"

"I can imagine, but try arguing with those two when they get their minds set on something. Lordy, what I'd give for just one son."

"Boss, are you telling me you're going to eat crow?!"

"If that means, indulging those two, then, yes."

"Dog-gone," Wyoming snorted.

"See here, Wyoming, let them have their way. When they discover how dirty, messy, and hard a job it is, they'll soon change their tune."

"All right, boss, you win. What's a day or two, anyhow?" Wyoming queried helplessly recognizing something inexplicable and infuriating was at work upon him. "We wouldn't have gotten much branding done at any rate."

"That's the spirit, son," Dixon said.

The two girls were not in evidence when Wyoming headed back to the bunkhouse where he was met by Chico.

"Ahh," Chico sighed. "What will we do, *Señor* Wyoming? *Señor* Reed no can ride."

Wyoming emitted a humorless laugh. "We got us two new partners, Chico ole man, and God help us!"

When Wyoming came to breakfast that next morning he found Annabelle dressed in overalls and top boots. It was hard not to stare at her slender lithe form. Her soft golden curls were drawn back and tied with a blue ribbon in a ponytail a style that he found so fetching. He sat down at the table just as Angelique entered the room dressed as was her sister. Annabelle smiled as she set a mug of coffee in front of him then went to stand next to her sister.

"Well," she remarked.

"Humph!" he snorted.

Annabelle grinned triumphantly.

"Has everybody gone loco?" Wyoming muttered.

They rode up into the wild reaches of Piñon Canyon, four of them leading a packhorse containing branding irons, medicine box, cooking supplies and food stuffs. But this time in place of the veteran Reed there rode two slight figures mounted on mustangs and driving the small *remuda*. The little cavalcade rode far up the canyon where Wyoming was certain no rider had ventured, and where dense brushy thickets never failed to yield calves and yearlings that had never smelled burned hair.

It happened just as Wyoming knew it would. Both girls turned out to be far less hardy and enduring then they had claimed. By midmorning they were drenched in sweat, covered with dust and bits of brush and cedar stuck in their chaps. They looked exhausted. Wyoming almost felt sorry for them...almost that was. There could be no room for pity. No, he'd have to steel himself. They needed to admit on their own how foolhardy their little venture was and go back home where they belonged. Besides he would never forgive himself if either one were to get hurt. So he never let them out of his sight. They were able to brand three cows that day. Wyoming was nearly worn out by mid-afternoon; not from beating brush, but from shouting orders at one or the other of the girls that from all practicable purposes went unheeded.

"Will you stop yelling!" Angelique burst out. "You're making me nervous, roaring like some grouchy old bear."

"I reckon I'll give orders any way I like, Miss Angie," he retorted.

"I reckon you can," snorted Angelique mimicking his drawl, "but that doesn't mean I have to listen."

"Yeah? I reckon I can just fire you—" he barked.

"You can't fire us—"

"Well, I can dam—dang shore quit though," he replied and touching spurs to his horse rode off down the canyon disappearing from sight. "Let them think about that," he grinned to himself.

"Quit?" Annabelle gasped giving Angelique a bleak look. "He wouldn't—"

Angelique silently stared in the direction Wyoming had gone for a moment, then turned to Chico who was leaning back on his hunches next to the small branding fire. She uncoiled the lariat rope tied to her saddle and shook it out trying to imitate the action she had seen Wyoming do, but the loop got caught around her foot and she cursed under her breath.

"Chico, how do you work this confounded rope—like you and Wyoming do?" she demanded.

Chico cocked his head stared at her for a moment before shrugging and getting to his feet. He walked to his horse and took down his rope. He shook out a perfect loop.

"*Señorita* Angie, you want to learn to use 'ees rope?"

"Yes," she said eagerly.

"Me too," Annabelle cut in.

Chico grinned. "*Si*, me teach you."

Both girls quickly dismounted, their fatigue apparently forgotten for the moment.

"*¡Mira!* You make a big loop, like this," Chico instructed, "It is all in ees…how do you say, *película de la muñeca*?" he said slowly rotating his wrist back and forth.

Watching him closely they attempted to imitate his action, awkwardly at first, but soon had the movement down pat.

"*Si, si, muy buena*, very good," he said with a broad grin. "Now, you swing ees loop over your head so it will stay big, like ees," and he twirled the loop over his head round and round, then suddenly sent it snaking out to drop easily over the empty pack saddle some twenty paces distant. A quick flick of his wrist jerked the loop taut.

"Gosh, Chico, you make that look so easy," Annabelle said.

He sauntered over and removed the noose from the pack saddle and returned to where they waited coiling the loop as he came. "Now, you try," he grinned.

For a moment he silently watched their clumsy attempts.

"Ah, *Señoritas*, no, no," he finally said, "You toss ees rope like a girl—"

"We are girls!" they retorted in unison.

"*Si,*" he laughed, "but you must throw ees rope like a man." He picked up a rock the size of his fist and holding it up so they could see, said, "You must throw the rope like you throw ees rock." And he whirled his hand over his head in the same manner he had twirled the rope and then let the rock fly. It struck the pack saddle and bounced off.

For the next hour the two girls practiced throwing rocks at a cedar stump, whirling their hands over their heads as though they held a lariat rope instead of a stone.

Peering from between the branches of a cedar where he sat his horse unseen, Wyoming watched curiously. "What the heck are they doing?" he muttered after a moment. He stared a little longer mystified. Then he grunted, realizing—Chico was showing the two girls how to toss a lariat rope!

"I'll be dog-gone."

He didn't know whether to be amazed or irritated. They didn't look like they were anywhere near giving up.

Wyoming deliberately stayed away using the time to ride further into the brush which proved to be the wildest reaches of the canyon so far. He spotted more and more cattle, a discovery which improved his mood immensely.

"A feller could work a month of Sundays and not put a brand on all them cows," he remarked to himself as he progressed further up the rough canyon.

In Wyoming's absence work, as it was, ceased. Annabelle withdrew to the shade of a cedar. She sat and took off her sombrero and laid it beside her. She ran one slim hand through her sweat-dampened hair before wrapping both arms about her drawn up knees. As she quietly sat there her eyes would slide often to the narrow trail down which Wyoming had disappeared.

"Chico," Angelique remarked setting cross-legged before the fire drinking coffee from a battered tin cup, "is that your name, really?"

"Oh, no, *Señorita* Angie, my name ees Juan Domingo Rodriguez. My mother, she have twelve children. My brother, he ees older, and he was born like me on the day of San Juan so we are both name Juan. So my father he call my brother, Juan *Grande*, and me, he call, Juan *Chico*. But everybody, they just call me, *Chico*."

CHAPTER EIGHTEEN

W yoming rode into camp and swung easily to the ground. Angelique watched him with wary curiosity as she sipped from the tin cup. Annabelle's disheveled head, however, bobbed up with a toss of golden curls and her jade green eyes brightened, an action strange and wonderful to see in one wearing rough and dusty male attire. Without speaking he poured himself a cup of coffee and squatted on his haunches in the manner of cowboys and took a long swallow of the bitter brew.

"Dang! Who made this coffee?" he demanded making a face.

"I did," Annabelle replied getting to her feet. "It's been setting on the fire since you rode off all hopping mad, so I suppose it has boiled away."

"Aw," he grunted and tossed the remains of the dark beverage into the brush. He got to his feet and brushed at the seat of his britches.

"*Señor,*" Chico said sharply. "Riders come."

Far down the canyon at the head of a draw Wyoming spied four riders. They were some distance below approaching at a brisk trot winding in and out of the sage and scrub-oak that dappled the rise. Shortly Wyoming's keen gaze recognized the riders.

"Chico, pull that rifle from your boot and slip off up in the brush. If shooting starts work that Winchester. Savvy?

"*Si, Señor,* me savvy," he said and mounting wheeled his horse disappearing in the brushy thicket.

"Girls stay back near them trees," Wyoming ordered. He thought they were going to argue for a moment, but after a slight hesitation they mounted and rode their horses to where he directed. "And keep your hats pulled low…and don't say anything."

Angelique made no response and Wyoming knew she recognized the slim red-headed rider next to Jed Ackers. Jimmy Anderson, Ackers and the lean unkempt Walters and the swarthy-faced Mexican, Jimenez made up the quartet. The four dark riders closed the distance quickly and drew up in a semicircle just opposite the fire. Ackers' bold eyes beneath dark thick brows swept over Wyoming lingering a long moment on each girl. They sat their horses, sombreros low on their foreheads. His gaze finally settled once again upon Wyoming.

"Wal, so here yu air," he said gruffly.

"Howdy, Ackers," Wyoming said coolly taking a step to one side, getting out of line with the others with a significance that could not have been mistaken.

"What kind of outfit yu runnin', McCord, a Greaser an' two gurls?" Ackers said with a harsh laugh. "An' rite pretty gurls, too, I reckon."

"Ackers, I'm not used to palavering with men like you," rejoined Wyoming bitingly. "I reckon you ought to turn around and ride out of here."

The color in the man's already ruddy face deepened.

"I reckon this is free range, McCord," Ackers declared.

"Not in your case, Ackers."

At that moment the unmistakable sound of a Winchester being cocked came from some hidden spot up the slope. Ackers' eyes flitted from the ivory-handled Colt low on Wyoming's hip to the direction of the sound. He gave an impression then of intense preoccupation, of an uncertainty, which he needed time to meet. Wyoming never turned a hair breath from the rider he was facing. If the shooting started he intended to take out Ackers first off.

"Ah-huh…Have it yore way," Ackers said in a cool hard voice, and whirling his horse about motioned with his head to his companions. Jimmy Anderson lingered his piercing gaze locked on Angelique. She kept her head lowered. He appeared as though he was about to call to the girl.

"Red, what's the hold up? Get yore worthless hide movin'!" Ackers yelled.

With a last hard look at Angelique, Anderson wheeled his horse about and joined the others. Wyoming watched until they disappeared in the sage and scrub-oak from which they appeared. Only then did he visibly relax. His glittering eyes moved to Annabelle whose face was ashen and her eyes darkly dilated with receding panic.

"You girls all right?" Wyoming asked.

Both girls let out pent-up breaths and gave jerky nods.

"Hmm," he mused thoughtfully, "have either one of you ever shot a gun?"

"Gracious, no!" Annabelle exclaimed looking wide-eyed at him.

Angelique wordlessly shook her head.

"Here take this," Wyoming said handing over his Colt to Annabelle—an action he had never done since that gun had become a part of him.

"I don't want to shoot your old gun. I don't like guns."

"If you want to ride with me you both gotta learn how to shoot," he said firmly. "Take it."

She hesitated for several heartbeats before she finally reached and clasped the Colt. She wrinkled her nose with revulsion.

"It's too heavy," she complained letting the gun fall upon her thigh.

"Be careful! Now you have to thumb the hammer—there on the back," he explained pointing. "Hold the gun high with your thumb on the hammer. Now throw it hard with a downward jerk. The motion will flip the hammer just as the gun reaches a level, and it'll go off, you bet—here, let me show you."

"Gladly," she responded handing the pistol back to him.

With a swift fluid motion he snapped off a shot. She flinched at the loud report, and her little mustang's ears sprang up.

"Now, let's see you do that," he said handing the gun back to her.

She took the Colt with a rather forbearing look. "Well, here goes," she said bravely, and with thumb on the hammer, threw the gun as she had seen him, aiming at the twisted trunk of a scrub oak.

"Ugh," she cried as the weapon leaped violently. Her mustang jumped straight up nearly unseating her. It took a moment to quiet him. "Here, take your old gun," she declared returning it to Wyoming. "It nearly kicked my arm off."

"Well, you hit the tree, anyhow, and that's shore fine," he drawled.

"Let me try," Angelique said.

Wyoming handed the Colt to her, and without hesitation she thumbed back the hammer mimicking his motion and the gun leaped in her hand. Bark splintered from the center of the tree. She turned and gave him a satisfied look.

"There," she declared. "Can I do it again?"

"Shore."

She thumbed back the hammer of the Colt and fired striking the tree nearly dead center again. She calmly handed his gun back.

"Well, I reckon you shore mean business," Wyoming said coolly eyeing her admiringly as he reloaded. "Let's ride for home"

"Why can't I carry a gun?" Angelique asked sulkily.

"Angelique!" Annabelle gasped.

Her sister ignored her penning an accusing eye on Wyoming.

"Well, I shore reckon if you're so determined," he grinned. It certainly wasn't a bad idea having the girl armed. Who knew in this wild country what a man, or in this case, a girl would run across even out for a relaxed ride; not with the likes of Ackers and his bunch around, and there was no argument, she certainly knew how to use a Colt he decided glancing at the bullet-marked tree. Too bad Annabelle was so opposed to guns.

Gathering up the supplies and packing the horses they were soon on their way down out of the canyon. The sun was dipping low in the sky. There would be no more work this day. They continued down the trail, always walled in by juniper, and patches of hickory pine, Manzanita and scrub oak. Cattle, wild turkey and deer fled before the clip-clop of the horses. Neither girl said a word, like Wyoming they appeared deep in thought. It had almost come to violence back there Wyoming knew. There was no doubt in his mind that Ackers was dangerous, but he wasn't worried that the man could beat him to the draw; not from the back of a horse, but one of the others; a lucky shot…he didn't want to think of what would happen to the girls should he take a slug. Anderson was young, hot blooded, but obviously saw himself as a ladies' man. Rustler, yes, but he didn't have the look of a killer. The beady-eyed Mexican on the other hand was one to watch.

The sun had dropped beyond the mountain range by the time they reached the ranch. The girls turned their horses over to Chico and went immediately up to the house, both visibly dog-tired. There was little conversation at the dinner table that night. Wyoming retired to his bed feeling good, satisfied that the two girls had learned their lesson.

When Wyoming woke the next morning the sky was a pale gray. He didn't rise immediately, but lay thinking. The encounter with Ackers and his bunch caused him some deliberation. The look on Jimmy Anderson's face worried him. He was moonstruck over Angelique. Wyoming pondered over the dire possibilities one by one and figured they didn't present any great obstacle to him! Of course, he could get shot in the back. He'd have to get back to the somber vigilance that had been natural to him in the past. For a long time now Wyoming had kept faith in the belief that it was enough just to be around Annabelle, but this was rapidly growing to be a fallacy. Having her near was no longer enough. It was turning out to be torment.

He threw back the covers and got to his feet. After dressing and washing his face he buckled on his gun belt. He hesitated as he reached for his sombrero mouth screwed to the side in thought. He walked to his pack and pulled out his spare Colt. He pulled the hammer to half cock and flipping open the loading port spun the cylinder checking to see that it was empty. He stuffed the Colt in his back pocket and with sombrero in hand stepped out on the porch.

The gray, rolling foothills, so exquisitely colored at that hour, and the black-fringed ranges, one above the other, and the distant peaks, flushed with the morning sun, all rose open and clear to Wyoming's sight, so wildly and splendidly expressive of the New Mexico he had come to love.

"Hey, sleepyhead," a voice called. "Time's wasting!"

He glanced down to see Annabelle striding briskly toward him.

"Well, well, somebody's in high spirits this morning."

"Sure am. Breakfast is on the table. Everybody's waiting. I came to fetch you."

"I'm on my way."

Wyoming started to step off the porch when he spied a rider approaching under the trees. Annabelle caught sight of him too and waited. Jack Ward rode into the yard. He dipped his hat to Annabelle.

"Mornin' Miss Anna, Wyoming," he said.

"Hello," she smiled in return.

"Howdy, Jack. What brings you out so early?"

"Say, I just heard about Billy," he replied resting one forearm on his saddle horn. "Thought I'd come over and see how he's fairin'."

"Get down and come on up to the house. I'm told breakfast's on the table. I reckon Billy's hobbled up there already. That hombre can shore pack in the grub."

Jack laughed and swung down from his horse. He fell in beside Wyoming and Annabelle leading his horse as they walked up to the ranch house.

Angelique glanced up as they entered the kitchen and seeing Jack Ward her nose rose in the air with mock drama before she turned back to the stove without saying a word.

"Why, welcome, Jack, have a seat," Mr. Dixon said. "Angie, girl, pour a cup of coffee for our guest."

With an indifferent shrug, Angelique placed a steaming cup of coffee in front of Jack as his eyes followed her movements with what appeared to be smoldering fire.

"What brings you?" Dixon asked.

"Wal, I heard about Billy's gettin' hurt an' come to see how he's fairin'," he replied slowly shifting his gaze to Dixon.

"I'm mendin'," replied that worthy. "But I reckon it'll be slow goin'."

"I don't guess you heard about the girls?" Dixon said.

Jack shook his head and glanced up at Angelique with telltale eyes.

"Hah!" he snorted. "They've been taking Billy's place."

"Takin' Billy's place?" Jack drawled, though surprise was evident in his eyes.

"You know I'm still not too keen on Anna and Angie chasing cattle like regular cow punchers," Dixon continued. "But they overruled me insisting that it had to be done. I still don't understand how those cattle thieves are robbing me blind, branding up all those 'mavericks' as you Westerners call them."

"Dada, a maverick's a calf that's lost its mother," Annabelle said. "I'm told that all ranchers brand mavericks, more or less."

"Miss Anna's right, Mr. Dixon," Wyoming said. "You see out on the range with mixed herds from different ranches there can't be no positive identification of whose calf it is unless the calf accompanies a branded cow, so if a calf or a yearling or even a two year old hasn't got the mark of one outfit, it'll shore get that of another, eventually. You see there's still a string of old cattle with Erickson's brand up in that canyon that belongs to you. I reckon we've put your brand on a heap of mavericks and that's going to rile that rustler outfit. They'll take to brand burning."

"Brand burning?" Dixon queried.

"Dada, Wyoming explained brand burning to me," Annabelle interjected. "Rustlers use a straight iron with a small hook on the end and amazingly they can change an original brand into something else by just burning another shape. Like changing the 'E' in Mr. Erickson's brand to make it a 'B' and drawing a box around it so it becomes a 'Box B'. It's very clever."

"My word, you're turning western on me," Dixon said admiration unmistakable in his tone. "But, Wyoming, couldn't you recognize any burning out of our brand?"

"Shore, I reckon I could—if we ever see it. That's the trouble," Wyoming replied. "That rustler outfit won't burn a strange brand on your cattle and then turn them out, as we've done. They'll throw a herd together and drive it pronto."

"You mean quickly? But where would they drive it to?"

"Probably into Arizona," Jack Ward spoke up. "I've heard there's government agents who'll buy up anythin' with no questions asked."

"Hmm," Dixon mused thoughtfully.

"Wyoming, if yu're keen to it, I reckon I could lend a hand with yur brandin'," Jack said, "At least for a few days."

"I'd shore be obliged, Jack," Wyoming said.

"Dada, are you sure we can afford another rider?" Angelique asked pointedly though she refused to look at Jack Ward.

"I reckon I'd just lend a hand, sort of one neighbor helpin' another," Jack drawled gazing keenly up at her.

"I see," Angelique shrugged apathetically but spoiled the effect utterly by sticking her tongue out at him.

"Say, that sure is generous of you," Dixon smiled, and then turned to take in each of his daughters. "Well, you girls are off the hook. With Jack here you won't need to chase anymore cattle."

"I'm not quitting," Angelique said forcefully.

"And neither am I," Annabelle added.

Mr. Dixon let out an audible sigh. He glanced at Wyoming, then Jack. "Boys, if you ever get married…avoid having daughters."

Annabelle and Angelique did the serving and during the course of the meal Wyoming's keen eye noted the way Angelique's jade-green gaze strayed often to Jack Ward—when she thought no one noticed. And when Wyoming ventured to look up at Annabelle, to see her strong, capable tan hands and her warm glance, sweetly expressive of—what? He wished he could read her mind.

Getting up from the table after they had all eaten, Wyoming motioned to Jack to follow him outside.

"What's up?" Jack asked as the two stepped out on the porch.

"Say, would you have an extra gun holster that would fit this here Colt?" Wyoming asked pulling the gun from his pocket.

"Shore," Jack said giving him a curious look.

"I reckon it's for Miss Angie," Wyoming revealed and went on to tell of meeting Ackers and three of his riders up in the canyon and how he had let both girls shoot his Colt. "Miss Anna shore shuns guns but Angie took to shooting like a duck to water and wants to pack a gun. I figured it wasn't a bad idea."

"I'll be damn," Jack ejaculated. "Shore, I'll bring a gun belt and holster with me when I come tomorrow."

CHAPTER NINETEEN

T he sun had not yet cleared the mountain ridge when they set off the following morning. They rode some distance along the canyon, which opened upward leading to the high mountain ridges. Wyoming abruptly turned in his saddle and looked from one girl to the other his eyes settling on the gun belt around Angelique's slender waist. She gave him a wicked smile. Jack Ward and Chico brought up the rear driving the *remuda* of twelve horses. On a grassy bench just where the pines began was a green bush-walled draw with steep ridges perhaps a mile deep forming a horseshoe-like enclosure having an entrance perhaps thirty yards across. A wash flooded by weeks of runoff from out of the mountains ran along the edge of the draw afforded plenty of water. One whole day was spent arranging a makeshift fence with a wide swinging pole gate to close off the opening to the draw.

"I reckon since Jack and me are old hands," Wyoming said that evening near sundown. "It'd be best if we worked in teams."

"I agree," Annabelle said. "And the fact that neither Angie nor I have much experience, one of us should join up with either you or Jack."

"That's what I was thinking," Wyoming replied trying to sound as casual as possible.

"That makes a heap of sense," Jack concurred.

"I reckon then I best team up with Miss Annabelle," Wyoming said. "Jack, how about you and Miss Angie partner up?"

Angelique gave him a sharp look, eyes glinting beneath the shadowy brim of her sombrero and muttered something under her breath. Jack glanced significantly at her and nodded without speaking.

"Chico, that leaves you with the branding fires."

"*Si, Señor,*" he grinned.

The next few days they worked the thick brushy reaches higher up in the canyon threshing out bunches of cattle, cutting out the yearlings and driving them down to the grassy bench they had enclosed. Calves and yearlings were making the dust fly along the mountain slope; wild old steers were crashing in the sage, holding level, unwilling to be driven down; cows were running and lowing for their lost ones. Melodious and clear rose the clarion calls of the riders. Here and there along the slope, where the sage oak clustered, a horse would flash across an open space; the dust would fly, and Wyoming or Jack Ward would peal out a lusty yell that rang along the canyon.

"*Go--aloong--you-ooooo.*"

Red cattle dashed pell-mell down the slope, raising the dust, tearing the brush, rolling rocks, and letting out hoarse bawls.

"*Whoop-ee!*" High-pitched and pealing came clearer yells that were purely feminine.

Wyoming drew rein watching Annabelle, giving in to reluctant admiration. She was becoming an accomplished horsewoman. Every time Wyoming or Jack threw a lasso, and every several times Chico did likewise, and once in half a dozen throws for Annabelle or Angelique, meant an added twelve dollars for the Dixon ranch. It was amazing how the thing grew. And likewise their appetite for work, and daring to take it in grew in proportion to their reward. But no matter how many catches were made, Annabelle refused to apply the branding iron, and Wyoming grudgingly refrained from chiding her for her squeamishness. Angelique though, showed no such qualms and readily applied the branding iron.

With few exceptions all the cattle were driven down the canyon to the hold pen. The range would one day run thousands of Triangle 'A' stock Wyoming visualized. They planned to spend the nights, as well as the weekends, at the ranch. But it became apparent to Wyoming that the farther up the canyon they rode they would eventually have to spend some nights in camp.

As the days and weeks passed, both girls lost a little of the fullness of their cheeks and the graceful roundness of form that even the loose and ill-fitting clothes they wore failed to hide. And each day they both endeared themselves the more to Wyoming for their courage and steadfastness.

Far up the canyon wide draws opened up choked with rocks and cedars and thickly covered with scrub oak and juniper and other brush hard on horse and rider. One morning Wyoming and Jack, with the Dixon girls and Chico trailing close behind, proceeded up one of these draws where water was plentiful in pools in the rocky streambeds. They at length struck a trail, which zigzagged steeply upward through pine and oak thickets. Wyoming hesitated deliberating a moment as he gazed up the faint overgrown trail. Often difficulties arose in the way of keeping Annabelle and Angelique from sharing real perils. To hint of danger a little too risky for either girl's strength or horsemanship was to normally invite failure.

"What do you think? That's shore rough going," Wyoming mused.

"Nothing ventured...," Angelique smiled flipping back the brim of her old sombrero, and before either Wyoming or Jack could respond she nudged her little mustang past them and up the steep incline, Annabelle close on her heels. Wyoming looked at Jack and gave a helpless shrug and the two spurred after them.

Clambering up the steep rocky slope they suddenly came out upon a wide level plateau sparsely timbered at the edge, but growing dense with cedar and juniper, which in turn led into the zone of tall pines. Beyond this and above rose the timbered faces of higher ridges that wound and sloped down from the opposite direction. Here the four riders reined to a halt staring in stunned silence. Cattle dotted the flat grassy table, lots of cattle, and deer and wild turkeys were seen scattering into the green. A swift amber-colored brook split one corner of the plateau. They no longer needed to thresh out the brushy thickets to flush mavericks, as had been necessary in the rough draws below. Here they could see calves, yearlings, steers and old mossy-horns.

"Build your fire, Chico, and heat up the irons," shouted Wyoming, excited at the prospect awaiting them.

Heating the irons took some skill. As soon as the iron turned the color of the ashes—not red hot, the brand would be burned on the calf or cow's hip. If the iron was too hot it would cause a sore that could become infected. If too cold, the mark would "hair-over" and leave no lasting brand.

The work began fast and furious. Chico ran from one spot to another with the hot branding iron. Soon the air grew rank with the odor of burnt hair and hide. The cattle for the most part were tame, having never been chased by a cowboy. Only the old wide-horned steers made any trouble. Wyoming's heart though was in his throat as Annabelle chased after a calf along the brushy and rock strewn slope. He had difficulty keeping his mind on his own roping as he tried to keep an anxious eye on her. As long as she stayed up on the level he wasn't as worried. She went after a yearling, tossing her lasso and missing. The animal darted into the brush opening upon a rocky incline. She spurred after him, gathering her rope for another throw.

Suddenly the mustang tripped. Annabelle jerked back on the reins, trying to bring the mustang's head up. The horse looked as though it would catch itself, but then stumbled and pitched forward throwing the girl head first down the rocky incline. Wyoming spurred toward her and leaped from his horse feeling his throat vibrate with a hoarse cry.

Annabelle lay still where she had fallen. Wyoming knelt beside her, searching for injuries, running his hands over her limbs, feeling her skull. She was wheezing, trying to catch breath that had been knocked out of her. She blinked at him in confusion.

"What happened?" she moaned.

"Horse tripped and throwed you," he managed. "Tell me your name."

"My name? Why are you asking me that?"

"Just tell me your name," he insisted.

"Annabelle Beatriz Dixon," she answered staring at him with round jade-green eyes. "Now that we know who I am…who are you?"

At Wyoming's expression Annabelle giggled and wrinkled her nose impishly. "I'm teasing. Really. I know who you are. I'm perfectly all right. I told you I was tougher than I look."

Wyoming glared at her; opened his mouth as though to speak, and closed it again. He held her across his lap one arm around her shoulders and her head resting in the crook of his arm. He stared down at her pale face against his arm, aware of its loveliness. He suddenly bent his face over her, eyes upon the sweet ruby lips so close.

"What are you doing?"

"I reckon I'm going to kiss you."

"You are not."

"Yep, I am. I reckon I deserve it for you scaring the daylights out of me like you did."

And he pressed his lips to hers in a kiss that started in defiance, but lingered in ecstasy. Slowly he redrew his lips from hers, stared down into her up-turned face. She laid still, eyes tightly closed for several heartbeats, and then slowly her eyes flickered opened. She stared up at him, her pupils like liquid jade.

"Anna!" Angelique cried skidding to a halt and leaping from her horse. Jack reined up close beside her where he sat peering with concerned eyes down at Annabelle. Wyoming straightened his face taking on a ruddy hue.

"I'm fine," Annabelle whispered huskily as Angelique dropped to her knees beside her. Couldn't her sister have waited a while longer before barging up? She'd been waiting for what seemed weeks for Wyoming to again kiss her.

Angelique stepped back as Wyoming helped Annabelle slowly to her feet. Then she reached and took hold of her sister's arm as if she thought she might fall.

Wyoming watched Annabelle closely and noticed that she was favoring one leg.

"You hurt yourself," he said.

"It's nothing," Annabelle replied limping to where her horse stood bridle down.

"Nothing my foot! Where are you hurt? Let me see."

She glanced back over her shoulder, hand tenderly massaging her left hip. "Not on your life, cowboy," she said cheeks taking on a crimson tint.

"We'll take the day off tomorrow and rest up," Wyoming said.

"Not on my account," she retorted, "I told you I'm fine."

"I reckon the horses need a break," he drawled, eyeing her.

She nodded. "All right."

Wyoming took hold of her little mustang's bridle and bent a keen eye examining him. Both of the horse's knees were skinned and bleeding but otherwise it appeared to suffer no other injuries. He got out the medicine jar and doctored the wounds then unsaddled the mustang. All the while Wyoming kept an eye on Annabelle observing her slow cautious movements.

When they arrived at the ranch Annabelle swung her leg gingerly over the cantle as she dismounted. Reaching the ground she caught herself and leaned for a moment against her horse's shoulder. When she walked purposefully toward the porch she was limping noticeably. Mrs. Dixon hurried out the door wiping her hands on her apron.

"Daughter, what's wrong?" she demanded. "You've hurt yourself!"

"Her horse tripped and pitched her," Wyoming spoke up swinging easily to the ground.

"Oh dear, oh dear. I told your father we should not have consented to this wild idea!" her mother cried. "Girls of your upbringing riding all over the country dressed like boys. Why, I've never heard of such a thing. Is it bad?"

"No, momma. Just a few bruises," she rejoined glaring at Wyoming.

"Angie, are you hurt too?" Mrs. Dixon demanded staring at her younger daughter.

"No, mama," Angelique assured her.

"Come inside Anna, and let me have a look," her mother ordered.

When Annabelle limped to the supper table that evening she was wearing a plain woolen dress buttoned tight at the throat, her golden curls looking freshly washed. Wyoming waited, saying nothing during the meal, but as soon as they left the kitchen he stopped peered intently at her. Though she tried to down play it Wyoming could see she was in pain.

"You took a bad spill so I reckon you ought to stay here and rest—"

"Like hob I will," drawled Annabelle, imitating his cowboy's laconic expression.

"Are you sure, Anna?" Angelique asked worriedly laying a hand over her sister's.

"Yes, I told you I was fine."

"Dog-gone! You girls are shore gonna give me gray hair before my time," Wyoming said impatiently. "I wish I could make you mind."

"Ha! You're asking for the impossible," Annabelle smirked.

"Yeah, I'm shore coming to realize that."

Annabelle slept fitfully. She ached all over, but each time she made to turn a sharp pain radiated down her left side centering upon her hip, and it brought tears to her eyes. She watched the sky lighten. She had been awake most of the night in constant pain. Over and over she cursed her stupid horse for falling, though she knew it really wasn't the poor mustang's fault, but it brought some meager comfort to blame something and her clumsy horse was the obvious recipient. The only bright spot in the whole incident, she sighed remembering, was Wyoming's kiss. It had been wondrously lovely—and had completely blocked out all thought of her throbbing aching hip…while it lasted.

Unable to spend another pain-filled moment in bed she slowly slid one leg over the side of the bed gasping as the sharp jolt of pain shot up her side.

"Oh God!" she cried helplessly.

Never had she experienced such agony. She couldn't even get to her feet let alone ride a horse. Tears spilled down her cheeks. The door swung open and Allison burst into the room still in her nightgown. She halted just inside the door eyes wide in concern.

"What's wrong?" she cried seeing her sister's tear-streaked cheeks.

"Oh, Allie, help me up," Annabelle moaned reaching out her hand.

Allison took her hand and started to pull, but Annabelle let out a jerky scream and Allison froze.

"Ohhh!" Annabelle whimpered. "On second thought, I better try on my own."

"I'm calling mama—"

"No—I can get up. Just give me a moment." With panting, pain-filled breaths she slowly got to her feet one hand heavily on her sister's shoulder.

"Allie, w-w-would you bring me a pan of warm water so I c-c-can wash?" she said through clinched teeth as she stood keeping her weight on her uninjured leg.

"Anna, you're not going to go with Wyoming—"

"Oh, no," she sighed. "I know my limits." A tear slowly trickled down her cheek.

Annabelle gingerly set about washing and found the more she moved about the throbbing in her hip seemed to ease. Shortly Angelique hurried into the room. She was still in her nightgown, golden hair disheveled by sleep having been summoned by Allison.

"Well, this settles it, Anna," she said in a firm no nonsense voice, "You're not going back out to the canyon."

"I'll not argue with you at the moment," Annabelle said with a helpless shrug. "I'm not giving up though I just need to rest a day or two—"

"Then I think I better stay here with you," Angelique said. "Now that *he* has decided to lend a hand I don't feel so compelled to."

"*He*? You mean Jack Ward?"

"Of course," Angelique growled. "Who else?"

"You don't fool me one minute, Angelique Dixon. I know you like him—"

"Ump-umm, my loco sister. Jack Ward may have dada and Wyoming fooled, but for me he's just a beastly jealous bully."

"Why, because he scolded you for riding off alone to meet that Jimmy Anderson—"

"That traitor! He squealed on me didn't he?"

"Who?"

"Don't play dumb you know who—Wyoming!"

Annabelle shook her head. "Don't blame him. He never said a word—and don't be angry with Allie. She just happened to let it slip."

"Ah," Angelique sighed bitterly as she sat down heavily on the bed. "You can be assured your little sister has learned her lesson. Jimmy Anderson turned out to be just what Wyoming said he was…a rustler."

Now, if she could just figure out what was happening to her heart where Jack Ward was concerned, she'd be right as rain! But she wasn't about to share that little detail with her sister.

CHAPTER TWENTY

August's glory of gold and green and purple began to fade. It rained off and on the next week enough to soak the frost-bitten leaves, and then the mountain winds sent them flying and fluttering and scurrying to carpet the dells and spot the pools in the brooks and color the trails. When the weather cleared and the sun rose bright again many of the aspen thickets were leafless and bare, and the willows and pines showed stark against the gray sage rises. Hills and valleys had sobered with subtle change that left them nonetheless beautiful.

Annabelle had recovered completely and was again riding. She seemed to have gotten past any trepidation related to her earlier hard spill and it didn't appear that any task frightened her. But for Wyoming he knew he could never rest with her out of his sight. Those few days before her accident had been a time of differing emotions for him. Her smile, her whimsical laugh, her quaint gestures, her voice, her words, the feel of her nearness, hands touching inadvertently as they worked, her excited laugh whenever her lasso settled surprisingly over a calf's head, the fetching way her nose wrinkled in disgust at the smell of burnt hide—had been well, wonderful. No, he couldn't deny that when he was near her, he felt happier, younger, more content and yet more excited, too, more at peace with himself and the world. It would be a pity, and he hoped it never happened that she would ever lose the innocent audacity that made her so beguiling. Yet the constant fear of her being injured again…or worse haunted him.

Mid-afternoon of the fourth day a great red-and-white-spotted herd of over five hundred yearlings was milling about in the makeshift enclosure ready to be driven into Santa Fe for shipment.

"I don't reckon we ought to leave this bunch unattended," Wyoming said as he and the others lounged on a soft cushion of needles in the shade of tall pines taking a rest from the hot dusty work. "They'd be easy pickings for Ackers and his gang."

He glanced at Annabelle. She sat with her arms wrapped about her drawn up knees, a dreamy gaze upon the distant ranges, and he wondered if she was already calculating the profit from the cattle sale.

"I reckon we set up camp," Jack grunted. "An' I shore could go fer some tasty trout fer supper. An' I know just the place; Cow Creek, no more than a half mile yonder," he said pointing with his chin. "Plenty of riffles, an' bend pools, an' shore undercut banks, and it just so happens I got fishin' gear in my bag."

"Anna, let's go," Angelique exclaimed excitedly rolling over on her knees and leaning back on her heels.

"I'm too tired,' her sister sighed. She was stretched out on the pine needles staring dreamily at the blue sky above. "You go ahead without me. You were the one who always liked to fish anyhow."

Angelique shot Annabelle a resentful glance.

"Wal, we'd have te dig up some nightcrawlers, maybe even catch some grasshoppers," Jack drawled seemingly interested in inspecting his lariat rope. "Nothing a greenhorn girl would be up to I reckon."

"Who are you calling a greenhorn?" Angelique demanded quite piercingly.

"Course minnows would be preferable to grasshoppers, but we'd need a net to catch 'em," he continued as though he hadn't heard her.

"Hah!" Angelique cried. "I've been fishing since I was a little girl I'll have you know, and I bet I can out fish you any day, you long-legged cowboy you!"

"Yur on," Jack declared tossing his rope aside. "It'll be like taking candy from a baby."

"Hah! That's what you think," she retorted leaping to her feet and sticking out her hand. "Bet!"

"You think it's safe to have them go off alone together; they just might drown one another," Wyoming mused.

Annabelle closed her eyes, making no reply as Wyoming stared after the two antagonists. After a moment he shifted gaze to the milling herd. Tomorrow they would drive the cattle into Santa Fe and make arrangements to ship the cattle. It wouldn't be hard to find a buyer. There was a demand for beef in the east, and it seemed to be growing. Maybe the price on the hoof had even gone up. If not, at twelve dollars a head they still had over six thousand dollars mewling lazily about in that corral. He seemed for a while lost in his thoughts.

"Hey, Chico, you lazy greaser, round up some firewood. If our fishing pards have had any luck we ought to have a fire blazing when they get back," Wyoming called.

The Mexican got slowly to his feet shoving his sombrero up on his head. "*Si, Señor* Wyoming," he grinned, "But maybe we open a can of *frijoles* make ready, what say?"

Wyoming laughed. "Let's hope their luck's good. I got a taste for some fresh rainbow trout."

A little more than an hour later Wyoming heard the sound of horses and presently Angelique and Jack came into view. They were still some distance away when Angelique's voice rang out clear and excited.

"Hello, we're back!"

"Did you catch any?" Wyoming shouted.

"You bet! I got five!" she said proudly.

"Chico, heat up yu're fryin' pan!" Wyoming ordered.

"*Si, Señor*, Wyoming," Chico grinned.

Angelique swung down from her little mustang and hurriedly untied a string of fish from the saddle. She handed them to Chico.

"Gee! That was sure fun," she said giving Wyoming a cool speculative gaze.

"Say, little lady, them fish shore ain't gonna clean themselves," Jack admonished.

"Ump-umm," she said shaking her head. "Not on your life. You lost the bet; you'll have to do the cleaning."

"Some fisherman yu air," Jack snorted. He handed Chico three more fish.

Wyoming pulled his saddle up under a tall pine and pushing his sombrero back off his forehead with his thumb leaned back using the saddle as a backrest as he watched Annabelle and Angelique tending the frying pans where the afternoon's catch sizzled.

The sun was setting in a cloudless sky when Annabelle yelled, "Come and get it!"

There was sudden silence wherein only the subdued clink of metal spoons against tin plates was heard.

Finished eating Wyoming glanced from Annabelle to Angelique.

"I reckon we ought to head back to the ranch. I'll come on back after I see you two home," he said.

"We brought our bed rolls," Annabelle said frankly, not meeting his eye. "You're going to want us when you drive the cattle in to Santa Fe, and we'll need an early start. So, we're staying here tonight."

"I reckon we'll shore be safe with three *hombres* to protect us," Angelique remarked.

This she said as she peered at Jack with a humdrum look in her eyes, though there was a hint of mischief in her voice.

Annabelle pushed her floppy-brimmed hat back off her forehead and the setting sun shown full on her suntanned face revealing a sprinkling of tawny freckles across her straight slender nose that he had not noticed before.

Once the sun dropped below the mountain rim twilight's shadows settled quickly. Stars blinked in the darkening sky, a night breeze rustled the pine branches, the sough of wind strange and mournful. Angelique sat quietly, knees drawn up to her chest, staring into the fire seemingly oblivious to Jack Ward seated across from her. He, on the other hand, seemed a weary, melancholy rider pondering to himself. Her aloofness worked upon him and her indifference, Wyoming decided, piqued Jack. Wyoming took pains unrolling his bed as he studied Annabelle out of the corner of his eye. She came up where he had laid out his bed and sat cross-legged on the pine needles across from him. He looked at her but said nothing.

"You're awful quiet tonight," she remarked.

"I reckon I was just thinking about tomorrow."

"Gee, me too. I'm excited," she sighed.

"Well, I reckon you ought to get some sleep. It'll be a long day."

"I know. I hope I can sleep. I've never spent a night like this, out in the open with no roof overhead." She leaned back on her hands. "The stars are so bright," she said, staring up at the black sky. "Can I ask you a question? Is that your real name, Wyoming?"

He didn't answer. A moment passed.

"Did you hear me? I asked—"

"Yeah, I heard you," he drawled. "It's been so long since I've been called by that name I had to think about it."

"You didn't! Really?"

"Randolph Lee McCord. That's my full handle. But I'd shore appreciate it if you didn't let that leak out."

"Hmm, Randolph huh," she mused. "I bet when you were a boy your folks called you Randy."

"Yeah, but its shore, Wyoming now."

"Why, don't you like the name Randy? I do," she said and there was a teasing note in her voice

"Girl, if you spill what I told you, I swear I'll—"

"What's wrong with people knowing your name?"

"It's Wyoming."

Before she could make a retort her head jerked upward.

"That sound. What was that?"

He hadn't been paying attention; his concentration instead had been on her.

"It wasn't a coyote," she affirmed. "I've heard them almost every night. I kind of like them. This was different, didn't you hear it; like the baying of a hound in the dead of night when death has come to some one—there!" she cried shivering.

There came a clear, cold, long withdrawing mournful wail.

He lifted his head into the wind. "Wolf," he said quietly.

"Oh. It sounds far away," she whispered. "I'm glad, but oh, it's strange and wonderful." She was silent for a moment. "May I roll out my bedroll here next to you?"

He made no reply as she stretched out on her bed and lay staring up through the trees, starlight glinting on the dark pupils of her eyes. The night felt warm, with a hint of summer in its balmy sweetness, the stars shown white through the pine branches.

"Good night…Wyoming."

Many minutes later he heard her sigh and turn on her side. After some time there came the sound of her soft even breathing, and he closed his eyes.

CHAPTER TWENTY-ONE

S unup found the cattle strung out in a long line stepping along at perhaps two miles an hour over grassy knolls tipped by cedar and grassy ridges, sloping down from walls of gray and green. For Annabelle, Angelique and Chico riding drag keeping the herd moving at a slow steady pace was a hot and dusty job. Wyoming and Jack became point, swing and flank hands all at the same time. This was where their experience became clear. When the drive started the yearlings broke out in a run and both riders kept to the front of the herd holding them up keeping them from stampeding. It became then a matter of keeping the herd strung out in a long narrow column with the leader pointed. This meant moving back and forth along the flanks and sometimes, one or the other of them, cutting through the herd at an angle to turn the leader when they attempted to veer from the path to which they were being driven.

It was late afternoon two days later when the last of the cattle was driven into the holding pens at the rail yards at Santa Fe. The drive, although hot and grimy, and for the girls exhausting, it had turned out uneventful. They had not lost one head, the final count being five hundred and seven. Wyoming left Chico at the pens and rode into town with Annabelle and Angelique. The place was alive with activity and for Wyoming the traffic in the wide street, the dust, the noise, the tramp of the throng, brought back memories of other like towns. Both girls insisted on accompanying him to the office of Mr. Fay Johnson on Lincoln Street. Since he had never done business with any local buyers, Wyoming relied on Hank Ward's counsel as to a reputable cattle dealer.

"Ladies, you best let me do the talking," Wyoming said as they tromped up on the dusty boardwalk before the cattleman's office.

Mr. Johnson was a tall slender man in his early fifties. He had a quick smile and the keen gray eyes of a Texan.

"Mr. Johnson," Wyoming said after introducing himself and the Dixon girls, "Hank Ward said we'd get an honest deal from you. We just drove in over five hundred head."

"Wal now, what yu askin'?"

"Fifteen dollars." Wyoming felt Annabelle's eyes on him.

"Wal, son, they're payin' sixteen in St Louis. I got te pay fer shipin' 'em, an' I reckon yu'd agree I got te make a little profit. Best I could do is thirteen dollars."

"Fourteen dollars, Mr. Johnson, they're fine stock and fairly fat," Annabelle broke in taking off her sombrero, letting her golden curls fall about her slim shoulders.

The old Texan gave her an appraising look, smiled genially. "Wal, Miss Dixon, yu got yur fourteen dollars. Thet's the best I can do."

"We'll take it," Angelique said. "And we'd like a certified check."

Johnson glanced at Wyoming. "The little Misses know their business," he grinned. "I'll have yur check ready first thing tomorrow morning, ladies, and I'll send my cowhands down to the pens to take charge."

"Thanks, Mr. Johnson," Annabelle replied smiling triumphantly up at Wyoming.

"I thought you were going to let me do the talking," Wyoming glowered when they reached the sidewalk.

"Sorry. I just couldn't help myself," Annabelle said.

"Right, we worked damn hard for those cows," Angelique added.

He stared in amaze from one to the other.

Angelique looked at him sheepishly. "Well, we did," she rejoined.

"Yep, we shore did," he grinned. "Say, since we can't pick up that check until morning we might as well stay the night in town and ride back in the morning."

"Fine," Annabelle agreed, flashing him a grateful smile.

"So how about dinner, ladies?"

"I don't know about you, Anna, but I'm ready for a nice bath," Angelique said.

"Oh, me too," Annabelle declared. "We'll meet you in the hotel dining room at six."

"It's a date," he drawled sweeping off his sombrero and bowing.

"I suppose you'll have to invite that lanky puncher who thinks he's God's gift to the female species," Angelique said.

"Are you referring to Jack Ward?" Wyoming grinned.

"Who else?" she retorted peevishly, but there was no genuine ring of sincerity in her voice.

"I reckon I could send him back tonight—"

"Oh, pumpkin-seed sunfish! The poor creature has to eat, I presume," she answered back, a little too quickly. "So, he might as well come to dinner with us."

Wyoming rode back to the holding pens to let Jack and Chico know that they had closed a deal and that the girls wanted to stay the night in town.

Reaching the hotel, Wyoming and Jack each checked in into rooms and ordered up baths. He forgot to ask the clerk what room the girls were in, and for a moment wondered if they were close by. Chico went to spend the night at his cousin's.

Wyoming and Jack entered the hotel dining room shortly before six and took a table near the wall. They ordered coffee and sat nursing the hot drink waiting for Annabelle and Angelique. It was nearly quarter past six when they caught sight of the two sisters. Annabelle stood poised in the doorway, Angelique at her side, their eyes searching the crowded room. They were still attired in their faded overalls and colorful shirts. In that brief interval before they spotting them Wyoming let his eager gaze devour Annabelle. She didn't appear in the least embarrassed by her masculine garb, and her loose-fitting shirt, open at her throat, did more than hint at her rounded breasts. She was bareheaded and her soft golden curls were swept up on her head and tied with some sort of cloth. Her eyes suddenly encountered his and she smiled and started his way dragging Angelique with her. Both he and Jack scrambled to their feet before they reached the table.

"Sorry we're late. We were trying to beat the dust out of our clothes so they would look halfway presentable," Annabelle whispered with a conspiratorial glance at her sister. "I bet you two are hungry. Have you been waiting long?"

Jack was quick to pull a chair out for Angelique and she sat looking everywhere but at him.

"Miss Anna would you mind sitting on my left?" Wyoming said positioning her chair. "I might have to, you know..."

Although her eyes bore a cynical expression, Annabelle wordlessly complied taking the chair on his left. Her face had a fresh-scrubbed look, and he noticed she had used a rolled up bandana to tie up her hair. Despite the old floppy-brimmed hat she normally wore her face had turned golden from days in the sun heightening the spray of auburn freckles across her nose. He suddenly recalled the first day he had seen her. She had been clad in a soft lace-trimmed blue gown, her skin white and as smooth as porcelain. She had been so dainty, so delicately lovely that day, a major factor that had inspired him to steal that kiss, but as he gazed at her now wearing a faded man's shirt, her throat bare, her cheeks richly tanned and showered with tiny russet freckles, he thought her never so beautiful.

"Why are you looking at me like that?" she asked her jade-green eyes narrowing with mock- suspicion.

He was caught off guard by her question, not realizing he had been staring, and he replied automatically before he could catch himself.

"You're shore pretty."

"Me?" she scoffed looking down at her faded shirt, but the color in her cheeks deepened and she picked up the menu card from the table and began to scan it absorbedly. "What are you having?" she asked trying to sound casual.

"My usual...steak and eggs."

"Hmm, I think I'll have something lighter. Their soup and sandwich looks good," she said laying the card aside as the waiter approached their table.

"Gee, do you believe it—seven-thousand dollars!" Annabelle exclaimed wonderingly after the waiter had left with their orders.

"Yeah, not bad for a month's work, and there's more to be had. But we got to be selective so as to build up a good-sized herd."

The talk continued, Annabelle obviously in high spirits delighted, he realized, at the thought of the money to be made. Before long their food arrived and conversation was abandoned as they all four ate with keen appetite. With supper concluded it was mutually agreed that it had been a long day. They exited the dining room into the crowded lobby. Among the rough-garbed and bearded individuals gathered there, freighters, teamsters, cowboys a young man, conspicuous because of the difference in his attire, at once caught Annabelle's eye. She recognized him immediately. Embarrassment and something of anger, accompanied her recognition. The man's sharp, cold, handsome features pronounced him about thirty years old. His black flock-coat and gaudy, flower-adorned waist-coat and long slicked-back black hair characterized him as a gambler, and none other than M'sieur Henri de Rousseau whom she had met by accident three years ago in New Orleans when she was sixteen.

At the time she had been lonely, longing for freedom and adventure, for love, and she had been foolish as to steal out to meet him on several occasions. Oh, she had never been bold enough to allow him anymore liberties than to hold her hand, and an occasional embrace. And once she found out he was a gambler and a rogue, she regretted her folly and ended the acquaintance. Or attempted to, but Rousseau had persisted, frightening her with his pushiness. Fortunately her father's health issues; having to sell the plantation and relocate west, had saved her further embarrassment and discomfiture, if not outright ruin. Annabelle had never heard from Rousseau after they left Louisiana and had, until now, forgotten the man. So it was a shock to see him here in this place. Suddenly recalling her past girlish indiscretion, her step faltered inauspiciously attracting the man's attention.

Rousseau's sloe-black eyes shifted to her. Initially he showed only careless interest, but then his eyes widened as he realized what he had first mistaken as a slim, lithe cowboy was actually a female.

And to his amaze and gratification a female he was well and avidly acquainted with.

"Well, well, and who can this be lovely creature be?" he espoused looking her up and down.

Annabelle suffered a moment of dismay. A quick assessment of this older man revealed that time had played havoc with him. Yet his hungry eyes betrayed that he had been hunting for her, and intended to make her remember. She was to blame for this. Whatever had been in her mind—to imagine she had been in love with this man?

"Annabelle Dixon, we meet again," Rousseau said with a gallant bow. "I have long dreamed of this moment." He stepped close and for an instant she thought he would attempt to embrace her. "You have changed," he breathed eyes boldly taking in her freshly brushed golden curls and snug pants and high top boots and shirt opened at the throat, garments which had, until this moment, become natural to her mind, but now made her feel like slinking off somewhere and hiding.

"M'sieur Rousseau," Annabelle said with more bravo than she felt as she attempted to make her interest sound casual, "Are you not lost, away from the gaiety of the French Quarter? What are you doing here in New Mexico?"

"Annabelle, you must know I have never ceased to search for you," he returned earnestly, and he did reach for her this time and caught hold of her hand before she could step away. "You alone have brought me to this wild west."

"Indeed," she retorted cheeks burning as she felt the heat of Wyoming's gaze while she struggled to pull her hand free. "I'm sorry if—if you overestimated my silly girlish flirtation as more than—what they were. But I have no wish to renew the acquaintance."

"Annabelle, I'd shore like to meet this feller,' Wyoming interposed in his cool drawl before Rousseau could respond.

"M'sieur Rousseau, this is my father's range rider foreman, Wyoming McCord," she introduced with relief as she managed to retrieve her hand. She immediately wrapped both arms about Angelique's arm and tugged her sister down the hall not slowing until they reached their room. Once inside both girls flopped on the bed arms still entwined.

"Anna, I can't believe he followed you out here," Angelique whispered worriedly. "What are you going to do?"

"I don't plan to do anything. I want nothing to do with him— nothing at all," Annabelle insisted standing and walking to stare out the open window. Stars were shining in a cloudless sky and a cold tang of mountain air caused her to shiver. A long moment passed with neither girl speaking. Annabelle jumped as a knock on the door interrupted the quiet.

Angelique leaped to her feet and hurried to the door. "Who is it?" she called.

"It's me, Wyoming."

Angelique opened the door and stepped back to allow the cowboy to enter, and then quickly shut it. Wyoming leaned a shoulder against the jamb keen eyes gleaming unwontedly.

"Say, Annabelle Dixon, it shore looks like you're responsible for that flashy gambler showing up here."

"I'm sure that's what he says,' she scoffed.

"Has he any hold on you?"

"None whatsoever, Wyoming McCord," she denied vehemently.

"I reckon I heard you tell him, but he shore was brazen, or thickheaded, 'cause he shore wanted me to know there was something between you."

"But there isn't! I—I admit that I flirted with him, but it was just silly—Oh, call it foolish girlish flirtation—and I had nothing more to do with him, and told him so, when I found out what kind of person he was."

"Well, all the same, the man's a fortune-hunter and way down on his luck. If I don't mistake my hunch, you're gonna hear more about this here girlish flirtation."

"Oh, Wyoming, you don't mean he will take advantage of that—that indiscretion to—to—"

"I reckon I do," Wyoming returned when Annabelle hesitated. "Cause the damn fool shore thinks you are—or was—sweet on him." He straightened, his keen gaze searching hers and she felt her cheeks warm in a heated blushed convinced that he didn't believe her.

Wyoming walked to the room next to his and knocked. An instant later the door was opened a crack. Seeing Wyoming Jack Ward stepped back and motioned him to enter. He was still fully dressed.

"Who's the flowery-vested card-sharp anyhow?" asked Jack.

"You heard as much as I did, Jack. I reckon he used to know Annabelle back in Louisiana. I reckon she flirted with him some, until she found out he was a gambler. And he's pestered her after that. It was plain that he means to take advantage of the early acquaintance. I reckon he'll shore make things unpleasant for her.

"How you figure thet? She told him plumb out she had no wish to renew the acquaintance."

"Yeah, I heard. It's a hunch, and I reckon I've not been in the wrong very many times.

"Speakin' of hunches; you figure on doin' somethin' about it?"

"*Quién sabe?* I might just have to set in on a game of cards with him."

Jack shot Wyoming a look. "Ah-huh, I reckon I savvy," he drawled after a moment.

"Say, Angelique wants to ride back to the ranch early in the morning before the bank opens."

"Yeah, I reckon we'll be leavin' right after breakfast."

"How are you and Angie fairing by the way?"

"I wish the heck I knew," Ward retorted giving Wyoming a keen look. "I confess, I reckon I'm done fer, Wyoming, pard. I'm shore loco about her, but she's shore got me stumped. One minute she sides up to me and next she won't even look at me."

"Ah, shore its hell," Wyoming swore.

He let himself out and sought his own room at the end of the hall. Once inside he took off his gun belt and stretched out on his bed. He supposed he couldn't outright shoot Rousseau, though it was tempting; Annabelle Dixon loathed violence no matter the justification. Hell, she didn't even want to touch his Colt let alone shoot it. Rousseau had pursued Annabelle all the way from Louisiana here to New Mexico. A man that determined wouldn't easily be turned away.

Wyoming and Annabelle drew rein before the small office of Mr. Fay Johnson the Texas cattle buyer the next morning. The tall slender Texan was waiting for them when they entered the door. Wide-shouldered, small-hipped, lithe, and erect, at fifty years of age he was yet an imposing figure. Hank Ward had told Jack that at one time Johnson had been a Texas Ranger. After shaking Wyoming's hand, his bold, honest gaze shifted to Annabelle and he smiled his gray eyes piercing and warm upon her.

"Good mornin', Miss Dixon," he greeted. "I have yur certified check just as yu asked."

"Hello, Mr. Johnson," she replied softly flushing like a chastened schoolgirl. "I'm sorry. I must have sounded overbearing yesterday."

"No, indeed. I reckon thet was good business sense," Johnson grinned amicably.

Wyoming glanced at Annabelle. Her gaze was fixed on the rough boards of the floor. Every since the encounter with Rousseau, she had been rather subdued, he realized, her green eyes wane and unfathomable. He wasn't certain he liked her this way. Not after the spirited and seemingly fearless girl he had come to know the last few months; sometimes headstrong and opinionated, other times mischievous and fun-loving, but always endearing in his eyes.

Mr. Johnson picked up the check from on top of his desk, eyes upon her. "Here yu are, young lady." He held out the check.

She took the draft, giving Wyoming a quick glance before looking away.

"Wal, thet's shore a find looking bunch yu drove in. I reckon if yu're looking to sell more, I'm always looking te buy," he remarked easily.

"Shore thing, Mr. Johnson, but I don't reckon we'll be up to selling anymore cows this fall. We still have a lot of branding to do," Wyoming replied, moving toward the door. "Well, we'll be moseying along. Thanks again, Mr. Johnson."

"Wyoming, let's stop by the bank I'd like to cash this check," Annabelle said once they were outside Mr. Johnson's office.

"Shore thing," he drawled and swung into the saddle. At the bank he followed her inside. He remained beside her as she stepped up to the teller and collected the cash.

On the ride back to the ranch Wyoming, a faint scowl on his face, remained quiet. Several times he was aware of Annabelle peering at him but made no effort to start a conversation. The gray, rolling foothills, so exquisitely colored at that hour, and the black-fringed ranges, one above the other, and the distant peaks, sun-flushed across the purple, all rose open and clear to Wyoming's sight, so wild and splendid. Tall pines on a small elevation, near the swift brook, and overlooking the ranch house perhaps a quarter of a mile below had come in sight when Annabelle riding along at his side finally broke the silence.

"Wyoming McCord, you're a—a bigheaded...jackass!" she suddenly cried.

"I am?" he exclaimed, piercing her with his sharp gaze.

"It was just a girlish flirtation."

"You never were in love with him?"

"Never!"

"Did you ever let him kiss you?"

"Gracious no! I flirted with him—a little."

"Ah-huh."

Wyoming's imperturbability lay only on the surface. Annabelle saw it in the blue flame of his eyes when he looked at her.

"Jack said you—oh, Wyoming, promise me you won't pick a fight with Rousseau. Promise me," she repeated, imperiously.

"Why should I, Lady?"

"Because—you—I just don't want anything to happen to you," she replied softly and setting spurs to her mustang broke into a lope leaving Wyoming behind.

A tremor ran through Wyoming's body. Thoughtfully he rode on. When he reached the ranch he saw that Annabelle had already given her mustang to Chico and had gone into the house. He took his time unsaddling Sparky and turning him into his stall. He poured a bucket of grain in the trough and tossed in a forkful of hay. He walked over to his cabin and dumping water in the pail washed his face and hands. He wasn't sure what to expect when he went up to the house.

CHAPTER TWENTY-TWO

A man, tall and lithe in the saddle, rode along the slope, with gaze on the sweep and range and color of the mountain fastness that spread out before him. He followed an old trail, which led to a bluff overlooking an arm of the valley. The trail came up back of the bluff, through a clump of aspens with white trunks and yellow fluttering leaves, and led across a level bench of luxuriant grass and wild flowers to the rocky edge. From this vantage point the rider could see below a wide swath of cattle tracks running east and west. The most recent tracks pointed west, proving that the last herd had been driven toward the uplands and into Arizona. Wyoming leaned his forearm on his saddle horn as he pushed his sombrero back off his forehead with a gloved thumb. He wagered that Dixon's rustled cattle left those tracks below.

In the months since they had sold that first bunch of cattle, straggling bands of fifty or so had disappeared. The activity of the rustlers had been difficult to uncover and hard to trace, and Wyoming suspected they had a spy watching them as to when and where they would be working so the thieves could work a different part of the range.

But then two days ago the rustlers had made their boldest move yet, driving off over one thousand head of stock that they had spent weeks chasing out of the brush. The rustlers would have no trouble selling the cattle, branded or not. Coming up with a fake bill of sale was of little concern, and in Arizona few questions would be asked. Something had to be done to combat the rustlers. He couldn't do it alone. And he was certain other ranchers were losing stock as well, perhaps on a larger scale than the Triangle "A". What was needed was a cattlemen's protective association. A group of honest cattlemen banded together for protection against rustlers. He vowed to talk to Hank Ward about just such an association.

Wyoming drew rein at the top of the ridge overlooking Hank Ward's ranch house. He sat there a moment enjoying the view. East rose the low foothills, which in turn mounted, step by step to the purple-sloped *Sangre de Cristo* Mountains. Wyoming started down the slope toward the ranch house having spied activity at the large corral west of the barn. As he grew closer he recognized Hank Ward, tall and thick-shouldered among a group of five or six others leaning or setting on the corral rails. Coming within earshot he heard shouts and catcalls and realized that a green bronc was being broken. And by the time he was within a few yards of the corral he could see through the swirl of dust a rider astride a pitching and bucking horse. Wyoming pulled up beside the fence and watched the flurry of movement as the bucking horse bound about the corral amid the gleeful shouts of the watching cowboys. The slim young rider was good, Wyoming mused as the horse's stiff-legged bucking soon slowed to a halt and it finally stood unmoving, legs spread, sides heaving.

Wyoming's easy gaze surveyed the watching group and happened upon a slender graceful figure sitting on the top rail of the corral. Alice Ward. She was dressed in a pale yellow shirt, overalls and boots, but no hat and her fair hair waved gently in the soft breeze. She didn't look his way, her gray eyes upon the rider who sawed the reins plow-horse fashion guiding the raw bronc next to the rail where she sat. With the lazy grace of his kind he slipped out of the saddle. He was tall, slim, round-limbed, with the small hips of a rider, and square, though not broad shoulders. His eyes appeared hazel, his features regular, his face bronzed. All men of the open had still; lean, strong faces, but added to this in him was a steadiness of expression.

"Wal, how'd yu like thet ride, Miss Alice," he drawled tipping his sombrero with forefinger and thumb in a cocky salute.

"Danny Roberts, just you wait!" Alice chided though her eyes sparkled merrily. "Some day there'll come a horse you can't ride."

"Ain't been born," the cowboy grinned.

"Ha," she mocked tossing her head back. She apparently caught a glimpse of Wyoming out of the corner of her eye and turned on the rail to peer at him. She had a pretty face, rather than beautiful, but strong and sweet—its striking qualities being a colorless fairness of skin that yet held a rose and golden tint, and the eyes of a rare and exquisite gray.

"Hi, Wyoming," she smiled brightly.

"Howdy, Alice," he drawled warmly.

"When did you get here?" she asked.

"Just rode up." He nodded to the young rider, who responded with a keen assessing look of unmistakable jealousy.

"Wyoming, this here is Danny Roberts," she said giving the young cowboy a rueful look. "He thinks he can never be throwed.

"There never was a bronc that couldn't be rode; and there never was a cowboy who couldn't be throwed," Wyoming grinned quoting an old cowboy saying.

"Ha, ha, that's what I told him." she laughed, wrinkling her nose teasingly at him. "Danny, this is paw's good friend, Wyoming McCord."

"Howdy," Roberts acknowledged.

"Howdy yourself," Wyoming replied, glancing at the lathered and trembling bronc. "Say, Danny, you any relations to Sid?"

"That's my paw," Danny said. "How come yu know him?"

"I stopped by your ranch a few weeks back. I reckon you were out."

"Wyoming," came a loud shout and he turned to see Hank Ward striding toward him.

"Mr. Ward," Wyoming said stepping from his horse to take his friend's hand.

"What brings yu?" Ward queried giving Wyoming's hand a vigorous shake.

"Something important," Wyoming replied.

"Wal, let's go on up te the house."

Taking a seat in one of the chairs on the porch, Ward motioned to Wyoming to be seated in one of the others.

"Alice, gurl bring some of thet cold lemonade fer Wyoming an' me," Ward called to the girl who had followed the two.

"Yes, paw," she replied and slipped fluidly into the house letting the screen door close quietly behind her.

"Now, what's the trouble?" Ward questioned.

"The bane of the cattlemen," was Wyoming's soft reply.

"Rustlers! Be damn!" Ward snorted.

"Yep, drove off more'n a thousand head of Triangle A stock two days ago."

Ward nodded solemnly. "Damn it, son. This business has gone on too damn long."

"That's what I wanted to talk to you about. Unless we band together, we'll never be able to stop these thieves."

"I shore reckon yur right, son. We've both losing stock, more an' more all the time. We've been particularly lax, mainly 'cause nobody's taken the lead. I think yu and I both know who's behind it, but we've no proof. Look, son, I know yu, an' what yu're capable of. Yu're the man te lead this enterprise and wipe out these damn thieves!"

Alice, carrying a tray containing a tall jug of lemonade and two glasses, interrupted their talk at that moment. She smiled shyly at Wyoming as she filled his glass from the frosty jug.

"Thanks, Alice," he said, and she smiled and blushed.

With one last lingering glance at Wyoming she turned and went back into the house. They talked at length, slowly nursing the cool drinks. When Wyoming bid goodbye some time later a tentative plan had emerged and another meeting was agreed upon, which would include other ranchers. Wyoming stepped off the porch just as Jack Ward rode up.

"Yu fixin' te leave?" he drawled.

"Yep."

"I'll tag along with yu," Jack said easily.

"Shore thing," Wyoming replied, swinging effortlessly into the saddle.

Toping the ridge the two riders started down the gentle slope. Cattle were bawling below them along the slope and on the grassy uplands below.

"How's things with Angelique?" Wyoming asked casually.

"Wal, I reckon I don't really know how she feels 'boot me. She flirts like crazy with all the cowboys, me included, but I don't reckon she's ever done bad with any of 'em," he said fiercely. "I know, 'cause I was jealous an' suspicious of her…An' I tried it. By Gawd did she let me have it, slapped me good. Thet queered me with her fer a long time. But lately she's been as sweet as can be. I reckon I jest can't figure her. Yu know what I mean?"

"Yea, I reckon I do," Wyoming grunted thinking of Annabelle.

They rode on in silence for a while.

"Jack, you're a good man, and Angelique shore needs a good man to settle her down," Wyoming said.

"Yu think so?" Jack grinned.

As they approached the house Wyoming saw two horses standing hipshot in front of the bunkhouse, and then he caught sight of two individuals lounging on the porch in front of the building. One sat with his back against one of the posts, the other stood shoulder leaning against the same post, one foot crossed nonchalantly at his ankles. The one standing apparently caught sight of Wyoming and Jack Ward. He stood erect squaring himself hand resting on his belt above his holstered gun. He must have said something to the one seated as he got slowly to his feet, separating himself a few feet from his taller companion. All this Wyoming saw in one quick assessing glance.

"Looks like yu got company," Jack drawled. "Recognize 'em?"

"Nope."

"Neither do I," Jack remarked.

Wyoming glanced toward the house; saw Dixon and his wife and Annabelle standing on the porch. Angelique stood next to Annabelle, one arm around her waist. Annabelle's arms were clutched tightly across her chest. He couldn't tell from this distance the expression on her face, but her stilted posture sent a tremor of apprehension inching up Wyoming's spine. Allison, who had apparently been watching for him hurried toward him from the side of the bunkhouse, the big hound trotting at her side. He drew Sparky up and Allison caught hold of his stirrup.

"Wyoming," she panted. "Those men want to arrest you; said you were a murderer. Don't go with them, they're—"

"Allie, come here," Mrs. Dixon cried hurrying to catch hold of the girl's hand.

The two men stepped off the bunkhouse porch and started walking toward them. For an instant sunlight glinted on something shinny on the taller one's vest. A badge! Wyoming gulped. Then all the iron of muscle and steel of mind gathered as if to leap.

"Wyoming, these—gentlemen," Dixon faltered peering at the slowly advancing strangers. "Damn it suh, they're here to arrest you! That shooting up in Colorado—"

Wyoming's eye went to Annabelle. She stared at him unblinking. It had finally come; he realized feeling a coldness seep over him. For over a year he had known that someday there was a chance his past would catch up with him. But for Annabelle he would have gone on drifting always aware of those footsteps trailing him but staying just far enough ahead. He had felt a wonderful gladness being here and that had allowed him to hope, to almost forget. Except that now time had finally run out.

"Which one of yu is Wyoming McCord?" the taller of the two men called his eyes upon Wyoming and it occurred to him that the man knew his identity even as he asked. A pallor showed under the man's coarse tan. He had hard, bright blue eyes and rugged features that fitted them.

"I reckon that'd be me," Wyoming replied coolly.

The shorter man had his gun drawn pointed at Wyoming. The man had a hard lean face of bluish cast under his short beard, and slits for eyes.

"Then I reckon we're hyar te arrest yu," the taller lawman said. "I advise yu te unbuckle thet gun belt and toss it over hyar." His eyes glowed with a coarse grim humor that failed to hide passion.

Wyoming slowly unbuckled the belt, but instead of pitching it where the lawman had directed, he tossed it onto the porch where it landed on the boards in front of Annabelle. She gasped and recoiled several paces.The lawman stepped forward; a pair of handcuffs dangling from one fist.

"Hyar, stick out yur hands," he ordered.

Silently Wyoming complied and the manacles were snapped tight about his wrists.

"Wal, folks, this hyar hombre shore must have fooled yu good…a murderer like him makin' out te be a pore ole range rider."

"Murderer?" came Annabelle's strangled voice.

Wyoming twisted in the saddle stricken eyes upon her. "Annabelle—" he choked, face suddenly pale. "You—believe—that?"

In answer, she whirled and with an inarticulate cry, fled into the house. Angelique turned eyes darkly dilated to Jack.

"Fetch our hawses," the tall lawman ordered catching the reins of Wyoming's horse.

"Wyoming—" Allison cried.

"Allison, hush! Go into the house," Mrs. Dixon ordered. "Angelique, take your sister inside, now!"

The girl didn't wait for her sister but whirled and raced off the porch sprinting toward the barn.

Wyoming stared straight ahead then, gaze unflinching as they started off leading his horse.

Annabelle stumbled into the house blinded by tears, so shaken and overcome by emotion that her mind seemed a whirling chaos. Wyoming was a killer, a murderer! Somehow she found her way to her room and fell upon her bed, only to struggle up, wiping at her eyes. Silly fool! That Wyoming had killed men was a well-known fact—gunslinger, Ed Hester had charged. She had known that, and though she hated it—she was astute enough to recognize that by western standards that did not make him a murderer. So why did she feel so wretched? Oh, she knew! She could not delude herself. His arrest by those deputies had put the stamp on his deception. He really was a murderer. His story about the shooting had left out a few little details, but it dove-tailed with what that one deputy had said. Once again she had a rending sickening agony in her heart. She had believed him, and he had betrayed her trust.

The heat of the day was slow in passing. Wyoming tried to keep his mind active, but he could not shake the cold feeling that settled in his bones. The look on Annabelle's face! She believed him a murderer. And the wave of sickness grew. What he had done dispatching Higgins and his ugly little henchman had to be done. He glanced at the two lawmen. His arrest by these men caused little concern. It would all come out. No judge would convict him of that shooting. Arresting him was not so terrible, no; it was the belief they had instilled in Annabelle of his guilt. That was the blow. It stung, it flayed. It was bitter. It raked over the old sore. Perhaps his reasoning was vain. Perhaps he should have left Higgins for the law to handle... but he was no murderer!

So caught up in his own thoughts he had paid little attention to where he was being led until he happened to look about. They had left the trail entering a thick grove of aspens surrounded by tall pine and spruce. Here they stopped.

The taller lawman slouched in his saddle. He peered at Wyoming, hate, motive, arrogance swept swiftly over his sharp countenance.

"Wyoming McCord, gun-slinger!" he sneered with a harsh laugh. "Burton said yu'd never throw down on a lawman, haw, haw." He pulled the badge from his vest and stuffed it in his shirt pocket. He gave Wyoming a long speculative look. "I still say I can take him, Clay—"

"No dice, Willy. Let's get it over with, like Burton ordered."

"You're no lawmen," Wyoming spat, color fading from his face. "You're on Bull Burton's payroll—"

"Haw, haw," Willy chortled, and his gun rose, leveled.

Wyoming dug his spur into Sparky's flank and as the horse leaped to the side Wyoming flung himself to the ground a split second before flame belched from the gun's muzzle. A sharp impact as from a violent gush of wind struck him and almost at the same instant he heard the distinct bang. Wyoming hit the ground hard. At the same instant the crack of a rifle sounded, once twice.

CHAPTER TWENTY-THREE

Wyoming's shoulder burned. He rolled to his hands and knees. Two bodies lay unmoving a few paces distant. Not far away two horses shifted nervously about reins dragging. He became aware of hot blood running down his left arm pooling on his handcuffed wrists. Tensing, he glanced up at the sound of horse's hoofs and saw Jack Ward. A moment later Allison's big gray hound trotted up to sniff at his bloody hand.

"Yu all right?" Jack called swinging easily to the ground. He held a Winchester in one hand.

"Plugged me high but I don't reckon it's too bad," Wyoming replied as with a shaking hand he felt for the wound. His finger came upon a tear in his jacket and shirt and a bloody hole in the muscle atop his collarbone. He glanced up at Jack as that worthy knelt at his side.

"How'd you get here?" he groaned.

"Followed yu; and yu can thank this little lady," Ward said as Allison leaped from Dottie and rushed to his side.

"Allie!"

"Oh, Wyoming, I was hiding by the bunkhouse watching for you to come. I heard them talking— those phony deputies. They were bragging how they were going to shoot you. Wyoming, they weren't real lawmen—"

"I discovered that…almost too late."

"I tried to tell Dada and Anna, but nobody would listen to me, and momma stopped me—wouldn't let me explain. She wanted me to go inside out of everybody's way—I think she was afraid there would be trouble. So I ran off and found Jack and told him what I heard. Aren't you glad?"

"You bet, scamp. I shore owe you. You saved my life."

"I know," she smiled proudly.

"Let me have a look at yur shoulder," Jack said reaching out a hand.

"Get these things off me first," Wyoming said, holding up his manacled wrists.

"Shore. I'll need a key I reckon. One of them stiffs must have it in his pocket."

Jack returned a moment later with a small handcuff key and unlocked the restraints and tossed them into the dust. He unbuttoned Wyoming's shirt and pulled it off his shoulder. "Reckon thet slug went clean through," he grunted.

"Use my—neck scarf," Wyoming said weakly and Jack untied the scarf, tearing and folding it into pads and pressing them over both wounds. With his own scarf he tied the pads on tight, looping it under Wyoming's arm and over his shoulder.

"Oh, Wyoming, they shot you!" Allison cried her small hand stole out to clasp his in a tight grip as Jack bound up Wyoming's wound.

"It ain't so bad, Allie," Wyoming said through clinched teeth. "But for you I'd be laying out there where them fellers are."

"I reckon thet'll stop the bleeding, but yu ought to see a doctor," went on Jack. "Can yu stand?"

"Shore—give me your hand," he replied.

With Jack's aid he labored to his feet and walked slowly to his horse. He stood a moment letting a wave of dizziness pass.

"Can yu ride? We'll head back te the Triangle A, and send fer a doc," Jack said.

"I don't reckon I'll be going back to the ranch—just yet," Wyoming muttered.

"Why?" Allison demanded staring up at him a puzzled look on her face.

"I reckon it's kind of hard to explain, scamp," he said fluffing her dark curls with his right hand.

"I know why," she sniffed. "It's cause of Anna. But you're not a murderer. And I'm going to tell her. That will make everything right."

"Ump-umm," Wyoming assuaged. "There's some things I reckon I have to do. But for now, get me to town."

"Thet's a long ride an' in yur condition I don't reckon yu'll make it thet far," Jack said shaking his head. "Best I take yu to my place, its closer."

Wyoming gave a jerky nod."Allie, you'll have to ride with us. I can't risk letting you ride back alone, and I reckon I could use Jack's help."

"What're we gonna do with these carcasses?" Jack asked indicating the two dead men with a jerk of his chin.

"If it's all the same to you, I say leave them lay."

Jack nodded. "I reckon we ought to search 'em though. There might be some questions asked if they're found carryin' badges even if they ain't real lawmen."

"You're right, Jack."

Jack dragged the two dead men into the bushes. He returned presently packing a heavy, fat wallet and a shiny silver badge.

"I opened this," he declared in amazement showing Wyoming the greasy wallet stuffed full of greenbacks. "Belonged to the tall one. He must have robbed a bank, he shore was heeled. Hundreds of dollars heah. What'll we do with it?"

"Shore, that's blood money, for doing away with me. Paid ahead of time, I reckon. We best hold on to it as evidence."

It was dark when they rode into the yard at Ward's place. Allison leaped off Dottie and rushed up to pound on the door.

"Allison!" Alice cried staring down at the little girl's anxious face. "Is something wrong—" She broke off as her eyes encountered her brother and Wyoming. "What happened?" she called hurrying toward them alerted by the ashen hue of Wyoming's face and bloody shirt.

"Get him into the house, he's been shot," Jack ordered easing Wyoming out of the saddle.

"Lay him on the sofa," Mrs. Ward instructed meeting them at the door.

"I'll get paw, and then head inte town for Doc Mills," Jack said and started off toward the barn.

"I'll be—fine," Wyoming panted, "If I—don't get—blood poison. The—bullet went—clean through."

No sooner had Wyoming stretched out on the couch when Hank Ward entered the room. He was silent for a moment glaring down at Wyoming.

"I'll jest be damn," he said forcefully. Jack told me yu'd been shot. Damnation! What the hell happened?"

Hank pulled a chair up next to the sofa, and flopped down, as with slow voice, Wyoming related the story…

"One feller—named Willy, the other—Clay—Two hombres pretending to be lawmen. They was acting under Bull Burton's orders. They wouldn't brace me—out right, so they cooked up a—scheme pretending to be lawmen 'cause they figured I wouldn't throw my gun on the law—They were right," he grunted, taking a deep ragged breath.

"Jack told me yu wouldn't let him take yu back to yur ranch," Ward said frowning. "What gives, son if I can ask?"

Wyoming closed his eyes. "Got to work some things out," he said hesitantly.

"Yu want me te let the Dixon's know what happened? I reckon they're pretty upset, them fellers makin' off with yu, an' yu not getting' a chance te tell 'em anything."

"No," Wyoming responded, perhaps a little too sharply.

"Hmm," Ward murmured shifting in his chair. "Wal, I reckon it's a shore fire bet now we're goin' te see te this cattlemen's protective association."

It was sometime later. The light had faded indicating evening. Wyoming heard voices and a moment later a man in a dark suit entered the room. He was a man in his mid-fifties with a thick pearl-gray mustache and corresponding griseous hair.

"I'm Doctor Mills," the newcomer said. "Let's have a look at you." The doctor carefully removed the crude bandages and unhurriedly examined the wounds. "Well, well, it seems you've been shot in this shoulder once before. This new entry and exit wounds nearly matched the old ones; only a half inch off. Looks like a clean through and through wound though. You're fortunate."

Wyoming lay there while the doctor attended to his injury. He was aware of others in the room. He saw Hank Ward and his wife and next to him Alice, and behind her, peering over her shoulder, Jack Ward.

"There, that ought to do it," the doctor said some moments later. "I'll leave something for pain if he needs it, but this boy is tough as an Indian. He'll be up in no time. He'll need his bandages changed in a day or so. I'll leave some dressings and ointment."

With a nod to Wyoming he turned and made his way out of the room. Wyoming fell into a fitful sleep. When next he opened his eyes, a kerosene lamp on the opposite side of his bed cast a pale yellow light in the shadowy room. His headache had departed but the pain in his shoulder was a burning ache. On the side table he discovered his gun belt and Colt. He wondered briefly who had brought it remembering he had tossed it onto the porch at Annabelle's feet. It had been impulsive, for the look of horror on her face; the fact that she could think him a murderer had angered him and…hurt. He lay wide-awake now deep in thought. He moved his shoulder slowly gritting his teeth at the pain. He needed to think this thing out. Obviously Burton was giving orders, but knowing what he knew, it was just as certain that Hester was behind the whole deal. He had to get back on his feet as quick as he could. The rustlers were evidently becoming desperate to resort to such a reckless scheme. The sound of the door opening disrupted his thoughts. Alice's head appeared from around the edge of the door.

"Are you awake?" she whispered. "It's near supper time. Would you like something to eat?"

"I reckon I could eat," he grinned.

"Well," she mused peering thoughtfully at him, "If you think you're up to it, I've fixed fruit, rice, eggs, toast, and coffee—"

"Alice, girl, you're an angel," Wyoming returned gratefully.

She blushed, and seemed momentarily flustered. She pushed the door wide and came into the room carrying the tray of food.

"You want me to put it on your lap?" she asked, and at his nod, set the tray down gently. "When you're done I'll come back and change your bandages. Doctor's orders, so don't frown. He left some dressings with me." She hesitated. "Unless you need me to feed you," she said blushing.

"Thanks, Alice, but I reckon I can still use my right hand."

She nodded, and left the room. Wyoming had no more than finished eating when Alice returned with strips of linen, a small green jar and a pan of steaming water. He lay unmoving looking up at her pretty face as she pulled back the blanket exposing his bandaged shoulder. She hesitated, staring at the bandages. Blood had seeped through the cloth, showing dark red.

"This'll probably hurt," she said, sensibly. "The bandages are most likely stuck to your wound."

With steady hands she began to cut away the strips of linen that served as bandages and then essayed to remove the blood-soaked pads. He closed his eyes. The feel of her cool fingers on his flesh was so soothing.

"Taking care of bloody wounds don't faze you?" Wyoming asked watching the confident movement of her small hands.

"Not really. I've seen enough between doctoring up paw and Jack and any one of the boys," she replied, "though it's mostly been cuts and broken bones, never a gunshot."

The pads were crusted with blood but fortunately were not stuck tight. She saturated the pads with warm water and pulled gently to free them. He heard her utter a tiny aggravated sigh, but didn't open his eyes. How soothing was the cool air to his hot skin and irritated wounds once they were removed. Gently she smeared cool salve to the wounds and slowly reapplied the bandages.

"There, it's done," she said.

"Thanks, Alice," he rejoined, smiling up at her.

"You're welcome," she replied getting to her feet and gathering up the old bloody dressings and water pan walked to the door. "I'll let you rest."

Wyoming watched the door close softly behind her and then closed his eyes. He woke later finding that his headache had departed and the pain in his shoulder was now only a dull ache. He fell back to sleep once again and when next he opened his eyes the gray outline of the window facing him showed and he imagined dawn was breaking. Besides the painful itching and contracting of his wounds he seemed to be doing pretty well, he decided. He lay there a while longer hearing the house stir with sound, and murmur of voices. He saw his overalls and shirt lying across the foot of the couch, laundered and folded. The bullet holes had been repaired. In all probability Alice's work. She was a sweet girl. She'd make some lucky fellow a wonderful wife. Sleep claimed him once more and when he woke he guessed by the shadow across the foot of the sofa that it was late afternoon.

There came the stomp of booted feet, and Jack Ward's head appeared in the doorway. "How yu feelin'?" he queried.

"Better. Say, how did my gear get here?" he asked nodding to his gun belt.

"Yu can thank yur little devotee. She brought them to me, said she had to slip out of the house with them before anybody saw her."

Wyoming smiled. Allison Dixon. How was he ever going to thank her?

Jack turned the chair around so its back faced Wyoming and straddled it resting his arms across the back.

"Paw's meetin' some of the smaller ranchers tomorrow evenin' to talk about gettin' that cattlemen association started. Reckon yu gettin' shot like yu was has everybody all in a lather."

"That's good news; you'll be at the meeting?" Wyoming replied.

"Yep. I'll keep yu posted."

The cattlemen association would provide enough riders that they could flush these thieves out of their hole. All they needed was for one to talk, implicate Burton and Hester...

"I'm wondering if you've heard any talk about those two hombres you shot," Wyoming went on.

"Nope, nary a word."

"I don't reckon that's strange," Wyoming said. "Burton's gonna hold his tongue, and wait for somebody else to make something of it."

"Yeah, that figures."

A light knock sounded on the door and Alice hurried down the hall to answer it. "Wyoming, you got a visitor."

Before Wyoming could speculate who it might be, Allison Dixon bound through the door.

"Wyoming!" she cried scampering toward him as though she would leap upon the sofa, but at the last moment fell to her knees clasping his outstretched hand. "I was so worried. I dreamed you— died—oh, it was an awful dream."

"Well scamp, you can see it was only a nightmare," he reassured her. "I'm alive and healthy—well nearly."

"Good." She sat on the edge of the sofa. "Hi, Jack," she said smiling at that worthy.

"Howdy, Allie," he grinned. "Where's that big ole hound of yur's?"

"Outside on the porch," she frowned. "Alice wouldn't let him in the house."

"Shame on her," he drawled.

"Wyoming, I told Anna what happened to you," she whispered leaning close.

"You did, huh," he said striving to sound indifferent.

"Yes. Don't you want to know what she said?" she asked when he made no further comment.

"I reckon you're about to tell me," he sighed.

"She cried," Allison said smugly.

"Is that a fact," he swallowed.

"Yep. And then she locked herself in her room and wouldn't come out."

CHAPTER TWENTY-FOUR

B y week's end Wyoming was feeling little the worse for his wounds. They were healing nicely. There had been several meetings of the newly formed cattlemen's protective association and Wyoming was pleased that the Texas cattle buyer Fay Johnson had been elected president. Johnson was once a Texas Ranger and evidenced no love for rustlers. He was an excellent choice Wyoming concluded. Hank Ward, however, was loquacious in his praise of Wyoming, contending that his presence was needed to ferret out the rustler gang. During this time Allison had come to see him several times despite Wyoming's firmness that she mustn't ride here alone.

"Oh, Wyoming, no one is going to bother me, besides Dottie knows her way here blindfolded. I couldn't get lost," she replied on one occasion after Wyoming had scolded her. "And don't you want to hear what's going on at the ranch since you've been gone? I still don't understand why you stay away. Your wound is nearly healed; you could ride over, couldn't you?"

"Shore, I reckon I could," he returned staring off toward the dark mountain range. They were seated side by side on the front porch.

"I'm just a little girl, but I know what's going on, you know," she sniffed and for a long moment neither spoke. "Anna had another visitor the other day," she said casting him a glance out of the corner of her eye. "He calls himself, M'sieur Henri de Rousseau—"

"Oh, yeah?" Wyoming queried dryly as he fixed keen eyes on her.

"Ah-huh."

"Did she—I mean—see him?"

"Shore," she said mimicking his drawling speech staring off into the distance as though that was the conclusion of her comments.

"Dog-gone, scamp, that Rousseau feller is no good four-flusher—"

Allison bounced up and down excitedly in her chair as she whirled to face him. "That's what she told him!" she twittered elatedly. "I was hiding under the porch, Caesar and me—in case she needed, you know—and did she tell him a thing or two—what does sycophant mean?"

"Dang if I know, but I reckon it ain't good."

"Boy he was hopping mad. He stormed off. I don't think we'll see anymore of him."

"I'm not so shore," he mused. "Say, you mentioned another visitor. Who else has come calling on your sister?"

"Which sister?" she answered offhandedly. "Jack's been over to see Angel most every night—"

"You know dang well which sister!" he interrupted.

"Ah-huh. Mr. Hester. He showed up two evening ago. She talked to him but I stayed with her the whole time, so—"

The screen door creaked and Alice poked her head out. "I fixed some lunch, are you two hungry?"

"Yes, ma'am," Allison said bounding to her feet.

"I reckon after you eat you better get on home," Wyoming said. "I don't want you out after dark."

Later he stretched out on his bunk in one of the unused cabins. He stared up at the ceiling. What was Hester up to? Either this crafty rancher had guessed his secret or had learned something from Annabelle. And in the passion of the moment Wyoming was inclined to the latter suspicion. He took a while getting to sleep that night.

The next morning found Wyoming again seated on Ward's front porch where he'd spent many hours the last few days, heedless of distant snow-covered mountain grandeur, deep in thought. Sooner or later the issue must be met, with himself, with Dixon, and with Annabelle. Was he to go back to the ranch, to work there, to eat and sleep there, to face Annabelle a hundred times a day? The prospect filled him with breathless tumult knowing the look of revulsion he would see in her eyes.

But slowly the turbulence began to lose the keenness of its edge replaced by a deep resolve. Annabelle was repulsed by the violence Wyoming represented, the men he had killed. He was well aware there were few graces to his character. He couldn't become a gentleman any more than a panther could become a house cat. So, he would ride away as he should have done those days gone, before he had stolen that fateful kiss. Reaching this decision had been a slow painful process that had its inception days ago as he lay half feverish but had at last come to its finale. There was something cold and deathlike in his soul, for it was then he knew he would bid farewell to Annabelle Dixon. But no matter what happened, of one thing he was sure—he would kill Burton and most probably Ackers. And that eventuality, of course, would put him forever outside the pale for her. Then—and only then—Wyoming McCord would disappear and never be heard from again.

That night he walked a ways from the house with the thick shadows all around him and the cold stars overhead; and he was sober in thought, reflecting in fruitless conjecture as to what the end of this strange and fateful adventure would be.

Through her bedroom window Annabelle watched her sister Allison ride into the yard and head toward the barn. Chico met her and held her bridle as she slid spritely to the ground. Allison had been to see Wyoming she knew and Annabelle's heart quickened its beating. What news would she bring? Had Wyoming mentioned her? She brushed at her skirts with nervous hands. What had this west done to her? She turned, walked to sit on her bed her mind in a whirl. She had unconsciously relied upon Wyoming's Western force—the bold and relentless violence which she knew his past contained, but then at the slightest provocation—she had failed him. Oh, the bitterness of it! She had believed the worst. The look in his eyes told it all. His disgust of her had been as plain as could be. He had quit her father, the ranch—her! What difference did it make what Wyoming's past was? Whatever he had been, he was honest and fine now; they had been partners—range riders together. And suddenly she knew; even if he had been a gunslinger, if all of it were true, she loved him so wonderfully that she would fight for him, and she would—win him!

When had she fallen in love with Wyoming McCord? She decided it didn't really matter when. It might have been when he stole that first kiss, when he'd danced with her, when he had taught her to drive a team of horses, and the kiss that accompanied it, when he gave Allison the little mare, Dottie...It didn't matter, she only knew that fallen she had. She had probably fallen in love with Wyoming on each of those occasions and a few more besides.

She leaped to her feet and jerked open the door to her closet. Within moments she had changed from her gown to shirt and overalls. She was pulling on her boots when Allison skipped into the room. The girl stopped abruptly staring at her sister's determined expression obviously surprised to see this change of mood. Allison flopped on the bed beside Annabelle.

"What are you doing?"

"What does it look like? I'm changing. I'm going for a ride."

"Who's going for a ride," Angelique queried poking her head around the door frame.

"I am," Annabelle replied getting to her feet and reaching for her sombrero. "What?" she demanded. "Why are you two looking at me like I've grown two heads?"

"Because you've shut yourself up in this room for the last week crying yourself silly. And you only came out to deliver a put-down to Rousseau and Hester, and suddenly you're going for a ride—that's why," Angelique returned. "So, where are you off to?"

Annabelle drew in a deep shuddering breath. "I'm going to—face up to—Wyoming," she said with almost grim resolve.

Her sisters stared speechless for a moment, and then in unison; "You can't go alone."

"I'll take Chico."

"Fine, but I'm coming along," Angelique said.

"Me too," Allison cried gleefully leaping to her feet.

"Do you have to pack that ugly gun?" Annabelle demanded.

"Absolutely," Angelique smiled beguilingly. "You'll just have to get use to it, sister dear."

Wyoming was almost to the house when a grind of wheels rolling down the gravel road drew his attention. He paused watching a buckboard approach and pull up in front of the house. He didn't know the driver, but recognized immediately the passenger, the tall eagle-eyed cattle buyer and now president of the newly formed cattlemen association, Fay Johnson.

"Howdy, Mr. Johnson," Wyoming greeted stepping up to the wagon to take Johnson's extended hand.

"Howdy to yu, Wyoming," responded Johnson. "Yu're just the man I was lookin' for."

"Well, I reckon you've found me," Wyoming drawled.

"Fay Johnson, get down an' come in," Hank Ward called stepping out onto the porch letting the screen door slam behind him.

Johnson met Ward midway up the steps to shake his hand. The three continued up to the porch where they settled in chairs lined against the wall beneath the window.

"Alice, gurl, trot out some lemonade fer our thirsty guests," he shouted back into the house, then turned his attention to Johnson. "So, what brings yu?"

"Came to see this young range rider," Johnson said keen eyes surveying Wyoming. "Son, are yur wounds healed?"

"Still a little tender, but nothing to hold me back."

"Good, good," he said pulling three cigars from a vest pocket. "Smoke?" he asked. "Fine cigars; come all the way from St. Louie."

Wyoming shook his head.

"Don't mind if I do," Ward said taking one of the proffered cigars.

"Well, now," Johnson went on puffing out a cloud of blue smoke. "I'd shore like to get our little confab over with." He afforded Wyoming another keen-eyed look. "There's rumor yu quit the Triangle A, son. Any truth in thet story?"

"I reckon it's a fact, sir."

"Ah-huh. An' if yu don't mind my askin', what air yur plans?"

"Are you wanting to know if I'm going to stick around and see the end to these rustlers?"

"Thet's straight talk, an' yes, thet's my concern."

"You don't need to worry, Mr. Johnson. I intend to see this job finished."

"Then yu've satisfied my concerns," Johnson said, letting out a relieved breath. "This particular range is due for a boom, an' it'll run a million haid of stock. It ain't none of my business, but there's shore a fine opportunity fer an enterprisin' young feller like yourself."

Before Wyoming could respond the pounding hoofs of a racing horse drew all three's attention. Wyoming leaped to his feet as he recognized Allison's little black mare Dottie. He bound off the porch in one striding jump racing to intercept the mare.

"Whoa, Whoa!" Allison cried and the black mare skidded to a halt throwing gravel.

Allison's face was deathly pale and tears streaked her cheeks. She threw herself into Wyoming's arms.

"Allie! What is it? What's wrong?" Wyoming demanded.

"Anna—Angel—they—they've taken them!" she sobbed.

"What?! Tell me."

"That man, Ackers, and Jimmy Anderson and—and two others. They surprised us—Oh, Wyoming they kidnapped Anna and Angel!

I ran, and—Oh, that Ackers, he shot at me!" she wailed pressing her trembling little form tight against him.

"Would yu look hyar," Ward grunted angrily running a soothing hand over the mare's rump. It came away red with blood. "A little lower an' he'd have crippled her."

CHAPTER TWENTY-FIVE

L eaning from the saddle Wyoming peered down at the fresh tracks in the soft dirt. He edged Sparky along following the scuffmarks. The girls, on their way to Ward's ranch had been set upon by at least four riders. The tracks of the horses cut up the ground, evidence of commotion. Allison had broken away and ran for Ward's place. And it was evident that Annabelle and Angelique had tried to flee also. But they were pursued and after a short distance caught and apparently dragged from their horses. As he was studying the sign Caesar let out a whiny rumble and Wyoming saw the dog pawing at something on the ground. Jack was nearest and stepped from his horse to inspect the object that had attracted the dog's interest. When Wyoming rode up Jack was holding a Colt .45 in his quivering hand. Wyoming quickly swung to the ground.

"I'll be damn," Wyoming exclaimed taking the gun from Jack. "That's the Colt I gave to Angelique."

"I figured it was," Jack said hoarsely wiping his hand on his chaps. "There's blood on it."

Wyoming looked down to see that blood smeared his own hand. He flipped open the loading port and spun the cylinder. There were two expended casings. Angelique had got off two shots. So, whose blood was on the gun, Angelique's or one of the kidnappers?

"My bet is Angie wounded one of them varmints. That's his blood," Jack said.

"That's my guess," Wyoming said. "She must have plugged one of them. I reckon when they caught up to her they wrestled the gun from her and threw it in the dirt."

A vision formed in Wyoming's mind; Angelique racing away on her mustang, twisting about in her saddle as she fired at her pursuers. Lordy, but the girl had spunk!

Stuffing the gun in his belt they returned to examining the signs. Six sets of shod hoofs led off west at a gallop. Still searching for further sign, the hound Caesar bound off nose to the ground. Wyoming followed. After a few hundred yards or so the tracks turned west to follow the rim of the valley, zigzagging among patches of aspen and pine. Once or twice, not far apart, the horses had been halted leaving a number of bunched tracks as six sets of hoofs stirred up the ground, which sent Caesar sniffing madly about before scampering off hot on the trail. There were booted foot tracks; one set Wyoming noted had a worn spot on the sole. He guessed that the kidnappers had put the girls back on their own horses; probably tied their hands he decided bending from the saddle to study the tracks.

"I reckon if these tracks keep on like they are they're head fer Cerrillos," Jack said huskily face ashen.

"What's at Cerrillos? Wyoming asked.

"Wal, there's a little mission church there," Jack mused giving Wyoming a hard glance. "But I don't reckon Anderson, an' shore, Ackers has marryin' on their minds—or ransom neither. More'n likely they're headed toward Cerrillos te try an' throw us off."

Wyoming nodded grimly. "I'll wager Ackers' the hombre who's been laying in wait up behind the house just for this reason—to get Annabelle."

"Acker's black-hearted. He'll maul Annabelle—violate her, the first chance he gets. An' Anderson's too damn green to realize Angelique's in danger of the same treatment—from Ackers or one of them others—"

"I reckon you don't have to spell it out," Wyoming choked shooting his friend a hard look. "Come on Caesar's hot after them."

Late afternoon the hound came on horse tracks that had left the well used track, and were now headed north.

"I reckon that hound's got a keen nose," Wyoming said. "You figured right, Jack. They've turned north."

"I reckon I'm loose in my head…but Wyoming, pard, I reckon I know where they're headed. 'bout a month back I was workin' a high draw near ten mile west of hyar when I came on several sets of hawse tracks mixed in with thet of a bunch of cattle. I shore was curious, 'cause we've been missin' cattle on a daily basis, mostly small herds of forty or fifty. So I followed. It was near sunset, an' I calculated I had gone a good twenty mile or so. It was new country te me. The trail led on te the northwest, an' was keepin' te the levels. I was shore in a quandary. If I started back right then it'd be way after dark 'fore I'd get back home, an' I shore didn't want te be ridin' this rough country at night. I figured I was goin' te be campin' out anyhow, so I kept on. Heck, I'd gone this far so I reckon I'd stick te it. About dark I came on a long oval where the sides were heavy with brush. At the upper end I found runnin' water an' decided te camp there fer the night. I didn't light no fire in case them cahoots I was trailin' was close by. I was up early an' 'bout a half hour after sunrise, I climbed to the top of a high ridge an' sudden like I spied a column of smoke driftin' up through the trees from down in the next valley. I got real cautious then, an' slipped ahead on foot an' peeked down through the trees. There was a cabin kind of huddled under an overhanging cliff. I didn't see nobody about, but there was four hawses in the corral, an' one of 'em was a fine lookin' paint thet I shore recognized as belongin' te thet greaser Jimenez thet used te ride fer old man Erickson. I reckon Jimenez an' the rest of thet rustler outfit's been usin' thet cabin as a hideout. I figure thet cabin is where he's headed fer with the girls," Jack Ward declared forcefully.

"Jack, I don't reckon I could find that cabin on my own. Let's head back to the ranch," Wyoming flashed. "Get as many of your riders as we can—and supplies. Knowing where we're headed might give us the edge we need."

Wyoming whistled for Caesar, who reluctantly broke off the trail and lumbered up to him. "Come on boy, it's gonna be a long trail we need to stock up."

Hank Ward was just coming out of the stables when the two rode up the big hound trotting alongside Wyoming's horse. Jack quickly apprised him of the situation.

"All the boys air out, but I reckon yu'll not wait. Go on, I'll send them out on yur trail as soon as they come in," Ward said, his keen gray eyes upon his son. "Get up te the house and have yur maw fix up some vittles te take along fer yu an' Wyoming. Be careful."

"Thanks, paw," Jack replied, "We'll leave a trail yu can follow at a trot."

"Wyoming, I'm going to take Allie back to her house," Alice insisted meeting them on the porch. "I'm sure her parents don't know what happened. I have to tell them."

"All right, Alice. How is Allie?"

"The poor thing is terrified for her sisters, as you can imagine."

"I reckon we better take Caesar with us," Jack said, "In case I'm wrong about where they're headed.

Once out on the range Jack led at a brisk trot, the hound keeping pace. Both men were armed to the teeth grim and cold and silent. Wyoming had deceived Jack, but he knew himself to be haunted. He knew the tumult under his wet and panting breast. Annabelle was at the mercy of Jed Ackers. He tried to shut out the terrible images endeavoring to overpower his thoughts, but they would not leave him.

Jack didn't intend to follow the outlaws' tracks, so as not to lose the dog or tire him out Wyoming lifted Caesar up in the saddle in front of him. The hound allowed the indignity but obviously didn't like it. Jack headed up around a high promontory back of Piñon Canyon bringing them out on a grassy range where cattle wearing the Triangle A should have been in abundance, but they only saw a few lone steers, some cows and calves. The rustlers had made a clean sweep of Dixon's stock, easy pickings for Ackers and his bunch. Hester and his accomplice Burton would have been cautious of stealing all a cattleman's stock. They came abruptly upon a waterhole fed by a spring, which showed signs of recent use. Here they came upon the kidnappers' trail. Wyoming bent from the saddle and let Caesar jump to the ground. The dog put his nose to the ground and began to sniff. A moment later he set up a whining howl. Jack went to investigate and saw the dog sniffing at a bloody bandana.

"Look hyar, one of them hombres' shore's been plugged. Looks like someone changed his bandages."

Suddenly Wyoming's gaze caught sight of something red far up the slope. Pulling his binoculars from his saddle bag he leveled it and adjusted it to his eyes.

"Ah," he grunted, "looks like a red cloth waving from a bush."

A moment later he was holding a silk scarf to his nose inhaling the sweet scent of Annabelle's perfume. "I reckon she must have seen her chance and tied it here knowing someone would be on their trail."

He brought the scarf to his nose, inhaled the fragrant scent again. Annabelle had courage, and all the affection, the love, for this girl came rushing into his heart. Late afternoon they came abruptly upon a set of four horse tracks that had left the well used track, and were now headed north. Dismounting, Wyoming bent to scrutinize the tracks.

"These tracks ain't more'n three hours old," he assessed.

They rode northwest. High ridges and narrow valleys alternated here. On the hilltops tall spruce and pine showed among golden-leaf aspens. The white flags of deer moved up every slope. Grass and water were abundant.

Wyoming peered up a wooded slope crowded with pine and interspersed with the tall white trunks of aspen, their yellow leaves rippling in the breeze. The gray trunks of trees uprooted by wind were scattered across a narrow rock-strewn runlet like huge sticks.

"If my memory serves me right, thet cabin is still a ways beyond thet ridge," Jack vouched pointing up through the trees.

The slope was easy of ascent, open in places, thicketed in others with tall aspen and pine and cedar growing at intervals. The trail here appeared to double back in a long slant, probably so Ackers' bunch could spy on whoever might be trailing them. They had covered their getaway cleverly by riding south toward one of the small towns. Although they risked being seen, once on the well-traveled roads their tracks would be impossible to distinguish by pursuers from any others. It would be easy then to duck off the trail and backtrack north, which they did. They hadn't counted on the big hound Caesar's keen nose.

Dark was coming on fast and Ackers' bunch still had a ways to go according to Jack. They would have to halt soon for the night; their horses were probably getting tired. The pursuers came abruptly upon a well-defined, hard-packed trail which led up along the crest of the ridge to the north and here shod hoof tracks of three horses intermingled with the tracks of the others Wyoming and Jack had been following. At this point the trail split. Five tracks went off in one direction and four in the other. Wyoming wondered which set was the one with the kidnapped girls. Caesar circled the spot once and then took off on the trail left by the four horses. They had travelled only a short distance when Jack let out an exclamation and Wyoming saw the small yellow ribbon entangled in a cedar branch. Jack spurred his horse ahead and snatched it up.

"I reckon this is Angelique's," he said.

They continued down the trail festooned by Angelique's yellow ribbon following Caesar. Twilight was rapidly approaching and coming upon a fresh flowing stream they halted calling the hound off the trail. Here they rested and partook of some of the fare Mrs. Ward had made up for them sharing with the dog. Both men were silent as they ate. After no more than two hours had passed they were again on the trail heading up a narrow aisle between wooded slopes. Wyoming and Jack had both hoped to catch up with Ackers' bunch before they had the girls all night fearing what they would suffer at the hands of Ackers. At the top of the slope they came across the tracks of six horses. The outfit joined up here with the tracks they were trailing and continued on.

Wyoming and Jack moved along more cautiously now ordering Caesar to stay close. The valley opened before them, narrow with scattered growth of cedar and pine. Few cattle were seen. Wyoming searched along the gray valley below for dust clouds which would signal Ward's pursuing riders, but no living object showed.

"There's the cabin, beneath them trees, see it?" Jack said pointing, and Wyoming saw the edge of a structure sheltered in the trees far below.

Just then a string of horses appeared out of a row of pine trees, moving toward the cabin. Twelve horses, nine riders and three pack animals. Four riders hung back some distance traveling slower than the others. Wyoming's eyes fixed upon two of the riders, small, mere bright dots in the saddle. That would be Annabelle and Angelique.

"There's another trail along this ridge that circles around to the east," Jack said, "I got turned around when I was up here before and just happened to stumble on it. I figure it'll bring us down to the other end of the valley. From there I reckon we could come up on the cabin from the far side."

They wasted not another second. In the next moment they were speeding along the ridge. The trail Jack had pointed out appeared open and hard. No dust would gust aloft to betray them, and they could not be seen from either valley. The ridge top widened to a big country and the trail kept to the middle of it. They ran their horses over the long level reaches and then slowed their gait over the rougher ground. A quarter of an hour's rapid travel brought them to a point where they had to cut across to the slope again. They found it long but good going.

They came out upon a timbered bench, and as luck would have it, there stood the cabin. The string of horses was still four miles at least down the valley, and at the pace they were moving it would be an hour or so before they reached the cabin. Somehow over the foregoing race along the level ridge they had lost Caesar. Wyoming whistled and called but there was no sign of the hound. The only thing now was for Wyoming and Jack to work their way down from the ridge. It was steep but appeared passable. Leading their horses they started down. Zigzagging through the brush and over benches, they came to a slant, which bothered Wyoming for the reason that though sliding down would be easy; they could not retrace their steps. Their range of vision here was restricted. Wyoming tried to see below. While he was searching out a way down, Jack started off leading his big bay and went sliding down the slant. He made it without mishap and Wyoming followed. Soon after that they got into rough ground and had to work along the shelves and back again. They lost valuable time. The sinking sun had gone down behind the ridge they had descended and shadows were thickening. Finally they crashed down over the last wooded barrier to level ground.

A stream flowed out from under the bluff. They left their horses to drink, and went ahead on foot. The main timber here was spruce, thin and spear-pointed, interspersed with aspen and brush. Wyoming could see the gold and purple of the valley beyond. The cabin stood out a little from the row of timber, marked by tall aspen trees and one low-branching oak tree. Wyoming was about to leave the woods when Jack caught his arm and pointed. He espied the string of horses half a mile below. Keeping the cabin between themselves and the approaching riders they ran across the open. Jack, with pistol in hand, rapped on the door. There was no answer. He glanced back at Wyoming who nodded, and pushing open the door he entered. Wyoming followed at his heels. Once inside, Wyoming glanced quickly around. Many frontier cabins consisted of only one room, but in this case, however, a partition extended across one end dividing the room in two. A doorway covered by a burlap curtain allowed access to the other half of the cabin.

Wyoming, with drawn gun pulled the burlap curtain aside and peered cautiously into the room. A metal-frame bed upon which sat a sagging mattress was pushed against one corner and beside it a scuffed table. An empty whiskey bottle sat on the table next to a candle stub covered with wax drippings. A saddle lay in the far corner, a bridle hooked over the saddle horn. Wyoming scanned the rest of the cabin. A cook stove that would also serve for heat sat out from one wall. A scarred wooden table with benches on two sides was situated in the center of the room, and in one corner was stacked several bedrolls and other cowboy paraphernalia. Shelves containing cans and other foodstuffs lined one wall. The place was well stocked and had probably been used by two or three individuals off and on for some time.

Wyoming figured that Ackers along with Anderson would bring the girls into the cabin first off, and he intended to shoot them on sight. They would hold up the others, unless they showed fight. It was Wyoming's idea that he could make at least one of them talk.

Through a chink between the logs Wyoming made out a flash of black and the next instant a thud of hoofs. Wyoming straightened and motioned Jack into the adjoining room. They had to be quick, for the horses were close. Gruff voices sounded plainly. Horses thudded up to the cabin, followed by the creak of leather and clinking spurs as the riders dismounted. Shortly there was sound of rattling spurs approaching the door.

Although Wyoming had contempt for Ackers, he still wanted steady nerves. And even in the lax months when all his efforts were in branding cattle, the habit of self-preservation still drove him, had forced him to continue his old secret practice of throwing his gun. And now as he waited, he felt it had been well worth it.

CHAPTER TWENTY-SIX

I n the cabin, Wyoming glanced at Jack who stood on the opposite side of the doorway. He could barely make out his features in the dim light. He peeked through the thin space between curtain and doorjamb. His hand tightened on his gun, waiting. The door opened and Wyoming saw the figure of a man silhouetted in the doorframe. He half turned and looked back.

"Billy, yu stay by the door. Charlie bring in some firewood while Jimenez starts a fire in the stove," the man said, then stepping high, with spurs jangling on the doorsill, he came in.

"Hyar, let me light the lantern, it's getting' kind of dim in here." A moment later the flash of a match being struck and then the bright flame from the lantern lighted the small room.

The man's voice was familiar and the lantern's light brought recognition—Jed Ackers! Close on his heels followed Ned Walters. Their garb, worn and soiled, did not lend itself to the look of prosperity.

Where was Annabelle and Angelique? Wyoming agonized, his plan suddenly hollow. They could make no move until they knew the girls' whereabouts. If Annabelle wasn't with Ackers, then who had her?"

"Let's get this hyar deal settled 'fore that swarthy-face gambler gets hyar with the gurl," Ackers said. "He's laggin' back but he'll be hyar pronto," Charlie said.

"I ain't hankerin' fer this deal," Walters said, "What yu figurin' anyhow?"

"I want the gurl," Ackers declared forcefully. "Jimmy can keep the younger one…fer now."

"Thet ain't hard te figure. Hell yu been undressin' them both with yur eyes every since we snatched them yesterday," Walters snickered.

"Yu best watch yur step," the man called Charlie spoke up. "That card-slick's a sly one. Yu notice thet sleeve gun he's carryin'. I reckon he knows how te use it."

"No matter," Ackers grunted impatiently. "We been livin' out hyar on the range, drivin' small bunches of cows night an' day fer the boss. I'm shore gettin' peeked."

Hell, Jed, yu ain't thinkin' of killin' him fer her—"

They're here," Billy hissed poking his head around the door frame.

"I'm out of this," Charlie declared, stepping over the high doorsill to disappear in the twilight shadows.

Wyoming's ears caught a soft thud of hoofs slowly approaching the cabin where they ended. Then there followed the creak of leather and the sound of booted feet hitting the ground.

"Don't touch me!" came Annabelle's shrill voice. "I'll get off the horse by myself."

"Tush, tush *chéri*," came a sultry voice. "You will soon get use to me, and find that you enjoy my embrace."

"Never! Let me go!" Annabelle shrieked, and peeking around the edge of the curtain, Wyoming saw Annabelle clutched in the Creole gambler Rousseau's arms, kicking like a little mule. Rousseau shoved her into the cabin. Her golden curls were disheveled, hanging down over one eye. Her dust-begrimed face showed tear-streaks. But no humiliated and shamed maiden could ever have possessed such blazing eyes. And Wyoming reveled in the courage that had sustained her. Still holding her arm, Rousseau pulled her toward the room where Wyoming and Jack Ward were hiding. Rousseau's face was flushed and showed the bloody marks of fingernails down one cheek. Jack's hand gripped Wyoming's arm, hard. Wyoming knew what Jack was thinking—where was Angelique?

"You men leave us now," Rousseau panted, jerking the burlap curtain aside and started to push the girl into the room. Walters got to his feet and disappeared out the door. Ackers made no move to leave.

Wyoming tensed, gun raised. Annabelle fought like a tiger in an effort to escape.

"I reckon not," came Ackers' laconic reply.

Rousseau halted, twisted his head to peer at Ackers, then gave Annabelle a hard shove and she stumbled into the room. Wyoming's hand shot out closing about her mouth and dragging her up against him.

"It's me, Wyoming," he hissed in her ear as he holstered his gun.

"Oh, God," she gasped into his fingers and immediately she slumped against him, her whole body trembling in obvious and wondrous relief. Wyoming, still holding her in his arms, stepped close to Jack Ward who was only a shadowy form in the duskiness of the room.

"Stay with Jack," he whispered in her ear.

She shook her head clinging to him.

Gently, but firmly, he pried her arms from around his waist and pushed her into Jack's arms.

"M'sieur Ackers, do you intend to challenge me for the girl?" came Rousseau's soft deceptive voice from the other room.

"I reckon I am. I aim te take the little *Señorita* off yur hands," Ackers replied.

"I think not," Rousseau purred. "I paid you well to kidnap the girl. Be satisfied with that. You can enjoy the younger one...when M'sieur Anderson is done with her...unless you are too impatient to wait your turn."

Wyoming whirled back to the doorway in time to hear bellowing thunder fill the cabin. A quick darting look and Wyoming saw Rousseau shudder, his gun, which had sprung from his sleeve, half leveled. Smoke and fire exploded from its muzzle, the bullet tearing splinters from the tabletop. Rousseau staggered backward crashing against the wall where he slid limply to the floor.

"Hah! Thought yu was fast with that little sleeve gun," Ackers chuckled, and he flipped his gun up to catch it by the handle, and sheath it.

Billy peeked cautiously into the cabin, then abruptly withdrew his head.

"Hay there, little *Señorita*. I reckon yu an' me air gonna have a fun time tonight," Ackers announced with a malignant laugh.

Wyoming stepped out into the room.

"Howdy, Ackers!" he said easily.

Ackers froze, his visage undergoing a marvelous transformation. Perception, surprise, hate, realization swept with violent swiftness across his countenance. And the last gripped him horribly. As clearly as if he had spoken he expressed wild fear and certainty of death. With an audible intake of breath, he crouched slightly, desperate as a wolf at bay, his eyes like points of fire. As he lurched for his gun, Wyoming's Colt leaped from its holster, booming in its outward lunge. Ackers died in the act of his draw, and he went hurling down as if propelled by a catapult.

In the next moment Charlie appeared in the doorway.

"Hands up!" Wyoming ordered and Charlie's hands went rapidly aloft, his face pallid.

"Step inside," Wyoming hissed, "quick now, line up against the wall. Get his gun, Jack."

Charlie complied without a word, and Jack jerked his pistol from its holster and stuffed it in his own belt.

"Where's the other girl?" Jack demanded jabbing the barrel of his Colt hard against the man's ribs.

"Out there, by the fire. Red's with her," he choked.

Jack peeked around the door frame. His gaze encountered Angelique. She sat huddled before the newly built fire, arms hugging her knees to her chest. Her small face shone white and wore an expression of torture. Anderson sat beside her, one arm about her shoulders. The sleeve of Anderson's left arm was rolled up exposing a bloody bandage.

"Billy, I ain't heard nothing fer a while, go see what's goin' on," Anderson ordered nuzzling Angelique's throat. "'sides, I need a little privacy while I see to my lady."

"Stop it! Get off me," Angelique cried. "Hadn't you a sister?"

Anderson let out a gruff laugh as Billy got to his feet and started toward the door. Jack stepped back out of sight waiting. As soon as Billy's slight frame appeared in the doorway, Jack's hand shot out and jerked him inside.

"Get over there with yur pard," Jack hissed, jerking the rustler's gun from his holster. Billy staggered over to line up beside Charlie an incredulous look on his face.

"I'll keep an eye on these two," Wyoming said, and Jack nodded grimly stepping back to the door in time to hear Angelique's angry cry.

"Get your stinking hands off me!" she hissed.

"Aw, I'm shore getting' tired of yu pushin' me away. Seems I been wastin' words on yu. I reckon there's only one way to tame yu, Angel Dixon an' by Gawd I'm goin' to do it—tonight," he flared passionately.

"You dirty monster," she screamed, the very embodiment of horror and scorn. "To think I—I once liked you!"

Twisting her head violently to avoid his groping mouth she suddenly saw out of the corner of her eye a shadowy form creeping toward them from the side the cabin. She froze with a smothered scream. In that instant a blue streak charged out of the shadow lunging at Anderson's throat.

"Caesar!" she gasped.

"Gawd Almighty!" Anderson bawled flinging himself backward as the snarling animal crashed into him.

Angelique staggered on weak trembling knees against the side of the cabin where she sank to her knees just as Jack Ward leaped from the doorway gun leveled at his side.

"Caesar, here!" Jack shouted and the big hound broke away to come trotting over to lick Angelique's cheek as her shaky arm slid around the dog's shaggy neck.

"Aggh!" Anderson bawled leaping lithely to his feet.

Howdy, Jimmy!" Jack sang out, though his mirth held a deadly edge.

"Yu! Aw hell," he gasped, the expletive terrible in its certainty, and with a spasmodic snatch his hand jerked downward to the Colt at his hip. Red flame shot from Jack's Colt and Anderson spun half around, sank slowly to his knees and then over on his face. It was only then Jack's haunted gaze found Angelique. Face grim, he knelt beside her. With a heart wrenching sob she flung herself into his arms. Slowly he brought his arms about her and laid his chin against her damp curls. They sat thus for a long moment before he spoke.

"Angelique, let's go inside. Annabelle's waitin' in there—safe. She'll be worried about yu."

She lifted her face to his. "How did you—where did you come from?" she whispered.

"Wyoming and me, we was hidin' in the cabin when yu got here."

"But how—"

"That big ole hound there led us here."

"Oh, Caesar," she sighed peering with misty eyes at the dog who stared soulfully up at her. She flung her arms about the dog's neck and kissed him soundly on his head. Then she looked up at Jack.

"I—I'm all right," she whispered. "He didn't—"

"Shore yu're all right," he interrupted softly "I heard. Brace up now. Yur troubles are over."

Annabelle slowly pulled the frayed curtain aside as Angelique stepped in the cabin door her eyes dark and tragic, her hand still clutching Caesar's scruffy neck. "Angie," she cried and rushed to her sister's side.

"Jimmy's—dead! And I—I didn't faint," Angelique whispered clinging to her sister. In the next instant she drew back. "Anna, are—you—"

"I'm fine. Oh, Angel, I—I knew we were saved when Rousseau threw me into that room—right into Wyoming's arms and suddenly both girls were crying and laughing at the same time. Wyoming turned eyes dark and grim upon them.

"Are you two all right?" he asked.

Both girls peered at him with large solemn eyes. Annabelle nodded, "We're both fine," she managed.

"Yeah?" he said, and one could sense the intense relief in his voice, but he never looked fully at her.

"Wyoming—" Annabelle faltered reaching out a hand.

"You best wait in here," he said. "I'll have Jack bring a lantern in so you won't be in the dark."

"Oh, Jack," Annabelle cried clasping his arm when that worthy entered carrying a lighted lantern. "Wyoming—he hasn't looked at me, really looked at me—once. What does he think? Oh, he doesn't believe—or care. Tell him, Jack—please, I'm—all right—that—"

"I'll tell him, shore," he whispered "But yu're upset. Don't try to figure things out now. In the mornin' we'll take yu an' Angelique back to yur mother an' Allie. That's enough to think about now."

He turned and suddenly Angelique's hand slid into his, clinging tightly, her face uplifted to his.

"I got te get back," Jack gulped. "Wyoming's waitin' fer me."

But it was not easy to unclasp Angelique's twining little hand or to turn away from her wide beseeching eyes.

"There were six of you, besides Rousseau, where's the other one?" Wyoming queried.

"How should I know?" Charlie retorted sullenly.

"Save us the trouble of hangin' him," Jack said.

"God Almighty!" Billy cried, sinking against the wall, face a pasty white. "Don't hang me—Please. I ain't done nothin.'"

"Yu're a cattle rustler."

"Yeah, I am, but I never was until thet Burton made me—"

"Shut up, Hicks!" Charlie snarled.

"You'll shore get your turn, rustler," Wyoming intervened.

Suddenly the door crashed open to admit three tall figures. Gun barrels glinted darkly in the shimmering light of the lantern.

"What took yu boys so long?" Jack cracked.

"Hell, boss," one of the men replied, darting a look around the cabin "We got hyar as fast as we could. An' I reckon we did all right gettin' a late start like we did."

"Wal, yu can put away yur guns boys, everything's under control. Wyoming, these hyar boys air three of my riders," Jack informed him. "That one's called Montana, an' that's Jimmy Dunn, an' Bud Talman."

"Get in thar with yu," ordered a voice from outside and a moment later the black-eyed Mexican Jimenez, with hands raised over his head, stumbled over the high doorsill, nearly falling before catching his balance.

"Howdy Jack. Caught this hombre tryin' te sneak away," the slim handsome rider holding a Winchester said.

"Good work, Danny," Jack acknowledged. "Tie him up with the others. I reckon we're gonna need another rope."

"Boss," spoke up Bud Talman. "I reckon yu ought te let us take over from here."

"Ump-umm. I reckon I better boss this party," Wyoming said. "These hombres have rustled their last cow."

"Maybe you should let my riders take the responsibility," Jack rejoined crossing to Wyoming and speaking in a low tone of voice.

"How so?" Wyoming queried.

"On account of—Annabelle, and—little Allie," he returned still in a low voice.

Wyoming glanced to where two pairs of huge haunted eyes peered from around the edge of the ragged curtain.

"I take yur meaning," he said. "But first I'd hear the truth about Hester and Burton. I reckon we can make this Billy Hick squeal."

"I savvy."

"Take them outside," Wyoming said. "And somebody build up that fire until its blazing so we can see."

Guarded by the new arrivals the three rustlers were marched out to the front of the cabin where the bonfire burned brightly sending sparks shooting up in the night sky.

"I reckon you best take the ladies off a ways," Talman said, "What's comin' won't be a fittin' sight fer their eyes."

Wyoming nodded. He circled the cabin and located his and Jack's horses and led them around to the front of the cabin. He recovered the horses Annabelle and Angelique had ridden and brought them back where Jack was waiting with the girls. All the while Caesar sat beside Angelique, head resting against her thigh.

"Ready," he said quietly.

Both girls gave jerky nods. Wyoming took Annabelle's hand and he led her to her horse.

The rider called Montana was in the process of shaking out a lariat rope. He tossed the loop over the head of the violently trembling rustler, Billy Hicks. He then threw the other end over a high limb of the oak tree and it dangled down, swinging slowly, menacingly in the firelight.

"Oh! Wyoming—they're going to—" Annabelle choked her eyes wide in sudden horrified realization.

"Get on your horse!" he ordered coldly. She obeyed. Angelique mutely followed.

"Give me a hand, boys," Montana called and two of the watching cowboys grabbed the rope end.

"Oh, Lord—please!" choked Hicks as the rope stretched tight raising him to his toes and holding him there a moment.

"I reckon yu love yur life, huh, rustler?" Montana said loosening the noose.

"God—yes!" Hicks coughed.

"Wal, what'd yu do to save yur life? Would yu talk?"

"Yes! I'll—tell all—I know," replied Hicks in hoarse accents of hope.

"Whose headin' this rustler outfit, Burton?"

"Burton gives us orders, but I know there's somebody higher up, a rancher, that pulls all the strings."

"Who's this somebody?" Talman questioned getting to his feet.

"I—"

"Damn yu Hicks!" interrupted Charlie. "Shut yur blabberin' mouth! Yu knew what yu was gettin' inte. Take yur medicine."

"I didn't neither!" Hicks shouted back. "Shore, I was in on thet first drive, before Dixon took over the ranch. But I swear I didn't know thet drive was rustlin'. Not till after. Burton told me then we was really rustlin'. An he's held it over me ever since. Lord—I'm shore glad te get thet off my chest!"

"Who's this rancher headin' the rustlin', Ed Hester?" Talman demanded.

"I've never seen Hester rustle no stock, but I know fer shore he sells burned brands. And I reckon I heard Burton talk, and I figure he takes orders from him."

"Hicks when we get back, will you talk in front of Hester and Burton?" Talman inquired.

"Yes."

Talman nodded to Montana, who whipped the rope so that the noose jumped from around Hicks' neck.

"I reckon we had better finish this deal tonight," Talman said. "Danny, prod thet first gent over here." Annabelle heard this last before clamping her hands over her ears as Wyoming grabbed the reins of her horse and started off. Jack had already ridden off in the night with Angelique.

CHAPTER TWENTY-SEVEN

Wyoming followed a worn path faint but visible in the darkening night up under the tall spreading silver branches of towering spruce and pines to a spot where he came to a stop far from sight of the cabin and the blazing bonfire. Final tragedy was still to be worked out before that fire, and he felt the steely ruthless clutch knowing what was to come. Annabelle said nothing as they rode, and he knew havoc still absorbed her. After seeing to the horses Wyoming spread his bedroll under the branches of a tall spruce on a soft bed of needles, Jack did the same laying his blankets next to those of Wyoming's. Caesar lounged before the fire.

"Heah yu are," Jack said cheerfully. "We're yur shore goin' to have a soft bed for yu two so yu can get a good sleep."

"Sleep. Will I ever again?" Annabelle said huskily her eyes upon Wyoming.

"Nature has a way of workin' things out fer a body," Jack assured her.

"Wyoming, will you stay close by?" she asked.

"Shore I'll set right here and hold your hand all night," he replied unable to keep his dark restive eyes from meeting hers. "I don't reckon I'm sleepy. But I can sleep setting up just the same."

Annabelle turned a strange look upon Wyoming. Her lips were trembling, the way they trembled when it was impossible to tell whether she was about to laugh or cry. The first hint of her old combative spirit or her old archness!

It was a wave of feeling that rushed over her. She closed her eyes; and the happiness she embraced was all the sweeter for the suffering it had entailed. Wordlessly she sank down on Wyoming's blankets staring with hopeful heart up into the star-lit sky as Angelique stretched out upon the blankets beside her. Something beat into her ears, into her brain, with the regularity and rapid thump of pulsing blood—not too late! Not too late!

Although the spectacle happening before the little cabin was no longer in sight, Wyoming's mind's eye saw it all. He had been at lynchings more than a few times. It was common practice; he realized begun to intimidate cowpunchers going bad. It seems it had not been very successful to that end. Watching Jack as he settled back against a tree a few yards from where the girls lay, he suddenly knew in a flash what the cowboy was thinking. His eyes never leaving Angelique's silent motionless form said it all.

Wyoming closed his eyes suddenly seeing this appalling spectacle with Annabelle's eyes. She had changed him as he now could see that Angelique had changed Jack. The law of the West was what it was; there was no altering it. But he realized with keen insight that the advent of women on this wild range could and would transform it.

The moon topping the trees sent stabs of silver light into the shadows beneath the tall spruce. Annabelle's breathing became deep and regular and he knew she had finally fallen asleep. As the long night wore on Wyoming sensed a gradual slackness of his own mood. He watched the slight sleeping forms. Annabelle's sad wan face, one little hand clasped in sleep in that of her sister, the glint of moisture clinging to her long delicate eyelashes, touched something deep within him. But he could not think how to meet the coming issue between him and Annabelle. She had failed him, had believed him a murderer. It was what continued to flay him—

Long hours Wyoming paced and sat under the cold white stars. Somewhere in that vigil a modicum of peace came back to him. Finally he slept. Day broke clear and beautiful. The rosy glow in the east reached out to turn the aspens gold, their leaves quivering delicately, softly in the soft morning breeze; the wondrous hue blazing against sky and forest. A hawk sailed across the blue opening above. All this Wyoming saw without feeling.

Annabelle stirred and came awake. She slowly sat up, one hand braced on the bedroll. A thick golden curl of slumber-disheveled hair drooped over one sleep-swollen eye. Her pretty face bore the pallor and strain of fatigue and fright, yet it appeared all the more bewitching for that. Jack had breakfast ready, the remains of the fare Mrs. Ward had sent with them. Afterwards he and Angelique walked off under the aspens side by side and Wyoming saw Angelique's little hand creep out to clasp Jack's. Wyoming tried not to look at Annabelle, but he could not escape the haunting eyes that followed his every move.

They struck off on the trail across country, as it was the shorter way, not waiting for the others. Of all the rides Wyoming had ever made, this one was the strangest, and seemingly the most endless. No one spoke. There were hours like years. But they passed, and the miles fell behind. Finally from the last rise they came in view of the ranch. The westerly sun sent golden rays across yard and buildings. They reined up before the house, and there standing on the front porch to meet them was Mr. and Mrs. Dixon, and Allison. Wyoming swung from his horse.

"Oh, Wyoming—you brought them home! ...Bless you! I can never—never repay you," Mrs. Dixon cried. As she hurriedly descended the steps Jack reached up to Angelique and she slid into his arms. Annabelle swayed in the saddle and as Wyoming wheeled about, she half leaped, half fell into his arms.

Her eyes remained open, staring up into his as he carried her up onto the porch, into the house and down the hall to her room. He laid her upon her bed and she sank into the soft mattress. Her mother bent over her as Angelique sat on her other side. Both girls wrapped their arms about mother's neck and hugged and kissed her, tears wetting the cheeks of both mother and daughters. Both girls slept the remainder of the day and all that night and well into the next day; thankfully, it seemed, theirs was a deep dreamless, exhausted sleep.

As the story of the rescue unfolded it became evident that the hound Caesar was a true hero and to Allison's delight the dog was granted the license to sleep in her and Angelique's room—indefinitely.

Near suppertime, two riders were seen on the lane leading to the house. As they came closer Wyoming recognized Hank Ward and, the Texas cattle buyer Fay Johnson. Wyoming walked out to meet them.

"Howdy, son," Ward said swinging down from his horse. "Glad yur back, an' from the look on yur face there must be good news—the Dixon girls are back safe and sound."

"Yep," Wyoming drawled. "Howdy, Mr. Johnson."

"Jack said the rest of the boys should ride in anytime," Ward said. "Fetchin' thet proof we're looking fer."

Dixon came out on the porch and was introduced to Johnson. "You gentlemen come on in, and have a cool drink," he said.

"Don't mind if I do," Ward replied. "Come on Johnson."

The slender Texan stepped effortlessly from the saddle and the two men gained the porch in long easy strides. Wyoming followed.

Seated in the parlor with cold drinks in hand, Ward leaned back in his chair, eyes bent on Wyoming.

"Wal, son, I'm powerful curious about this little rescue escapade, an' that proof Jack Ward mentioned," Johnson said.

Wyoming nodded, face serious. Slowly the story unfolded. The wild guess as to where Ackers was headed with Annabelle fortunately had turned out to be a sound deduction. He told of reaching the cabin before Ackers and his gang arrived with Annabelle and Angelique, the gunfight between Ackers and the gambler Rousseau, which resulted in Rousseau's demise, and then his own killing of Ackers and the capture of the remainder of his gang. It did Wyoming good to talk. It was a relief to get it off his chest.

"One of the rustlers, with a little persuasion decided to talk," Wyoming said. "But I'll wait 'til your ride Talman and the rest bring him in, so as he can talk, and you men can judge for yourself. I'll say this though; he's implicated the man at the top of this rustling business."

"Wal, wal," Ward drawled. "Seems like yu've done most all the work. We might not need the association after all."

"Maybe not in this particular incident," Johnson agreed, "but shore in the future. I reckon we ought te stick with our plan. Rustlin' never goin' te end."

"Yeah, I reckon yu're right," Ward agreed.

The sound of hoof beats drew their attention and peering out the window Wyoming saw Talman and his four riders rein up before the house in a swirl of dust. Slumped wearily in his saddle was the rustler Billy Hicks.

"I reckon they're here now," he said.

"Let's take our little palaver down te yur cabin," Ward suggested. "Might not be somethin' the women folk would want te hear."

"Agreed," Johnson said, and Dixon nodded in concurrence.

In Wyoming's cabin Hicks was seated in a chair facing Ward and Johnson. Once he started talking it was like a floodgate. For Ward and Johnson's ears he fully implicated Burton, and the rancher Ed Hester.

"Wyoming, I reckon we've heard enough," Ward said. "I'd like te ride with yu to brace Burton and Hester."

"Thet goes fer me too," Johnson enjoined.

"Well, I figure on heading there right this minute," Wyoming replied.

About mid-afternoon Hicks led the way out of a winding wooded gulch down upon the open range. Following close behind rode Wyoming and five heavily armed riders. A mile or so down the gray-green slope of sage and manzanita and straggling groves of aspen stood a picturesque and sturdy cabin. This was the ranch where Bull Burton and Ed Hester held forth. It had belonged to a rancher by the name of Seth Winters before Hester bought him out, much like he had Erickson, before selling that ranch to Dixon. And this place was undoubtedly being altered making ready to be offered for sale, as had been Erickson's ranch.

Wyoming studied the Hester ranch cabin. He could see no activity, not even one horse, but Hicks informed him that there was a wide porch on the side facing away from them, and most likely it was there they would find either Burton or Hester, or both men.

"Hicks, how many in Hester's outfit?" Wyoming asked.

"Now? Wal, most likely only two, me an' Ned Walters. I reckon the rest are back there at the cabin where yu left 'em," he said pale of face.

"What's yur plan, Wyoming," Ward asked.

"I reckon me and Hicks and Johnson, will ride on in. Jack, you and Montana and Talman go around to the west side of the cabin where you can cover us."

"Agreed," Ward said.

"All right," Wyoming said. "Let's ride."

As soon as Jack and his two riders had moved into position, Wyoming led the others, riding down the slope at a brisk canter keeping the line of aspens between them and the cabin. Rounding the corner of the cabin Wyoming's gaze swept the scene. Ed Hester sat in a rocking chair tilted back on its runners, a slender Mexican cigar in one hand. Ned Walters was seated on the porch dangling chaps over the edge of the boards.

Startled Hester sat unmoving, the cigar hanging from his mouth. His eyes moved from Wyoming to Hank Ward and then back to Wyoming.

"What the hell—?" he sneered getting slowly, deliberately to his feet. A long barreled pistol rode high on his hip. "Yu got business here, McCord?" he demanded. Then his eyes darted to Hicks, who sat his horse with a sort of fatal resignation.

"Well, Hester, let me acquaint you with some facts. Ackers is dead. So is Anderson and Charlie and your Mexican—"

"What's thet te me. I don't know those men," Hester denied hoarsely.

"Yu're a liar!" Hicks said. "I'm tellin' it all! Yur the one headed this rustler—"

"Who the hell are yu, callin' me a liar? Who is this fool?" Hester said coldly looking at Ward.

"Hicks, come up here," Wyoming ordered, stepping from his horse and walking to the bottom step leading up to the porch. Hicks quickly dismounted and came up beside Wyoming.

"Yu know this man?"

"Yes, sir, I do," Hicks said.

"Who is he?"

"He calls himself Ed Hester."

"Have you rode for him?"

"No, but I rode for his partner, Bull Burton."

"Do you know what became of the cattle Hester here sold Dixon?"

"Yeah. They was rustled. Three big drives and some little ones. I was in all of them, only I didn't know the first drive was rustling. Afterward Burton told me it was and said if I didn't help with the other drives, he snitch me off to the law—"

"I'll not stand fer anymore from this lyin' bastard!" Hester snarled. "One more word an' I'll bore yu!"

Hicks swallowed hard, eyes on the ground.

"Did Burton lead any of these drives?"

"Yeah, the first one."

"What'd you do with the cattle?"

"Drove them over here, and Hester—"

"Damn you! I warned yu!" And Hester's hand flashed to his holstered gun.

A red flash of flame sprouted from Talman's rifle and Hester clasped his chest and fell without a sound.

"I had te shoot, boss! He'd of bored Hicks shore, an' he was unarmed."

"I'll be a witness te thet," Johnson said.

Wyoming nodded.

"What'll we do now," Jack said.

"Rider comin', hell bent fer leather," Montana shouted.

Down the long slope perhaps half a mile distant, a horseman approached running hard.

"Prop Hester up in his chair," Wyoming ordered. "Montana, you and Talman get out of sight behind the cabin. The rest get inside."

"Walters, stay where yu are!" Jack said jerking Walters' Colt from its holster. "If yu open yur trap, yu're a dead man."

Wyoming leaned back in the shadow of the cabin wall, watched the rider pound up to the porch. Gravel and dust flew as he jerked his mount to a halt. Bull Burton leaped to the ground and started up the steps to the porch at a run.

"Hell's te pay, Ed. Ackers an' Anderson—daid! An' Chaffin too—hanged, all of 'em!" He broke off as his eyes encountered Hester's lifeless body.

"What the—" he hissed, and then Wyoming stepped out of the shadows.

Burton gave a sickening gasp, and threw up his hands, his face contorted in terror. "I won't draw on yu, McCord," he cried.

"Well, Bull, I reckon that don't matter. You're a dead man anyhow," Wyoming retorted. "Hicks here spilled his guts."

"It's a rope for you—rustler!" Hank Ward said. "Talman, toss a loop over Burton's neck."

Like a snake the noose glided out to drop over Burton's head. Talman gave the rope a whip snapping it snug.

"Good God, yu're not goin' te—hang me?" Burton cried.

"Wait," Wyoming spoke up. This crude justice brought home to him now its futility. He wanted an end to it. "Fellers, if it's all right with you, I've got a proposal."

Johnson nodded. "Go ahead, son."

"Bull, I reckon you've got a decision to make. Take your choice. Hang or leave New Mexico."

"I'll—get out," he panted, tearing at the noose.

"Ah-huh. Just as you are. And if I see you again on this range neither Johnson nor anyone else can save your neck. Take Walters with you."

Moments later Burton and Walters were seen riding hard, heading west.

On the slow ride back to the Ward's ranch, Jack rode along side Wyoming.

"What do yu think, Wyoming?" Ward drawled. "I asked Angelique to marry me."

"Dog-gone! You did?"

"Yep, on the way back from thet old cabin. And—she said, 'yes'," he replied as though he still couldn't believe his good fortune.

"Jack, I'm shore glad for you and Angelique too."

Restless Wyoming paced in front of one of Ward's spare cabins where he had taken up residence. Finally he sank down on the porch steps as dusk began to fall. A coyote wailed from somewhere out in the twilight's darkening shadows. In the week that had passed he had had ample time to think. Annabelle had betrayed him, profoundly, and that hurt in ways Wyoming couldn't begin to label, much less describe. However, not once had he felt betrayed from his reasoning mind. What was he to expect. She wasn't Western, couldn't understand, maybe never would, and yet how could he dismiss her way of thinking, her reprehensions? How could he bear her any ill will when something inside him was changing? He hadn't wanted to stay, take a part in the range justice meted out to the rustlers that he had done, not once but on many occasions. He began to see now that that form of vindication was no longer an option or even a need. The rule of law was coming, and coming speedily; and the rule of the gun was fading, with as much rapidity.

His ears caught the pounding of horse's hoofs and a moment later Jack Ward rode into the yard. For a moment he sat peering at Wyoming before stepping from the saddle. He sat down on the step beside Wyoming.

"I just came from Dixon's place," he said holding out a wrinkled envelope. "I brung yu a letter."

Wordlessly Wyoming took the crumpled envelope his heart pounding. In the dim light from the house he saw his name scrawled across the front of the missive in an immature hand. Slowly he got to his feet and walked to stand near the window where the light was stronger. He tore open the envelope and extracted the folded sheet and painstakingly read:

Dear Wyoming,

I miss you so very much. Caesar is sad also. I think he misses you too. Dada is beside himself, though Jack has been a big help, but he could really use your hand. Anna cries when she thinks no one sees her. I just thought you ought to know. I love you.

Allison Dixon

It hit him, hard nearly taking his breath away. Allison thought Wyoming no longer loved her, didn't miss her, all because her sister had hurt his feelings. What matter hurt feelings or dignity compared to love. He loved Annabelle no matter how she had hurt him. Because of his foolish pigheadedness, his stubborn pride, he hadn't even allowed her to explain. He looked over at Jack who still sat on the porch step.

"I reckon I'm going for a ride," he said and started off toward the barn. Jack watched him go a smile on his lips.

Lights blazed in the front room of the Dixon ranch house when Wyoming rode into the yard. He swung to the ground. The door sprang open and Allison bound out on the porch.

"Wyoming!" she cried and threw her little arms about his waist. He hugged her tight, a lump rising in his throat.

She abruptly slipped from his embrace and put a finger to his lips.

"Hush," she ordered, and then taking his hand in both her small ones she led him to the porch steps. "Sit down, and don't move!"

Without another word she disappeared back in the house. With a strange sort of calmness settling over him, Wyoming settled on the step elbows resting on his knees. Shortly he heard the screen door open and soft footsteps behind him. He didn't look back but his heart began to pound in his chest. Something brushed his shoulder and he turned to look. Annabelle clad in a white gown of some sort of shimmering material stood next to him.

"Wyoming," she said her voice low. "May I sit beside you?"

"Shore, I reckon," he blurted. He had to steel his nerves to keep himself from snatching her to him.

She settled beside him on the step, her hip brushing his. "Wyoming—can we talk?"

"I've been doing a lot of thinking," he returned. "Annabelle Dixon, you believed me a murderer."

"I did…" she replied after a hesitation. "I shouldn't have, but they were lawmen—or so I thought, and they were so sure. God forgive me! I did believe it the truth. When they rode off with you—that very instant, I knew I was wrong. I knew you couldn't be—" Her eyes shown with a poignant haunting.

"You believed I was a murderer," he accused relishing Annabelle's distress and at the same time hating himself for putting her through it.

"What more can I say?! I do not deny it. I could have lied," she cried, near frantic. "Oh, God…Wyoming McCord, I've loved you from the first moment I laid eyes on you. From that first wondrous kiss I've loved you—and—I love—you—now," she cried, brokenly. "Terribly! And—and if you do not—love me—"

Wyoming could hold out no longer. He drew her to his breast, and her arms lifted, stole around his neck.

"Then you—forgive me?"

"Annabelle, sweetheart—I love you. There's no need to talk forgiveness," he moaned,

He touched her cool sweet lips with his own. And she responded blindly giving her lips in kisses that broke off only to be renewed with terrible sweet urgency until at last her lovely face fell back in the hollow of his arm. And it was no longer white or tragic.

"Annabelle, will you marry me?" he asked huskily.

A tear slipped from beneath her eyelid, glided slowly down her cheek.

"Yes. Oh, yes!"

"You're crying. Why are you crying?" he asked softly, stroking her hair.

"Oh, Wyoming I'm so—so happy," she signed snuggling closer. "But we'll still be pards, I mean, I'll still be your right-hand cowbo—girl, won't I?"

"Annabelle Dixon, you'll be my wife," he replied forcefully.

"Yes," she whispered. "Randy...darling."

The End

Printed in the United States
By Bookmasters